DEATH BENEFITS

DEATH BENEFITS

A SOUTHERN FRAUD MYSTERY

J. W. BECTON

A WHITELEY PRESS, LLC, BOOK

A WHITELEY PRESS, LLC, BOOK

Copyright © 2012 by Jennifer Becton
www.jwbecton.com

All rights reserved. No part of this book may be reproduced in any form, except in the case of brief quotations, without written permission from the author.

ISBN-13: 978-0-9837823-6-0
ISBN-10: 0-9837823-6-9

The characters and events in this book are fictitious or used fictitiously. Any similarity to real people, living or dead, is coincidental and not intended by the author.

Other Works by J. W. Becton

The Southern Fraud Mystery Series
Absolute Liability
Death Benefits
At Fault
Moral Hazard
Shock Loss
Sunset Clause
"Cancellation Notice": A Southern Fraud Short Story

For

Bert Becton

ONE

The course of his life had already been set—written on his soul as if chiseled in cold, hard stone—and that meant that the bodies would never quit coming.

He'd never be able to stop them.

Resigned to his fate, the man in the baseball cap paused only for a moment to look into the night sky. The oppressive heat of summer had finally begun to taper off, but fall had not yet arrived. During this in-between time, reality seemed suspended somehow—not quite summer, not quite fall—and he felt nothing, neither anger nor pleasure, as he undertook his task.

He simply pushed the limp, lifeless body onward to its final destination.

It was what he must do.

Two

"A dead body, a car fire, and a potentially fraudulent death benefits claim," Ted Insley announced far too cheerfully for eight o'clock on a Monday morning.

Too cheerfully for anytime, really, but especially for my first day back at work at the Georgia Department of Insurance after a two-week medical leave.

"And good morning to you too," I tossed back, looking up from my laptop monitor where I'd been catching up on my long-neglected email. I watched my boss saunter into my office, place the new case files in a neat stack on my desk, and take a seat.

Ted chuckled as he picked some imaginary lint from his trousers and leaned back into the beam of sunlight that streaked through the window. His silver hair and starched white shirt seemed to glow, and I squinted at him as he said with exaggerated formality, "On behalf of the Georgia Department of Insurance, welcome back, Special Agent Julia Jackson. We've missed you around here."

"I've missed being here," I said as I crossed my arms in front of me and tilted my chair back. A shrill squeak of springs filled the room, almost as if the furniture were heckling me for bending the truth.

Well, I'd mostly missed being there. Even if I were already mourning the loss of freedom my little mandatory vacation had provided, I could at least be happy about one aspect of my return to the DOI: it meant I'd officially been cleared in the shooting that ended my last fraud investigation.

I knew my actions had been justified. After all, an armed gunman had broken into my house and tried to kill me, but in a society fraught with frivolous lawsuits, you just never know what might happen. I half expected the guy's widow to sue me.

That would have been a disaster.

Of course, the news of my being cleared in the shooting didn't fully assuage my conscience. I was still coming to grips with what I'd done—I had taken a life—but at least I knew I wasn't going to be tried for defending my own.

And I wouldn't be confined to my desk either.

"So...," Ted began in an overly cautious tone that had me cringing after only one word. "How are you feeling? Are you healing well?"

He looked pointedly at my left arm, where the bullet had made its impression, and then at my head as if it might conceal a ticking time bomb.

Geez, I wasn't exactly okay with killing another human or being shot myself, but I was definitely not fragile either. I was just...wounded. I forced my thoughts away from the bandage on my arm and smiled brightly at Ted. "Me? I'm just fine."

I hated having people tread carefully around me and despised having them question my ability to cope with a difficult, yet regrettably normal, aspect of a law enforcement officer's career. But what I loathed even more was the fact that I had been asking myself the very same questions that Ted was dancing around now.

"I'm perfectly okay. Thanks for asking," I repeated in a firm tone that was meant to reassure both of us.

It appeared to work on Ted.

"Excellent! The timing couldn't be better." He gestured at the files. "This big case came in late last night, and we need someone on the scene today. I was running out of investigators."

I smiled to myself, understanding what Ted had not said. If I hadn't been cleared and healed enough to come in on this lovely Monday morning, Ted himself would have had to go into the field and investigate the case on his own. Although he was a former field agent, Ted was much more suited to—not to mention comfortable with—sitting behind a desk in a nice clean office where everything was ordered and regular. These days, he avoided the field as much as possible.

"Big case, huh?" I asked, already curious about the files in front of me.

"Well, nothing like the last one. No one's been abducted. But there is a body." Then he added soberly, "It's not pretty."

Even though I'd taken two weeks off and was supposedly recovered from the shooting, I was surprised that Ted would assign me a case involving a dead body.

Why not a nice staged car accident or a simple homeowner's insurance scam? Heck, even a medical con would be better at this precise moment.

Still, I began to thumb through the paperwork in front of me. I scanned the cover sheets and flipped through the rest of the pages, stopping when I saw a few photographs of a burned car leaning unevenly on the shoulder of a wooded road. I shut the folder before I saw any bodies.

Still a bit early in the day for that.

"It's not a problem, Ted," I said, hoping that was the truth.

"I was reluctant to assign it to you"—he looked at my arm again—"given the circumstances. It's not the ideal case for your first day back, but I really need you on it. Everyone else is busy handling the backlog of investigations that accumulated while you were gone."

I restrained a sigh. There was no denying that this backlog of cases was the result of my time off. I knew Ted wasn't trying to be a jerk by handing the death benefits case off to me, but I wondered if he might be testing me, making sure I was really capable of continuing with my duties after what happened.

Well, if that were the case, I would prove to Ted, everyone at the DOI, and even myself that I was more than capable of doing my job.

Determined, I flipped the pages of the files again.

"If it makes you feel any better," Ted said, his tone still tentative, "you'll have help."

I raised my eyes to meet his. "Help?"

"Yeah, you remember those new policies mandated by the Atlanta office?"

I nodded. The new policies had also been the result of my last case. When it became clear that I'd been the target of an abduction and an attempted murder, the DOI went into cover-your-ass mode.

Their first mandate was that DOI investigators must be armed at all times during the course of their duties, which explained the Smith and Wesson M&P .40 caliber pistol strapped securely to my hip as I sat at my desk.

Now, apparently, they'd added more stipulations to their new list of rules.

"All major DOI investigations must be run by no fewer than two agents," Ted said as if quoting from the official memorandum. "This death benefits claim qualifies as a major case."

"So I've got a partner?" I translated.

Ted nodded, his expression uncertain as he looked away from me. I wondered if he thought I'd complain about this new mandate.

I leaned back, causing the chair springs to shriek in protest again and wondering if I should protest too, but truth be told, I didn't mind the idea of working with a partner. I sure could have used a partner beside me when I was staring down the barrel of a revolver two weeks ago.

"Who? Gershman?" I asked, thinking he'd likely pair me with the other investigator in the Mercer, Georgia, office.

"Me," a deep voice said.

It was clearly not the voice of nearing-retirement-age Webb Gershman.

I looked up to find Mark Vincent lingering just inside the threshold of my office door, and I took him in for a beat. Tall, broad, and all business, Vincent was the quintessential military man, and even though he was currently dressed in dark jeans and a sport coat, there was no mistaking him for a harmless civilian.

Nope. Not at all. There was a Sig concealed under that jacket, and years of personal protection experience meant he was deadly accurate at 100 yards with his weak hand only.

Well, maybe not 100 yards with a pistol, but with a rifle? Definitely.

I looked purposefully back at Ted, who seemed to be gauging my reaction, so I did my best not to react.

"Special Agent Vincent requested a transfer from Atlanta," Ted explained, "and you worked so well together last time…."

Of their own volition, my eyes darted back to Vincent's face, trying to read his intentions there. He'd requested a transfer? I studied his stoic expression. Nothing. He was a complete blank.

And yet I'd witnessed that face so full of longing and pain that it hardly seemed possible that it could ever be void of emotional cues.

My first thought, which managed to teeter on the border of hope and abject fear, was that he had asked to move to Mercer for me. After all, we had shared a bit of a moment after the shooting, but I forced myself to think logically. His son, Justin, was attending college nearby. Yes, that was it. He came for his son, not me.

Why would anyone make a drastic life change after working with someone for just a week and a half? That would be highly unlikely and, frankly, a bit presumptuous.

But given what I knew—and it was admittedly not much—about Vincent's strained relationship with Justin, he would make such an extreme choice for his son. He would probably move to Antarctica if it meant a relationship with Justin.

Surely that explained what he was doing in my office.

Somewhat relieved, I turned my gaze back to Ted. He said Vincent and I had worked well together, and that was true enough. We had similar investigative styles, and I felt comfortable with him. Not only was I sure he'd have my back, but somehow he'd managed to make me feel freer when I'd been working with him than when I'd been going it alone.

Odd. That was hardly ever the case, at least in my experience as a law enforcement officer.

"Excellent," Ted said as he slapped his palms on the knees of his perfectly creased trousers and smiled. "Vincent is already settled into the office next door, so unless you have any questions, I'll let you two take it from here."

Vincent stepped farther into my office, and his increased physical presence caused a palpable shift in the balance of power. Ted seemed to disappear into the bright sunlight as Vincent addressed me, and we became the only two people there, the two most powerful, a team.

"I emailed you a link to the digital pictures of the fire scene and a few other items that have trickled in during the last half hour, but I'm still working on getting a copy of the life insurance policy in question. How long do you think you'll need to get up to speed?"

Resolute, I flipped open the top folder, which was marked "Theodore Vanderbilt."

"I'll do a preliminary read-through now," I told Vincent. "Why don't we meet for lunch to discuss where to start?"

Vincent nodded his assent and added, "That should give me time to compile all the pertinent financial and police records. And get that policy out of Americus Mutual."

From the pale wash of sunlight, Ted said, "Good, and if you two need any assistance, don't hesitate to call me."

Translation: I'll be in my office enjoying my cushy management position.

Both Vincent and Ted left my office then, and I took a deep breath before delving back into the world of fraud and, apparently, death.

A gruesome case began to take shape before me.

The deceased, Theodore Vanderbilt, had owned the U-Strip-Em Auto Salvage, an automotive junkyard, and the We-Shred-Em, a metal recycling center, both located in Cranford County, Georgia. At approximately 3 AM Saturday, his 1986 Ford LTD was found engulfed in flames on Highway 403 with his body in the driver's seat. The scene seemed to indicate an accident, but the burn patterns had raised suspicions among the fire personnel.

Overwhelmed, the Cranford County sheriff, Bart "Tiny" Harper, had requested the help of a state arson investigator. Eva Sinclair from our sister office, the Georgia Department of Fire Investigation, had been sent in. Eva was the source of most of the photographic evidence in the files, and apparently she was still in Cranford County working to determine the source of ignition of the fire. At the time of the writing of her initial report, she had not been able to rule out arson.

Cranford County Coroner Morton Ivey had removed the body under Eva's supervision and transferred it temporarily into refrigeration at Cranford General Hospital's morgue. When Ivey had been unable to determine the victim's identity or the cause of death through the limited methods available to him, the body had been moved to the Georgia medical examiner's office at the state crime lab to undergo a full autopsy. The unclear circumstances of death, along with widow Kathy Vanderbilt's prompt phone call to Americus Mutual Insurance and her demand for the life insurance money even before the death certificate could be issued, had moved the whole investigation to DOI jurisdiction pretty damn quick.

Lovely, I thought as I turned to my laptop and found the place on the server where the rest of the fire scene photos were stored. Taking a deep breath, I forced myself to look at each one closely. The photographs began with general shots of the area—a wooded two-lane road surrounded by tall pines and a few mature oaks—and became progressively more specific in the details they captured.

In a way, it helped to start out vague and become more specific. Each shot prepared me to deal with the next, and it piqued my curiosity to learn what had actually occurred.

From what I could tell from the photographs, the condition of the burned Ford LTD was certainly suspicious. If the accident scene in the photographs were taken at face value, the fire was the result of a front-end collision with a pine tree. Supposedly, Theodore Vanderbilt had crashed his LTD into a tree, passed out, and then been consumed by flames that started in the engine compartment.

And it was a rather realistic scenario. Accidental car fires often begin in the engine compartment, where flammable fluids can combine easily with the heat of the motor and ignite. Most damage occurs there, and then the flames spread to the rear portions of the vehicle.

However, the photos of the LTD told a different story. Most of the damage seemed to occur inside the passenger compartment, so that meant the fire was likely centered there. And because the rugs and fabrics in automobiles are treated with heavy-duty flame retardants, making interior fires notoriously difficult to start, this hinted at a purposeful blaze. So even if Vanderbilt had hit the tree, passed out, and happened to drop a lit cigarette, a small ignition source, the interior wouldn't burn. A larger flame and some sort of liquid accelerant are usually necessary to start an interior car fire.

That was a pretty major hitch in Kathy Vanderbilt's death benefits claim.

I flipped to the next picture, wondering what else it would reveal about the claim, and discovered the first detailed shot of the burned body. It was almost hard to believe that such a thing had once been a living, breathing human. The remains looked like something from a horror movie set: fleshless, mouth open, lips burned away, the face was frozen in a permanent scream.

I closed my eyes for a moment.

But only a moment.

Then I began to think logically about what these pictures told us. We could certainly rule out a simple disappearance scam. Usually, those dumbass cons try to fake their deaths by hiding long enough for their beneficiary to receive the insurance money, and they are in for a long haul because a life insurance payout without a body can take up to seven years. And if they actually manage to remain hidden for that long, miracle of miracles, the dead arise and walk again, only now quite a bit richer.

And usually with a new name.

No, we were dealing with a body, and that opened the door to multiple possibilities. If I were wrong about the origin of the fire and it had been the result of a front-end collision, then Theodore Vanderbilt was likely rendered unconscious, and then the car had caught fire, burning or asphyxiating him before he could awaken and escape. Or he may have died of a heart attack or stroke while driving, causing the car to collide with a tree and ignite.

But if the scene had been staged and the fire set purposefully—and this seemed the more likely scenario as far as I could tell—then that could signal more disturbing events.

Although it was rare, Vanderbilt could have chosen to commit suicide by fire.

Or he could have been murdered, and the fire was used to cover up the evidence. Perhaps Kathy Vanderbilt had killed her husband in order to collect the insurance money. So we could also be looking at arson and murder.

But I am not a fire investigator or a homicide cop. I investigate insurance fraud, and though my cases sometimes take me into the realm of other crimes, my primary job in this instance was to determine if Kathy Vanderbilt's death benefits claim was legit. If so, the insurance company had to pay up. If not, then someone was going to prison.

I finished looking at each picture of the fire scene, and when I closed the photo viewer, I leaned back and sighed. Originally, I'd taken a job at the DOI in the hopes that I'd be dealing with boring—and safe—white-collar crimes, but I was beginning to realize that even the insurance world could become grisly and uncomfortable. And the fraudsters out there were often desperate and dangerous people, no matter where they fell on the social spectrum.

Earlier, I'd been hoping for a dull fraud, a crime of numbers, not bodies. But in this case, we were dealing not only with a potential arson but with a horrible death as well.

Already, I felt the familiar pull of justice at my heart. The images of death I'd encountered were horrific, but my need to unearth the truth forcefully overcame the lingering feelings of guilt induced by my own brush with violence.

Three

"First, we need to get our hands on Theodore Vanderbilt's life insurance policy," I said to Vincent between bites of chicken salad croissant and tomato soup.

We were sitting in the heart of downtown Mercer on the outdoor patio of Hugo's, a café owned by a French expat and designed to mimic European sidewalk restaurants. It served an oddly satisfying combo of French cuisine and good old-fashioned Southern lunchtime fare. At noon, the place was always packed with workers desperate for an escape from their offices, and now that the summer weather had begun to melt slowly into autumn, it was even more pleasant. The patio offered a bit of a breeze, the sound of birdsong, and a view of the Yoshino cherry trees that lined every street in town.

"What's the holdup?" I asked. We couldn't do much of anything until we knew the stipulations of the life insurance policy and who—other than Kathy Vanderbilt—might stand to benefit from Theodore's death. We should have had access to the policy the minute the insurance company had requested DOI intervention.

"Hell if I know," Vincent said. "Apparently, there was some bureaucratic snafu at Americus." A national insurance giant, Americus Mutual was the company that supplied Theodore Vanderbilt's life insurance policy. And that was about all we knew so far, except that Kathy's death benefits claim had hit their switchboard bright and early Saturday morning.

Vincent continued, "Jackasses in their office gave me the runaround, claimed some kind of Internet outage, so I called the adjuster's cell myself. We're supposed to meet her sometime this afternoon to get the hard copy of the policy."

I studied Vincent over my sandwich. He should have looked ridiculous in this setting. His large form appeared even more hulking when it was parked on a dainty metal chair, and his hands looked bigger when they were holding a delicate water glass. Yet somehow his movements managed not to be awkward at all. He looked perfectly natural and unself-conscious.

"But the conditions in which the body was found are troubling," I said. "If the fire was set purposefully, what was the motive? What needed to be hidden?"

"Hell," Vincent grunted, "we don't even know for certain it was Theodore Vanderbilt in the car."

"We need to put a rush on the autopsy report," I summarized.

"Yeah," Vincent said. "While you were getting up to speed on the case file this morning, I put a call in to the state crime lab. Our body has been pushed to the front of the line, but they probably won't be able to get to it until tomorrow at the earliest."

"That should be fine. We have plenty of other ground to cover," I said as I watched Vincent finish off the last of his sandwich and wondered if he were aggravated by the wait. He seemed to have a talent for moving things along when it came to bureaucracy, but even though suspicious deaths and unusual circumstances were always moved to the front of the autopsy line, there was still a line.

Whatever his secret to motivating functionaries, it hadn't worked this time, and though I didn't ask, I was curious to know his back-channel methods.

I figured I'd learn his secrets eventually—when he was ready—and I wouldn't try to force him to talk sooner because I didn't want him to return the favor, so to speak. I sure didn't want him digging around in my little storehouse of clandestine affairs.

"All right," I said as I pulled my phone from my belt to check the time. "Why don't you see if you can firm up the meeting with the Americus adjuster?"

Vincent stood, extracted his phone from his coat pocket, and winked at me. "Meanwhile, you take care of the bill."

I glared up at him with mock ferocity. "You don't want to start this kind of war with me," I said. "One of these days, when you least expect it, you'll find yourself footing my bill for the most expensive surf-and-turf dinner you've ever seen."

He laughed, totally unconcerned, and as he strode out of the dining area to make his call, he shot over his shoulder, "I'm counting on it."

I rolled my eyes, but I settled the bill anyway. And afterward, I whipped my phone from my belt again, this time to call Tripp Carver, a detective on the Mercer Police Department Violent Crimes Unit and my long-extinguished flame. Because Vincent would probably be a few minutes with the Americus adjuster and I knew we'd be busy the rest of the day, now was my best bet for a little privacy.

With the DOI case suddenly looming before me, it was becoming clear that I needed to find another way to continue my quest to discover the identity of my sister Tricia's rapist.

Confession time: I hadn't spent my two weeks of medical leave resting. Instead, I'd been working the new lead in Tricia's case.

The only new lead I'd had in seventeen years was a single fingerprint, which had been discovered in conjunction with an aggravated assault case in Orr County.

Enter Charlie Atkins. Good ole Charlie had the misfortune to be arrested for participating in the beating of a local bar owner while his accomplice—and presumably the owner of the fingerprint in question—fled the scene.

So after Atkins had been released on bond to await trial, I made him my permanent mission.

I learned everything I could about him through the initial police report and arrest record, and then I staked him out.

Yes, I'd been following a recent divorcé and likely felon all over Middle Georgia. I'd sat for hours in front of his crappy apartment complex and in the parking lot of a franchise store where he was employed as an accountant.

And it was terribly dull.

But it was all done in the hopes that Atkins might come into contact with his unknown associate and thereby reveal to me the identity of the man who'd raped my sister.

Was I unwise for staking out a man charged with aggravated assault? Clearly, he was dangerous, and clearly, I was alone. But it was a calculated risk. After all, I had a great deal of experience with solo surveillance. A lot of insurance investigation involves sitting at a distance, watching unobtrusively, and waiting for the moment when the subject makes a mistake.

And that's just what I'd been doing for the past two weeks.

Waiting for Atkins to make a mistake.

So far, nothing.

But after all those years of running the latent print from Tricia's file—all those years of hoping that one day her attacker would get caught committing another crime, enter the system, and allow me to discover his identity—I wasn't going to waste my chance.

Here's what I'd discovered so far: Atkins was handy with a golf club. He toted his bag for thirty-six holes both weekends I'd been watching him, and he also kept the clubs in the trunk of his car just in case he needed to beat anyone senseless. Yup, he and his friend had used golf clubs to assault that poor bar owner for something as innocuous as announcing last call earlier than the pair had preferred.

So yeah, Mr. Atkins was a thug—pure and simple—but he dressed nicely and had a decent job, so he probably fooled a lot of people.

As for the probable rapist, I'd learned little. Witnesses at the bar that night said Atkins had been with another man whom they described only as Caucasian, average height and weight, with a graying crew cut, very clean and well groomed.

Apparently, he was only remarkable in his grooming habits, but coming from the patrons of a third-rate juke joint, I had to take that description with a grain of salt. Clean-cut and well-groomed to that clientele could mean as little as "washed himself daily."

That was all I'd been able to learn in the first real break in my sister's cold case in seventeen years, but unfortunately, I no longer had the time to follow Atkins all day in the hopes of his meeting up with Tricia's rapist. It had been a long shot in the first place.

Now, I had the greatest temptation to use my position as a state law enforcement officer to worm my way into the local PD's investigation. Between my badge and my existing friendships in the area, it would be fairly easy to do. But I'd already skirted the boundaries of legality in some of my methods for keeping my sister's cold case from freezing over, and I didn't want to do anything else to jeopardize the prosecution's future case, so I decided to approach the investigation through official channels.

Mostly.

If possible.

Hence my call to Tripp.

I shook my head at the thought of asking for his help. Tripp had always had a hero complex when it came to me and my family. Even our romantic relationship, I'd realized years later, had been based mostly on my youthful need to be saved and his need to be a savior, and I'd worked hard to end this unhealthy aspect of our relationship. I did not want to go back to being a damsel in distress in his eyes.

Plus, I had absconded with a few bits of evidence—the latent fingerprint, for example—from Tricia's case file when I'd been laid off the Mercer PD during the citywide budget cuts three years ago, and though I didn't mind if my reputation ended a bit sullied in the name of justice, I didn't want anyone else's reputation—especially Tripp's—tainted alongside mine.

Of course, I wasn't asking him to do anything even remotely illegal.

In fact, I was asking him to do his job and investigate a new lead on a cold case. Tripp had contacts in the Orr County PD whom he could inform of the connection between their aggravated assault case and my sister's cold rape case. It would be easy for him to request their help in learning the identity of the owner of the latent print on the golf club.

Resolved, I exited Hugo's, found a quiet spot around the corner, and dialed Tripp.

His low, husky voice came over the speaker. "Hey, Jules." He sounded relaxed, and I imagined his feet propped on his desk as he leaned back to chat. "What's up?"

"I'm back at the DOI this morning," I said. I figured I'd start off with a bit of chitchat before hitting him with my big request.

"That's good," he said, his voice hesitant. "Are you sure you've given yourself enough time, you know, to recover?"

Not unfamiliar with the necessity of taking a life in the line of duty, Tripp had been concerned over my reaction to the shooting last month. He might cover it with bravado in front of his police buddies, but he felt the same weight that now clung to my back: the responsibility for a life beyond my own.

But I also had another burden—the responsibility for finding the bastard who had effectively killed Tricia's spirit and destroyed my family in the process—and that would always keep me trudging forward, keep me in the world of law enforcement for as long as it took. I was willing to face anything if it meant I could find justice for my sister and for those whose lives had been ruined.

But once justice had been served...well, who knew?

"I wouldn't have come back otherwise," I said, infusing my voice with confidence. "But it's nice to know you're concerned."

"I'm always concerned about you, Jules," he said.

And that was true. He'd always been there for me, and I was counting on him being there for me now.

"Listen," I said, drawing out the word as I tried to figure out the best way to approach him. I could remind him of our history—both romantically and professionally—but it felt like manipulation, and I didn't want him to agree to my proposal out of guilt. I wanted to give him the option of saying no without fear of endangering our friendship.

So I said it bluntly: "I've got a lead on Tricia's cold case."

"Yeah?" Tripp asked, sounding more excited than I'd expected.

"One of the latent prints from her file turned up a match over in Orr County in conjunction with an aggravated assault charge. Two guys beat a bartender with a driver and a nine iron."

"Nice," Tripp said, adding a long whistle. "Did the print come with a name?"

"Unfortunately not," I said. "Our suspect fled the scene, but the other—a Charlie Atkins—is out on bail and waiting for trial."

I decided to confess about my stakeout of Atkins, painful as the prospect was.

"I've had Atkins under surveillance for the past two weeks."

"You've what?"

I could tell by Tripp's tone that he was ready to talk some sense into me. "I know what you're going to say," I said, hoping to avert the lecture, "so let's just skip that part and I'll tell you what I learned."

I heard Tripp sigh heavily. "Fine," he said through gritted teeth.

"It's not much, really," I admitted. "As I said, Atkins is out on bond for an aggravated assault in Orr County. A latent print from the weapon used in the assault—a golf club—matched the one in Tricia's file. Witnesses of the assault said another man participated but fled the scene before police arrived." I paused, sucking in a breath to make the pronouncement I'd been afraid to speak, even to myself. "It could be him, Tripp."

"Yeah," Tripp said, "but it might not be. Were there more than two sets of prints on the club?"

"I don't know," I admitted. "All I know is that a set of prints from the club matched the one in Tricia's file. And that makes it appear as if Atkins knows him." I paused again, feeling suddenly defensive. "I had to follow him, Tripp. He's the best lead to Tricia's rapist."

"I understand, but for God's sake, Jules, you can't just stalk a man around town. It's dangerous. Not to mention illegal."

I chose not to comment on the illegal part and instead relayed the rest of my information. "I followed Atkins, but so far nothing." I took another deep breath, preparing to drop the big question, but Tripp didn't let me.

"I know a guy in the Orr County PD," he said. "I could make some inquiries. Maybe talk to the DA, get him to work a plea deal—reduced charges or sentence—with Atkins in exchange for the name of the other suspect."

All the breath left my body in a great whoosh. I hadn't realized how badly I'd wanted his help. "Would you?" I squeaked.

"That was what you were about to ask, right?"

I could hear the smile in his voice, and I grinned back even though I knew he couldn't see me.

He knew me too well, but I wouldn't admit it to him. I only said, "I can't tell you how much I appreciate it, Tripp. Really."

"I know, Jules, but you should also know by now that I want to help Tricia just about as much as you do."

"I'll email you all the info I've got," I said as I checked my purse to make sure I had my flash drive. I was careful always to keep my personal investigation separate from my official work, so I'd send the info to Tripp from my personal email account as soon as I got back to the office.

"All right," Tripp said. "I'll do what I can."

"I know you will," I said.

A good cop to the core, Tripp always played it by the book. I was the kind of cop who played mostly by the book but also scribbled her own notes in the margins.

"But remember," Tripp added, breaking my train of thought, "this could turn out to be nothing. The print could have belonged to the guy who sold Atkins the golf clubs or a caddy at the club. It might not be the other assault suspect."

"I know," I said. But it was a start.

"You told your sister anything about the print?" he asked.

"Nope," I said without the least compunction at withholding the facts from Tricia. "I don't plan to say anything until I'm sure I've found the guy."

"Yeah, she is a bit"—he searched for the word—"fragile."

"Yes," I agreed. "Thanks for everything, Tripp. Let me know when you hear something."

"Will do. And take it easy for a while, will ya? I don't want to be called to your house for a shooting ever again."

"Believe me," I said, "I don't want to relive that scenario either."

"Good," Tripp said, as if our agreement would make it so, and then we hung up.

Fragile. It was as if Tripp had reached into my mind and spoken my very thoughts. Tricia was fragile now—that was certain—but she hadn't always been that way. When we were kids, I'd looked up to Tricia. She was everything I wanted to be: smart, funny, popular. I'd tagged along after her, and she'd never tried to ditch me.

I could still picture her that night as she drove off in her Z28, her blond ponytail hanging over the seat back as she headed to some post-football game party. Lots of jocks and cheerleaders: not my style.

When she'd come home later that night, battered and bruised, our family changed forever, and I began my quest to save everyone.

So far, I hadn't been successful in saving anybody, including myself.

Seventeen years later, my sister was an alcoholic, my mother was stuck in the past and totally in denial, my father was mostly absent, and I had organized my entire life around the event that caused it all.

But now, I might be on the verge of freeing my entire family.

And Tripp was still there to help me.

I stared blankly ahead for a moment, bringing myself out of the past, and went to meet Vincent in front of Hugo's. I found him leaning against the trunk of one of the cherry trees. Together, we turned toward the DOI office, which was located three blocks over.

"Are we set with the adjuster?" I asked.

"She's in the field this week, so we're meeting her at her current location, which is staking out a gas station off I-16."

"We're meeting at her stakeout?" I asked, not sure I liked the idea. Not only was I loath to sit in a surveillance vehicle—I was all too familiar with the stench a car acquired when one sat in it for days on end hoping to catch a suspect in the midst of a con—but I also didn't want to jeopardize the adjuster's anonymity.

"Apparently, she's got a good location that won't arouse any suspicion," Vincent said. "Plus, she sounded bored."

Four

Vincent and I were headed straight to no-man's-land, which is basically anywhere on I-16, the most desolate, boring stretch of highway in the state of Georgia. Only when the road reached the coast with its white sandy beaches, live oaks, and Spanish moss did drivers realize why I-16 had been created in the first place. The Georgia coast was magical.

Unfortunately, Vincent and I weren't going to make it anywhere near the beaches. We'd be stopping somewhere in the middle of a vast section of flat nothingness.

Super.

And to make the trip even more exciting, Vincent had managed to talk me into driving, and I was currently fighting to keep my mind focused on the uninterrupted blacktop before me and not slip into a driving coma.

I searched the horizon for anything—other than the billboards that dotted the roadside—that resembled civilization. Even a truck stop would be comforting.

Vincent and I had studiously avoided any sort of personal conversation so far while he kept his head buried in the files, occasionally reading portions aloud to me. I'd just perused the same information that morning, but I appreciated his recap anyway. It told me what facets of the case had stood out to him.

"Cranford Police responded to a report of a car fire at approximately 3 AM on Saturday," he said. "The call came in from Luis Pedroza, a passing motorist with a cell phone who was returning home from his shift at the diaper plant. He lives on

Highway 403, which is fortunate for us because that road is apparently not highly traveled at that time of night."

"Convenient place to set a fire," I said. "If it were set deliberately, that is."

Vincent continued his summary without commentary. "First responders were a couple of guys from the Cranford Volunteer Fire Department, who found the 1986 Ford LTD fully engaged, seemingly as a result of a collision with a tree. Flames were visible in the passenger compartment, and upon approach, the firemen discovered a body in the vehicle."

"Did they try to extricate him?" I asked, jumping ahead.

Out of the corner of my eye, I saw Vincent shake his head. "Says the body was already dead and badly burned. Standard protocol dictates that the firemen keep the flames back but try to leave the body in situ to preserve any remaining evidence. Once the fire was extinguished, the local LEOs—the sheriff and a couple of deputies from the Cranford sheriff's office—put in a call to the Georgia Department of Fire Investigation. Everything was photographed before the body was taken to the morgue at Cranford General and ultimately to the medical examiners at the state crime lab."

"And Kathy Vanderbilt did not go to the morgue to identify her husband's body?" I asked, finding that a bit odd from my initial reading. Unless Kathy had somehow identified the body, we wouldn't know for certain that it was Theodore Vanderbilt in the vehicle until after the autopsy. He could have loaned the car to someone else without Kathy's knowledge, or he could have been carjacked.

We couldn't assume anything.

"You saw the photos. There was no point in having her look at the body," Vincent said as he flipped a few pages. "The victim was burned beyond recognition—no clothing survived either—but Kathy was able to identify her husband's wedding band and watch, which he'd been wearing when he left the house, and to confirm that he had been driving the Ford LTD that night."

"Ah, and when did Mrs. Vanderbilt call Americus Mutual about her claim?"

"Thanks to 24/7 claims departments, she made the call fifteen minutes after she'd been notified of the accident."

"That was quick." At least she'd waited those fifteen minutes for the sake of appearance. Can't seem too eager.

Another strike against Kathy.

"The company dispatched"—Vincent paused as he searched the file—"Janice Winder. Given the suspicious circumstances surrounding the discovery of the body and the Cranford sheriff's lack of access to sufficient labs in the area, it didn't take long for the company's fraud department to flag the file, and here we are."

"Yeah, here we are." I glanced sidelong at him.

"You okay with this?" Vincent asked.

After my conversations with Ted and Tripp, I was prepared to defend myself, tell Vincent I was ready to face anything, even the goriest crime scene, but then he gestured between the two of us. He was not asking about my preparedness for the task at hand. "About you and me?" I asked, looking back at the road. "As partners, you mean?"

"Yeah," he affirmed. "Ted sprung it on you pretty quick this morning."

I shook my head. "It was a surprise, yeah, but not necessarily an unpleasant one."

He settled deeper into the seat and closed the file. "Well, I'm glad you didn't turn him down because right now Ted would be sitting there instead of you, and managers and I don't seem to get along."

Shocker. Vincent wasn't the kind of man who could be managed.

I laughed. "I'm sure Ted is glad too. He doesn't seem to be interested in getting his hands dirty."

"Yeah, he's a good guy, but he's more suited to an administrative position than to field work. Besides, I don't trust managers to watch my back," he said.

I nodded, all the while hoping he could trust me to keep him covered. Wasn't I supposed to freeze up now that I'd been traumatized?

God, I sure hoped not.

We lapsed into silence until I turned off at the appropriate exit.

At the intersection, I looked in both directions. To the left were stores and restaurants, and to the right was the more industrial section, with auto body shops and sprawling warehouses.

"Which way?" I asked.

"North," Vincent said with a gesture toward the left.

"Really?" I asked. I had fully expected him to guide us to the industrial section of town, which was usually where the larger fraud cases occurred.

"Ms. Winder is in a grocery store parking lot."

"Dandy," I said, knowing we'd probably all be crammed together in the investigator's car. I hoped she was in a big car at least.

Using his phone's GPS, Vincent directed me through a tangle of streets, and we ended up in front of a large chain grocery store with a gas station in the parking lot.

"She's in a silver Toyota Corolla."

Great. A compact.

We drove around the busy lot for almost five minutes before we found Janice and her Corolla.

I took a spot nearby, and we walked toward the car. Janice hailed us.

Apparently, this wasn't a stealth mission, and we had "law enforcement officer" written all over us.

Or maybe it was just Vincent.

"Hey, y'all," Janice said as she laid aside her camera and smiled up at us from the car. She was a large, dark-skinned woman with the long-lashed eyes that gave her a 1950s movie star aura.

I showed her my badge and leaned in to shake hands. "Special Agent Julia Jackson." I nodded my head to the right. "Special Agent Mark Vincent."

"I'm so glad you picked today to come out here. I was dying of boredom. These stakeouts can take forever." Janice hit the automatic door locks and said, "Hop in so we can talk while I watch."

I went around the car and took the passenger seat while Vincent wedged himself in back. For a surveillance car, it was pretty clean, with only a few snack food wrappers and Coke bottles to be seen and, fortunately, no odor at all.

I turned sideways in my seat so I could see both Janice and Vincent.

"Who are you surveilling?" he asked.

"Chad Jevons. Employee at the Olde Time Soda Company, a bottling plant east on I-16. He's on worker's comp, but we've gotten reports that he's employed unofficially and being paid under the table at that gas station." She pointed across the lot at a small no-name brand gas dispensary. "I've already gotten a photo of him working the counter, but I'd also need a shot of him doing some kind of physical labor that proves he's faking his injuries."

"You're not worried about being in such an exposed position?" Vincent paused and looked around as if he suspected snipers were lurking behind a nearby minivan.

I looked at the mothers and children shopping at this time of day and laughed. Clearly, they were all armed enemy combatants.

I rolled my eyes at Vincent. Apparently, he had spent a little too much time on protection details in war zones.

Janice echoed my thoughts. "You kidding me? No one has given me a second look. Hell, I bought a bottle of Coke from Chad himself to get the first photo. I'm not dealing with a genius here." She picked up the camera that had been sitting in her lap and angled herself back toward the gas station. "Now, you're here to talk about that car fire in Cranford County, right?"

"Right," Vincent said from the back seat where he was situated in such a cramped position that his knees were nearly folded up to his chest. "We read the preliminary report and requested copies of all the Americus files, but we haven't heard back."

There was Vincent being polite and not repeating his earlier assertion that the company was full of jackasses.

"And," I said with an arched brow at Vincent, "we wanted to come out and get the full story in person."

"Yeah, those boys at the home office are having computer problems," Janice explained. "Frankly, it's been a relief. No email for days." Then she turned to me and added, "The full story ain't much to tell. The claim smelled funny from the get-go."

"Why was that?" I asked.

"First red flag? Timing. Survivors don't usually call until the death certificate is in hand. And they don't threaten the customer service rep when they make their claim."

"She threatened someone? How?" Vincent asked.

"I believe the gist of it was that she wanted her money, and she wanted it yesterday. Didn't want to wait on any death certificate, and she'd come get the cash herself if necessary."

Lovely, I thought. Kathy Vanderbilt sounded like quite a classy lady.

"The second red flag?" I prompted.

"Once I read the police report and contacted the arson investigator and the volunteers who were first on the scene, I suspected this claim was going to turn into more than I could handle. When I met the coroner at the morgue to see the body, I was sure."

"Why was that?" I asked, now watching the gas station along with Janice, hoping to catch sight of this guy Chad.

I guess surveillance had become a habit.

"The Cranford coroner said he couldn't use fingerprints to ID the body, and he couldn't find a cause of death without a full autopsy. And add to that the whole accident scene." Janice looked between us and explained, "If you take the body out of the scenario, it was a textbook car arson. Seen 'em a thousand times. Flames in the passenger area, nine times out of ten, some joker is trying to dispose of his vehicle. Maybe he's behind on his payments and wants them to go away or he needs to make a quick buck off the vehicle by stripping and burning it. That's Claims Adjusting 101."

"But there's no crappier car than a 1986 Ford LTD," Vincent said. "This probably wasn't done for the auto insurance payout."

"You're not kidding," I said, looking away from the gas station and refocusing on Janice. "They probably wouldn't even bother having comprehensive or collision coverage."

"So there's only one chance in ten that the fire was a result of the accident," she continued. "I can handle a staged accident, but I have a very big problem if this was some psycho torching up his buddy. And homicide is someone else's turf."

"Homicide?" Vincent asked abruptly—and maybe a touch too forcefully—from behind me. "What makes you say it was homicide?"

Janice and I both turned to look at Vincent. "Don't get your panties in a wad, Special Agent Vincent," she said. "I'm just speculating."

I lowered my eyebrows at him in the hopes that he would ease up on the tone a bit—Southern ladies do not like to be barked at military style—and he raised one shoulder in an almost sheepish shrug.

Not that he could ever really pull off sheepish. Not with that wolfish look always in his eyes.

"What makes you speculate that it was a homicide?" I asked more gently as Janice and I turned to face the gas station again. "Anything specific? Or just a hunch?"

"A hunch, I suppose you'd call it." She seemed to consider her words and shook her head. "No, it's not even really a hunch. Probably I've just watched too many crime shows on TV is all. Nothing that dramatic happens in real life. But with a life insurance policy that size, well, I wouldn't write off murder as a possibility, even if it is pretty remote."

"Tell us more about the policy on Theodore Vanderbilt," Vincent said. He was still issuing commands, but at least this time his tone held an air of restraint.

Without taking her eyes from the station, Janice reached toward the pocket on the driver's door, pulled out a file folder, and waved it in my general direction. "I made copies of everything we've got. In there, you'll find the original policy, and it's a doozy. Five hundred grand with a double indemnity rider."

Vincent whistled at the figure.

"Yeah," I agreed, flipping the pages of the policy. A double indemnity rider clause had been added to Theodore Vanderbilt's standard life insurance policy that would pay twice the benefit if his death were caused by an accident. This included murder by someone other than, and not in collusion with, the beneficiary of the policy, but it excluded suicide, death caused by the insured's negligence, and death by natural causes.

On its own, the $500,000 life insurance payout was incentive enough to fake a death, but with the double indemnity rider, which would pay a cool million on an accidental death, a whole other world of possibilities opened up.

The beneficiary of the policy—Kathy Vanderbilt, according to the papers in my hand—would collect that sizable sum if her husband's death were ruled accidental or murder and it was proven that she had not been involved.

So it behooved Kathy Vanderbilt for her husband to have perished in a car accident or even through foul play. It behooved her so greatly, in fact, that she had a motive to make her husband's death appear accidental even if he'd died of natural causes or taken his own life.

And as Janice said, it also provided her plenty of motive for murder.

"We're going to need to find out exactly how Mr. Vanderbilt died," I said, voicing my thoughts aloud.

"And that's exactly why I'm glad I'm not a part of that claim anymore," Janice said. "I'm a company fraud inspector, not a detective. The most involved I ever got in the forensics world was the time I sent some washed checks to the questioned documents expert at the state lab. I don't do dead bodies and autopsies." She gestured across the parking lot. "I take pictures of people faking injuries and look at bashed up vehicles now and then. That's all. If something looks like a big case, I send it up the ladder. Company policy."

Conversation lulled, and we all seemed to be looking at the gas station again, hoping Chad the faker would make an appearance to liven up the trip.

A few moments later, I shut the folder and passed it back to Vincent. "Looks like we've got all we need," I said to Janice. "We'll get out of your way."

"No problem, and let me know how the claim turns out. I'll probably still be here waiting for this dude to make a mistake." She sighed. "God, these cases take forever."

I couldn't help but pity Janice as we left. She'd be cooped up in that car for hours, maybe days, waiting for Chad to show that he was perfectly capable of working, despite his claims of injury.

As Vincent and I reached the Explorer, I unlocked the doors but hesitated before getting inside. I looked at Vincent. "Make yourself scarce for a few minutes, would you?" I said. "I'm going to give Janice a hand if I can."

Vincent eyed me curiously but nodded and shut the passenger door without climbing in.

"I'll pick you up here when I'm done."

I hopped in the SUV, cranked it, and drove to the gas station, parking off to the side of the building so that Janice could get a good photograph.

A thrill shot through me at the prospect of this minor deception. I don't know why. I'd done much more dangerous things in my seven years as a cop. This should hardly register on my thrill meter, but it did in a nostalgic kind of way. It was fun, like going back to my childhood and playing kickball. Sure, I'd played more challenging games as an adult, but there was something about going back to the basics.

As I walked across the parking lot to the convenience store, I adjusted my jacket, making sure that my gun and badge were covered, and I paused at the glass door to check my reflection. With my DOI paraphernalia out of sight, I looked pretty much like any other Southern businesswoman, except my hair was a little less sculpted and I wasn't wearing nearly as much makeup. Although I didn't go so far as to break my mother's hard-and-fast rule about never leaving the house without "putting my face on," I'd given up on trying to be a cop and attain true Southern belle style long ago. I kept things simple, and that's how I planned to play this little con on Chad the faker.

I spotted Chad—or the man I assumed was Chad based on the fact that he was the only employee in sight—sitting behind the counter on a stool and watching a game show on a small black-and-white TV. He looked like the kind of guy who'd gotten distracted by booze, cigarettes, and perhaps drugs in his early years. His face wasn't sad exactly, but his unfocused gaze hinted that he liked to float through life without much direction or ambition.

Sadly, I was familiar with that look.

But that was neither here nor there. My job was to motivate him properly.

I glanced around, assessing, and smiled when I saw a large display of bottled water. Shrink-wrapped cases were stacked in the back corner of the store, and with twenty-four bottles per case, they looked heavy.

Plus, they were on sale.

Deception and a deal. Couldn't beat it.

I walked to the display, leaned down, and hefted one case, making a great pretense of struggling to the counter under its supposed weight. Actually, it wasn't a complete act. My wounded arm was still gaining strength after the shooting, and putting too much strain on it didn't feel so great.

I dropped the first case in front of the register and leaned over it, making sure to give a little sigh of distress.

Chad turned away from the TV, and his expression transformed from annoyance to amusement as he looked from the case of water to me.

I definitely had his attention.

"Whew!" I said with a giggle. "That's heavy."

"Yes, ma'am," Chad said. "Water weighs more than you think."

"Mind if I leave it here while I get a few more?"

"No, ma'am. You leave anything here you'd like," he said to my chest.

I smiled and batted my eyelashes brainlessly and then managed to make two more similar trips. Chad watched me all the way.

"That all?" he asked me over the stack of three cases of water as he rang up my selections.

"Yeah," I said, pouting as I handed him my credit card. "I don't know how I'm going to get all this in my SUV, though. That wore me out!"

"Aw," he said, leaning over the counter toward me and winking. "I can give you a hand…with anything you'd like."

I squelched a grimace as Chad came around the counter, hefted all three cases of water at once, and followed me out the door.

"Which way?" he asked over the water.

"Over here," I said as I led him to my SUV and hit the door locks.

I didn't open the lift gate for him, hoping he'd give it a try. That would make an excellent photo op.

Without a single wince of pain, Chad the faker balanced the water in his right arm and yanked the door latch with great aplomb.

Seriously, it was just too easy.

This guy was perfectly capable of returning to work, I thought, as he dropped the cases of water in the cargo area, slammed the lift gate, and leaned against it.

"You havin' a party or something?"

"Nope," I said, stepping around him to the driver's seat and rubbing away the pain in my left arm. "I'm just helping out a friend."

"Your friend must be really thirsty," Chad said.

"Nah," I said and then added cryptically, "she just really wanted to go home."

I shut my door and cranked the engine, leaving Chad the faker shrugging behind me.

Vincent was waiting where I'd left him, and when I pulled beside him and opened the window, he smiled as I leaned over to talk to him.

"Looks like Janice got what she needed," Vincent said, gesturing to the empty spot where her Corolla had been parked. "You probably saved her a couple days of surveillance."

I grinned at Vincent as I popped the locks on the SUV. "If only all insurance investigations could be wrapped up that easily...."

Five

"Want to head to Cranford County?" I asked as Vincent opened the passenger door. "That will give us a good look both at the incident itself and at the insurance repercussions it caused."

He slid onto the leather seat and slammed the door behind him, and just watching him made me conscious of the throbbing in my arm. With the water-bottle scam and the hours of driving, I'd probably pushed my injury too hard today, and I wasn't done yet. Before pulling out of the lot, I groped in the back seat for my bag. I was totally game for hitting the fire scene, but there was no need for me to be in pain.

I popped two pills of ibuprofen and realized I probably should have been subtler. Vincent was studying me with a wrinkle of concern between his eyes.

"What?" I asked, hating my defensive tone.

"You're hurting," he said. "Admit it."

I considered lying, but I figured it was useless. He'd caught me fair and square. There was no point in pretending. "Well, I was shot. I'll be fine as soon as these kick in." I jiggled the pill bottle at him before dropping it back into my bag.

"Yeah," Vincent said, his voice laced with a healthy dose of skepticism. He checked his watch. "It's after five already. You'd tell me if you needed a break, right?"

No, I thought.

"Of course," I said.

"Humph," Vincent said as if he didn't believe me, and I felt a twinge of guilt. "Look. I can read you pretty clearly. Your jaw is clenched, and there's tension in your shoulders. If we're going to be partners, we've got to be honest with each other. At least about stuff like this."

"Humph," I echoed.

"Don't worry," he assured me. "I don't expect to hear all your dirty little secrets." Then he winked and added, "But I wouldn't stop you if you have anything to confess."

Vincent was leaning toward me with a mixture of concern and amusement on his face, and I smiled at him despite myself. He had a point. We were partners, and we were supposed to be watching each other's backs. We were supposed to protect each other, and that was more difficult if one of us was impaired.

But I was not impaired. I was sore.

I told him so and added, "I'm fine to walk the fire scene if you are."

"Fine by me," he said, still looking skeptical.

To put an end to the discussion, I threw the SUV into gear and left the parking lot. Once I was back on the road, I decided to change the subject and ask for some honesty of my own. And I wasn't going to mince words. "So on the topic of confessions: what made you request a transfer to Mercer?"

I could feel him looking at me, possibly searching for something in my expression, but I kept my eyes on the road.

"Justin," Vincent said. "He spent a lot of time at the lake with me, decided he liked it, and now he's taking up space in the guest room permanently."

I looked at him now and gave him a wide smile. I didn't have all the details, but I knew he was trying desperately to form a relationship with his son. "That's great, Mark," I said, meaning it. "I'm really happy for you both."

Vincent's blank expression seemed to falter a bit when I used his first name. I'd said it without thinking, but now it felt a bit like I'd seen him in his underwear. And no matter how appealing that image might be, it seemed too intimate for partners who most often used each other's last names.

I looked back at the road.

Before either of us could say another word, my phone trilled and I grabbed it from the cup holder, eager for a distraction from the conversation.

My mother.

Not the distraction I'd hoped for, but I'd take it.

Maybe I'd get lucky. Maybe she was calling to find out how I was feeling after my first day back at work. I had been shot in the arm, after all. Checking up on me would be a nice, normal, motherly thing to do, but the days of my mother being nice and normal were long since over, and I had no such luck.

"Hey, Mom," I said in a fake cheery voice as I shrugged an apology to Vincent.

"Oh my God," my mother said, clearly panicked, "you've got to get downtown now. Your sister's had an accident."

"Had an accident?" I repeated, not comprehending what she meant. I clicked the volume button on my phone up a few notches. "She was in a car accident?"

"Yes, an accident, but not in her car...." My mother's voice trailed off into silence, and I knew she was crying. My chest tightened as I listened, and I could feel Vincent looking at me, curious. "She fell. She's at the Mercer Med Center. They say she needs emergency surgery right away!"

"Fell?" I repeated, not sure how a simple fall could result in such a serious injury. "Emergency surgery?"

"Yes, fell," my mother explained. "Down some stairs at that bar downtown. You know the one where the musicians used to hang out in the seventies."

I knew the one. And it was on the tip of my tongue to ask what in the world my sister had been doing in a bar before the end of a workday, but the sad truth was that I already knew.

My sister was an alcoholic, and no matter what I did, I could never manage to disentangle myself from her chaotic life. I tried not to be an enabler, but that was easier said than done. I managed to stop sending her money, I didn't give her a comfy place to live, and I tried not to get my hopes up every time she had a good day. But I had vowed to do one thing for Tricia, and that was to bring her rapist—the man who had begun her downward spiral—to justice.

Beyond that, I saw her at our family dinner each Sunday—well, family dinner minus my father—and generally tried to keep myself from getting sucked into her drama.

But I knew I couldn't stay away. Tricia was hurt and needed surgery. I had to go to her. "I'll be there as soon as I can," I said into the phone and then disconnected.

With a quick glance at Vincent, I explained what had happened. "I've got to get to the hospital. Find out what's going on. Let's skip Cranford until tomorrow when we've got our meeting with Eva."

Vincent nodded and seemed to be waiting for me to say something else, explain what was going on, but I didn't.

My mind was already playing over the possible reasons my sister required surgery. She could have hit her head, broken a leg, or sustained internal injuries. The jitters took a firm hold of me by the time I dropped Vincent at the DOI and arrived at Mercer Med. I rushed into the emergency room, convinced that Tricia was at death's door, and went straight to the front desk.

"Tricia Jackson," I said between gulping breaths.

The woman seated there, a middle-aged Latina wearing muted green scrubs and an impassive expression, turned her unconcerned eyes on me and said, "Let me check the computer." She tapped deliberately at the keys with long, manicured nails. "She's in surgery," she informed me with her eyes still on the screen.

Exasperated, I plunked both elbows on the tall counter in front of me. "Okay," I said, drawing out the word. "What's being operated on exactly? What injuries did she sustain? What's her prognosis?"

The woman looked at me from under her brows, and I could tell by her expression that she was about to tell me to calm down—or stick it—when I heard my mother's voice behind me. "Baby girl, over here."

I turned and found my mother leaning out of a waiting area. She looked as she always did—perfectly dressed in a boxy suit from the 1990s and poufy sandy blond bangs—but as usual, her pulled-together—if out-of-date—clothing was an illusion. Her wide, watery eyes told the true story.

I walked up, trying to appear calm and composed, and gave my mom a big hug. She clung to me for a long time, and I let her, even though she was crushing my injured arm and I really wanted to hear what was going on.

"Oh, I'm so glad you're here," my mother said as she let go of me.

"I am too, Mom," I said, even though I wished with every fiber of my being that this weren't happening right now. Or ever.

My mother led me to a vacant corner of the sterile, beige waiting area, and I watched as she wiped the tears from her eyes with her fingertips.

"Mom," I said gently, trying to keep her in a serene frame of mind while simultaneously extracting information from her. "Can you tell me what is going on? Why does Tricia need surgery?"

"She fell down some stairs at that bar, and her ankle...." She paused to wipe her eyes again. "Her ankle was all messed up."

I looked at her. "All messed up? What does that mean? What did the doctor say?"

"It's broken. It looks horrible, all swollen and blue. They said the fracture was cutting off a blood vessel, and if she hadn't come in right away like she did, she could have lost her foot—" My mother's voice broke in a pitiful strangled sound that was somehow echoed by the strangled feeling around my heart.

We gathered ourselves for a moment, and then my mother continued. "They sent me out here to wait. The surgery should be starting any minute now."

I let out a big breath and tried to think logically about Tricia's injury. No head wounds or broken back. No fractured vertebra. No brain swelling.

It was just an ankle, and the doctors said she'd come to the hospital in time to save her foot.

Relieved, I decided it was time to get a few more details about the situation. "When did all this happen?"

"Late this afternoon. Tricia called me around five from the emergency room, and she was crying and in awful pain."

And she was already drunk by 5 PM.

"She spent the whole afternoon at the bar?" I asked. I hadn't meant to sound so disappointed, but that's how it came out.

My mother brushed her bangs out of her narrowed eyes. "So she was at a bar today," she said with a huff. She dropped her voice and added, "Do we have to talk about this now?"

"Was she drunk?" I asked, ignoring her wish to leave it alone. I couldn't skip the fact that my sister, who was supposedly working at a salon with the intention of doing hair for a living in the future, was drinking in the middle of a workday.

"No!" my mother whispered. "She was just a bit tipsy."

I wanted to roll my eyes, but I knew that my mother, bless her, wanted to help Tricia, and she seemed to think the best way to do that was to put a happy face on the problem. No matter how often my sister ended up sloshed and pulled over for DWI, my mother always believed it was a gross injustice. Her daughter was a good girl. A Southern lady doesn't get drunk.

She was just like any other mother, I guessed. She wanted to see the good in her children, and she didn't want to see them hurting.

Too bad it never seemed to pan out for her.

By eight o'clock, the late-summer sky was nearly dark, and Tricia was still in surgery. My mother and I had heard nothing from the doctors yet, and even though we tried to distract ourselves with hospital cafeteria food, it did no good.

We just sat there together, making me even more aware of the one who was missing from the picture: my father. I knew my mother wouldn't like it, but I had to ask. "Have you called Dad?"

My mother looked away, giving me a good view of the back of her head. "No."

I studied her hair as if it might reveal her thoughts. I understood why she hadn't called. After Tricia's rape, my father had left. It was as simple as that.

Neither my mother nor my father handled Tricia's rape well at all. My father turned angry and quiet, while my mother became an empty socialite intent on staying in the before time. The before-rape time. She clung to the past, while my father shook it off with a surprising vehemence.

He filed for divorce, got a house about half an hour south of Mercer, and kept mostly to himself. He'd show up now and again when we needed his help, but that was it. He had come to visit me after the shooting, and he took care of removing all traces of that awful night from my house, but that was the first time he'd come for me and not my sister.

I wished it weren't that way. Like my mom, I wished we could go back to the past and have a full family Sunday meal. Have a normal family life.

That would never happen again, but it still wasn't right for my mother to keep important information from him. My father deserved to know his daughter was in the hospital.

I stood up. "I'll call him."

My mother looked as if she wanted to protest, but she remained silent and only nodded.

I stepped into the hallway to make the call, and my father answered on the third ring.

"Hey, girl," he said by way of greeting. That was as affectionate as my dad's nicknames ever got, but I didn't mind. I knew that somewhere in there he cared about me.

"Hey, Dad." I paused, trying to figure out how best to break the news of Tricia's accident, and decided to be blunt. That was my father's usual MO, so he'd probably appreciate it. "Mom and I are at the Mercer Med Center with Tricia. She broke her ankle and is in surgery."

For a moment, he didn't speak, and I could imagine how his face had gone impassive and hard like it always did in a crisis. "What happened?"

I filled him in on the details, omitting the part about the drinking and the bar, and then told him all I knew about the surgery.

When I finished, there was a long silence on the line. "How is this being paid for?"

I leaned against the hallway wall. I hadn't even considered money. My sister had no health insurance. My mother couldn't afford to pay a premium for her, or she definitely would have. My father, on the other hand, staunchly refused Tricia any sort of financial help, which he considered enabling. And probably rightly so. As for me, I was conflicted. I certainly couldn't afford to pay for her health insurance on my salary, but I often wondered what I would do if I could.

That was irrelevant now.

"I don't know how the hospital will deal with the bill, but they were obligated to help her. The fracture was pressing on a blood vessel. She could have lost her foot."

My father paused again and finally asked, "Do you need me to come?"

This was a tricky question. Did we need him here?

No, I thought, we didn't. If my mother couldn't handle the situation, I knew I could.

But did we want him here?

That was a resounding yes. At least on my part.

Still, knowing it was probably the best decision for both Tricia and my mother's emotional states, I said, "That's okay, Dad. Maybe you can visit after surgery or once she gets home and settled. I'll call you when we know more."

"Good," he said and then added softly, "And if something changes or if something goes wrong, you call me right away. I'll be there."

"I know you will."

We hung up and I lingered in the hall for a moment. I knew I should feel hurt at my father's reluctance to come to the hospital to see to his own child, but I only felt relief. My mother and sister were volatile enough already, and I didn't want to add my father to the mix. I didn't know if I could handle a full-family meltdown right now.

When I returned to the waiting room, I found my mother talking with a man in surgical scrubs. Assuming him to be Tricia's surgeon, I hurried toward them, hoping to hear the details firsthand.

"Oh," my mother said. "Here's Julia, my other daughter. Julia, this is Dr. Janowski, the orthopedic surgeon who operated on Tricia."

Tall with dark features, Dr. Janowski had a young face, a warm smile, and a firm handshake. "Pleasure," he said.

"How's my sister?" I asked without preamble.

"Miss Jackson came through the surgery just fine," he said, "but we did have to take a few precautions to minimize the possibility of complications."

I blinked at him. "Complications?"

"I'll be happy to explain everything." He gestured to a door at the far end of the waiting room. "Let's speak privately."

I nodded, slightly concerned at the sudden need for seclusion, but my mother and I followed Dr. Janowski to the door, which opened into a small room with four chairs, a side table and lamp, and a box of tissues.

That box of tissues set off all my warning bells.

Dr. Janowski closed the door and then turned to face us. "First, let me assure you that we were able to repair the blood vessel, and Miss Jackson's foot is receiving normal blood flow."

I felt myself release the breath I'd been holding, and my mother flopped into a chair, relief written plainly on her features.

Then Dr. Janowski continued, "X-rays revealed that Miss Jackson suffered a trimalleolar fracture and a tibial plafond fracture." I stared at the doctor, waiting for the translation from medical jargon to plain English. He smiled and explained, "She broke three bones in her ankle where the tibia connects to the foot, and I was able to repair it, using a metal rod and screws."

I considered his words for a moment. "That sounds like an awful lot of damage for a fall down a few stairs," I said.

"Your sister's injuries were exacerbated by the condition of her bones."

My mother looked horrified, and her hands flew to her mouth in a gesture that would have been comical if it had been happening anywhere else but here. "But I gave her plenty of milk as a child," she protested.

Dr. Janowski looked momentarily surprised, but he managed to conceal it well. "I'm sure you did, but I'm afraid her condition is caused by too much of another, adult beverage and not from a lack of milk in her developmental years."

I watched as my mother's face went completely blank. Denial time.

Well, I wasn't joining in.

"Tricia is an alcoholic," I said flatly. My mother seemed ready to protest again, but I held up a hand and continued, "What does that have to do with her bones?"

"Alcohol inhibits calcium absorption, and we often see signs of malnutrition in heavy drinkers." Looking at my mother, whose face had turned white, Dr. Janowski quickly moved on. Smart choice. "The presence of alcohol in the bloodstream also changes the way we prep a patient for surgery, just to be safe. As a precaution, we intubated her to help her breathe, so when you see her in a few moments, she'll be in the intensive care unit on a respirator."

"ICU? A respirator?" my mother said as shock registered in her wide blue eyes. "For ankle surgery?"

"Yes, ma'am. As I said, it was a precaution, and she'll have the best respiratory therapists working with her to help her get back to normal soon."

Jesus, I thought. Could this get any worse?

As is often the case, the answer to that question was yes.

Dr. Janowski turned to me. "Because your sister has a long-term history of alcohol use, we'll also be watching for withdrawal symptoms and delirium tremens. I'll order some medication to help ease the transition, but she'll still need to be monitored closely."

Great, I thought. This was going to be a disaster.

Six

He remembered them all. Maybe not their names, but definitely the important things like how the life had left their bodies, the moment he had closed their eyes with his own fingertips, the dull thud of their lifeless bodies hitting the earth.

No, he'd never forget them. Not one. Somehow, these people seemed like family. He sneered at the thought. Yeah, like family. He'd treated them all just the way his family had always treated him. He shuffled them right out of his way and dumped them out here where no one would ever think of them again.

No one would remember but him.

In his experience, family was always the first to forget. The first to look at you and not really see you. The first to push and push until something snapped inside.

He remembered the exact moment something snapped in him, and that was years ago when he was just a little thing.

Early on, his daddy had started taking him in the woods with a rifle, telling him to take a shot at anything that moved. "Toughening you up": that's what his daddy had told him he was doing. He didn't want a wimp for a son. No, he wanted a son who could look death in the face and feel nothing.

Absolutely nothing.

Turns out that making your eight-year-old son slaughter a goat will do the trick. It had toughened him up right quick.

His eyes slipped shut as he recalled the event as if it had just happened, and it wasn't the look of innocence in the goat's brown eyes as he pulled the trigger that he remembered the most.

No, it was the look of giddy pleasure on his father's face as he'd forced his son to watch him field strip the critter afterward. To prepare him for the future, he'd said. His old man had explained each stroke of the knife over the still-warm flesh and seemed to revel in the blood that began to cover his hands and shirtsleeves. His daddy had wielded that gleaming blade like a madman and mocked his son for the tears that streaked down his cheeks. Then he'd laughed as he'd tossed the mutilated body into a trashcan and told the boy to clean up the rest of the mess.

From that day forward, he'd hated two things more than anything else in the world: his father and the darkness his father had unleashed within him.

To this day, he hadn't been able to get away from his father or that blood-stained darkness.

And he'd never killed anything with that rifle since.

But he still used the knife—that shining, dangerous, beautiful knife.

SEVEN

I jolted awake around 6 AM and found myself in my own bed with Maxwell curled in a ball at my hip. He eyed me with his silent green gaze as if to tell me to settle down and go back to sleep.

I reached down to scratch his head and said, "Oh, I'm sorry, am I disturbing your slumber?"

Maxwell turned away, burrowing his head back into my side.

Cats had it so easy.

The events of their lives didn't cause them to lose any sleep. They seemed perfectly content with any eventuality—save a lack of tuna—and were able to keep their sleep schedules on track.

Me? I wasn't going back to sleep anytime soon, so I got up and padded down to the kitchen to start coffee. Soon the rich, dark aroma filled my house, and a warm cup steamed in my hands.

I had plenty of time to get ready for the day, so I didn't rush. I considered turning on the TV for company, but after flipping through a few inane morning talk shows, I decided against it. Who could stand that level of saccharine cheer so early in the morning?

I winced. Not me.

Instead, I peeked out my front window in the hopes that Helena St. John's light might be on. She was often up at this hour with baby Violet.

I peered across the street through the morning mist. Helena's house was the image of the quintessential American dream: a white Cape Cod-style structure with a big oak tree in the front yard. The only thing missing was the white picket fence.

And inside was Helena, my best friend who was in the process of living her dream. She had a successful law career, a beautiful daughter, and a husband who adored them both.

It's not that I envied her life exactly.

No, my dreams were very different. Undefined, actually.

I envied that she knew what she wanted in life.

Aside from catching my sister's rapist, I wasn't sure what I wanted.

An image of Vincent flashed in my mind, and I squelched it immediately.

Those types of thoughts would not do.

Instead of ruminating on my life situation, I returned to the kitchen, poured two travel mugs of coffee, and went across the street.

I tapped softly on Helena's front door. If no one was up and the light had been left on by accident, I didn't want to disturb them, but as I'd hoped, Helena opened the door with Violet on her hip. She looked me up and down, rolled her eyes at the MPD t-shirt and sweats I'd slept in, noticed the coffee, and said, "Oh girl! You must have read my mind. I'm dying for coffee. Tim's still in bed, so he's no use, and someone"—she looked pointedly at her daughter—"demanded her breakfast first. Now get yourself in here."

I smiled, glad she was as eager to see me as I was to see her. Somehow we managed to exchange burdens. She took the coffee, and I got a squirming baby.

"Hey, Miss Violet," I cooed at her as I smoothed the pink floral t-shirt across her tummy. "What are you up to today?"

"We've been eating breakfast, and later we'll be helping Mommy organize her home office," Helena said for her daughter. "But now we're ready for playpen time."

I smiled. "Let me get her settled. You do what you need to do."

"Deal," Helena said. "Just make sure she has her purple elephant toy. It's her favorite."

I headed back to Violet's nursery, found the stuffed elephant, and returned to the breakfast room, where the playpen was set up in the corner.

Expecting the baby to object when I put her down, I lowered her slowly and then handed her the elephant. Violet gave me a large, watery smile and took the toy in her chubby fingers.

"Violet's such a good girl," I said. "Babies don't normally play so well on their own."

Helena nodded. "It's Tim's genes, I'm sure. To hear my mother tell it, I was never able to get along like that at her age."

"Tricia didn't like to play alone either," I said as Helena directed me to a vacant chair at her kitchen table. "Me, I didn't mind."

"How is Tricia?" Helena asked.

I could tell she was trying to be careful. Even though I hadn't shared the full history of my family with her, she knew enough to comprehend that I never really wanted to talk about my sister.

"Not so well, actually," I said, keeping my eyes focused on my coffee mug. "She's in the hospital recovering from a broken ankle."

"Good lord," Helena exclaimed. "I hate to hear that. She just can't catch a break, and I sure wish something would happen to help that girl."

I couldn't agree more with what Helena said. I did wish something would happen for Tricia, but I didn't think anything, not even a conviction for the man who raped her, was capable of yanking her out of the downward spiral her life had become.

We lapsed into thoughtful silence, which I broke by asking, "Organizing your office, huh?"

"Yeah." She leaned forward, her almond-shaped eyes conspiratorial and whispered, "I haven't told anyone yet, except Violet and Tim, but now that Violet's a bit older, I'm starting a new job on Wednesday!"

In my excitement on her behalf, I leaned forward too. "Really? Where?"

"The US attorney's office," she said, still whispering as if the house might have been bugged by rival lawyers.

"Wow! That's great news!" I said, continually amazed at my best friend and her meteoric rise in the law world. I was also truly happy for her. The US attorney's office was a big step up, and one that she deserved.

"That's right," she said as she preened just a little. "You're looking at the newest assistant US attorney for Middle Georgia. I still can't believe it! I'll be working downtown, right between the MPD station and the courthouse."

"No one deserves it more than you, Hels. You're a hard worker and a great attorney." I smiled at her broadly. "Now, tell me everything."

Helena chronicled the process that led to the job offer, but then she paused, coffee midair, and a shadow passed across her features. "Of course," she said finally, "I wouldn't trade this year with Violet for all the high-profile criminal trials in the world, but I've been itching to get back in the courtroom."

"I can understand that," I said, nodding in what I hoped was an encouraging manner.

"I didn't. Not at first," she confessed, eyes wide and moist. "I felt awful for wanting to go back to work, especially at such a time-consuming job. I love my little girl, and the last thing I want is for her to feel as if I abandoned her."

I picked up my mug and took a long sip while trying to find the words to express my thoughts on this subject. I mean, I had plenty of mommy issues myself, so I could certainly understand Helena's worry. But this was a much different situation from my family's craziness.

My own mother had not abandoned me in any sort of traditional sense. She hadn't thrown herself into a career or vanished completely, but since Tricia's rape, she was not the same person. She seemed to have turned off the mothering part of her life, at least when it came to me, and I had become the parent.

I put down my cup and said with firmness, "To be perfectly clear, you aren't abandoning Violet. You know that, right?"

I looked at her hard, as if my eyes could force logic into her head.

If only that worked, my job at the DOI would be a lot easier. People would confess their fraud in less than five minutes.

"Yeah," Helena said with a longing glance at Violet, who was rolling on the playpen floor and chewing on the stuffed elephant's trunk. "I know that, and it's not as if a stranger will be taking care of her. Tim's momma will be watching her during the day. But I just don't want to miss anything. Violet won't be a baby forever."

"No," I agreed, "she won't. But you know you can be in the house all the time and still miss things. Important things."

"That doesn't make me feel any better!" Helena said with a laugh.

I rolled my eyes. "You know what I mean. No human being can be there for every single solitary event in their child's life. That's just not how it works." I studied her, making sure she understood what I meant before I continued. "You're trying to find a way to balance your role as a mother with your career as a lawyer. And maybe at first you'll mess up and end up overdoing one or the other, but eventually, you'll reach equilibrium. And being a happy, fulfilled person is a good example for Violet to follow."

I spoke as if I had experience in that department. The sad truth was that I had been trying to reach a balance between my personal desires and my quest for justice my whole life. I certainly hadn't figured it out, but I truly did believe that one day, I would reach equilibrium.

Helena would have it figured out before I would.

We sat in silence for a while—I guess we were both contemplating balance—and then Helena stood, walked to my side of the kitchen table, and threw an arm around me. "See, this is why I keep you around."

I laughed. "I only speak the truth. You're a great mom, and you'll be a topnotch US attorney."

Helena pulled back and returned to her seat.

"I'm glad you're feeling so confident about my new job because I'm nervous about going back to work full-time."

I was about to tell her she was being silly, but she interrupted me.

"I know it seems ridiculous, but I can't help it. I've been out of the courtroom a long time. I need a little confidence booster."

"Like what?" I asked.

"A new wardrobe. Hey, why don't we go shopping Sunday?" She looked me over pointedly, her eyes raking down my ugly gray t-shirt.

I was tempted to demur—I wasn't big on shopping—but Helena's hopeful expression changed my mind. This was what friends did for one another. They went shopping together and reminded each other that it wasn't the clothes that provided confidence but the attitude of the person who wore them.

Shopping was something I could do. It was a whole lot easier than catching criminals.

"Sounds fun," I said, mostly meaning it.

"Great!"

We sat back to finish our coffee and finalize our plans until I had to get ready for work. Vincent and I had a busy day ahead in Cranford County.

Eight

Vincent and I met at the DOI, and after a quick drive to Cranford County, I was pulling the SUV to the shoulder of Highway 403, where a couple of sheriff's department cruisers, a pickup, and a white van with emergency light bars and the Georgia Department of Fire Investigation logo were already parked.

"We're fortunate that the Department of Fire Investigation was called in right away, and Eva is one of the best arson investigators on staff," I said to Vincent as I hopped out of the Explorer.

Two young Cranford deputies were lingering on the periphery of the fire scene—obviously having pulled guard duty—and I nodded to them in greeting as I walked straight over to DFI investigator Eva Sinclair, whom I'd met on numerous occasions.

Fraudsters were always setting stuff on fire, so the DOI and the DFI often worked in tandem on these types of cases. In addition, city officials and sheriffs can request state arson investigators, and though they don't ordinarily investigate isolated vehicle fires, the presence of a body made this case a high priority, especially since Cranford County was not equipped to handle such an inquiry.

Fire was the quickest way to destroy evidence, or so criminals thought, but Eva was good, and she'd racked up a record number of successful prosecutions.

I was glad to see her.

With a last name like Sinclair, Eva should have been born with red hair and a flaming temper to match, but she had nothing of the stereotypical Scottish appearance.

Instead, she was more like a Nordic goddess: tall, blond, and composed. Wearing a pair of black cargo pants, military-style boots, and a tan polo shirt with the DFI logo embroidered on the front, she was the picture of calm efficiency as she greeted me. I wouldn't call her particularly beautiful, but she radiated a certain power that I admired, and the two men beside her were obviously under her spell already.

"Hey, Eva," I said, extending my hand for a quick shake. "How's it going?"

"Oh, you know," she said, gesturing around at the pine-tree-lined street with the clipboard she held. "Fun, fun, fun in exotic locations. Have you met Sheriff Harper and Fred Thomas of the volunteer fire department?"

I shook the sheriff's hand and then greeted Fred, who I knew from the reports as one of the firemen who'd extinguished the blaze. He owned the Bait and Tackle, a nearby hunting and fishing supply store.

I introduced Vincent, and after everyone exchanged the obligatory salutations, we gathered in front of the taped-off fire scene, taking in the carnage that used to be a Ford LTD.

"Well," Vincent said, deadpan, "we can definitively rule out an auto insurance claim as the motive. This car's Blue Book value couldn't have been more than five hundred bucks."

"I think you're being generous," I said with a laugh. "Blue Book was probably two-fifty, tops. But maybe he could get five if he sold it for scrap."

Vincent grinned at me and then turned back to the car. He ran a hand from his chin to his cheekbone, and I swear I could hear the sound of his stubble scratching against his palm as he studied the scene.

The LTD was scorched to say the least. All the windows were completely gone, and tiny rectangular cubes of shattered safety glass littered the ground around the vehicle. Paint had burned off sections of the side panels, and the whole vehicle sat unevenly, probably because the tires had not sustained consistent damage at all four corners.

We walked toward the perimeter for a closer look. The driver's door was open, revealing what used to be the passenger area. No one was going to be sitting there anytime soon. The seats had been reduced to metal and springs.

All the plastic that had made up the dashboard and door panels had melted into a black ooze, revealing the scorched sheet metal behind it. Part of the steering wheel had melted, and ash and debris were everywhere.

How in the world could a car fire leave that much junk behind? And the smell....

"What's that smell?" Vincent asked as if reading my thoughts.

"Does it smell like barbecue?" Eva asked.

"Yeah, kind of."

Oh, God. I definitely did not want to know what it was.

"That's the odor of burned human remains," Eva said matter-of-factly.

"It smells a lot like smoked pork," Fred affirmed.

"You're kidding," I said, wishing desperately that I hadn't heard that. I might never eat barbecue again.

Ever.

"I wish we were kidding," Eva said, "but humans have a great deal of similarity to pigs, at least when it comes to physical properties."

I looked at the burned-out car and the total destruction before me and thought back to the pictures I'd seen of the body.

Maybe humans were even more like pigs than Eva realized. Only a pig would set out to destroy a body in such a heinous fashion.

That is, if this fire were ruled arson.

I stepped back from the tape where Fred Thomas was subtly ogling Eva as she spoke with Sheriff Harper.

"You were the first responder on the scene?" I asked, pulling his attention away from Eva's backside. Aside from being an obviously classy and discreet person, Fred was short and squatty, but sturdy enough.

"Yes, ma'am," he said, scratching under his baseball cap and leaving the bill tilted up. "Mike Symmes and I took the call around 3 AM."

"Describe the scene when you arrived," Vincent said.

And here is where Fred Thomas confirmed the myth about outdoorsmen and fish stories. He stuck out his chest, which actually did more to display his beer gut than his pecs, and began his embellished tale.

"The LTD was fully involved when we pulled up. Flames were shooting out the windows at least two hundred feet high." We all looked up toward the treetops as if the flames might appear now.

The tallest pines were about half as tall as Fred claimed the flames had been, and none of them showed signs of being singed more than halfway up the trunks.

"Two hundred feet high?" Vincent repeated, eyeing him seriously.

"Well, maybe not that high, but flames were visible not only in the engine compartment but also in the passenger area," Fred said, sobering. "And we were able to see a person in the front seat, so the victim became our first priority."

I nodded, and trying to keep Fred on track, I asked, "Was the victim responsive?"

"Not that we could tell, but at that point, our goal was to get him out of there. We ran a 1-and-3/4-inch hose, and Mike kept the flames off the guy so I could work on extracting him, which is dangerous work." He leaned toward me and waggled his shaggy eyebrows. "Cars don't just explode like they do in the movies, but you've got to be careful of other hazards, like fumes and bumper struts blowing off and taking out a knee. Normally, we keep back from the vehicle until all the flames are extinguished."

"So Mike manned the hose and you approached the vehicle?" I prompted.

"Yes, ma'am. First, Mike washed out the underside of the car to keep flammable fluids from catching and to cool the gas tank. Then I was able to approach as he aimed the stream through the driver's window, which was already open. I was planning to carry the victim a safe distance away and render what aid I could until EMS arrived."

"But that's not what occurred?" I asked.

"No, ma'am. I would have," Fred said, "but the victim was already deceased."

"Even at that point in the fire, you were certain?"

"I don't mean to be crude, ma'am, but once the flames had been knocked down and I got the door open, I saw there wasn't much of him left. I didn't want to risk moving the body, given its condition. When we discover a body in that state, we do our best to preserve what we can by keeping the flames away and leaving the body where it is until EMS or the coroner arrives. Plus, removing a victim from a burning car is dangerous for the fireman."

"So you extinguished the fire?" Vincent prompted.

"Yes, sir, but when the EMS arrived, there was nothing to be done, and soon after the coroner declared him dead."

Sheriff Harper jumped into the narrative here. "At this point, I put a call in to the state arson investigator. We don't see incidents like this much in Cranford—we get more domestic violence calls than anything else—and we don't have the equipment to handle a fire investigation of this scale."

"When did you arrive on the scene?" I asked Sheriff Harper.

"I rolled in while Fred and Mike were knocking down the last of the flames. That was around 3:30 AM."

"Was anyone else present? Any onlookers?" I asked.

"Well, it was late, you know, so the crowd was pretty slim. Luis Pedroza, the man who called 911, was there and also a couple of boys from the volunteer fire department."

"Sometimes the newbies like to come out and watch, so they can learn from us veteran firefighters," Fred interjected.

Vincent's focus remained on the sheriff. "Have you followed up with the witnesses? Canvassed the area?"

"Of course," Sheriff Harper said, turning to Vincent. "I sent a team of deputies out the next morning. They spoke with Mr. Pedroza and the volunteers. Mr. Pedroza said there was no one else around when he came by on his way home from his shift at the diaper plant, and no one passed the site while he was waiting for the fire truck."

"And the volunteers?" I prompted.

"They didn't see nothing but the fire," Fred said. "Trust me. A fireman's first love is the flame."

"Any other witnesses?" Vincent asked, looking down the isolated road.

No cars had passed since we'd arrived, and only a few driveways were visible, but the houses were set a good distance back from the road and tucked behind the pine trees. The vehicle's location was almost totally isolated, so I was guessing the number of possible witnesses would be pretty low.

Sheriff Harper confirmed my suspicions. "I sent the team to the houses adjacent to the fire scene, and they brought back a big fat nothing. Everyone was asleep at that time of night. No one saw the blaze, much less noticed anyone coming or going on the highway."

Eva, who had been riffling through the papers on her clipboard while Vincent and I spoke with the first responders, stepped beside me. "Sheriff Harper requested a state arson investigator at the ungodly hour of 4 AM Saturday morning, and I arrived around 5."

"I thought you were based out of the Atlanta office," I interrupted, confused. "How'd you make it so fast?"

"Oh!" Eva said, smiling at me, her eyelids crinkling so much that her blue eyes almost disappeared. "Didn't I tell you? I've been promoted to lieutenant, and Sophie and I are moving down to the Middle Georgia sector. We're staying at a hotel in downtown Mercer until we can buy a house of our own."

"Congratulations on the promotion," I said as I looked behind me toward Eva's van for Sophie, her accelerant-detecting partner and yellow Labrador retriever. "Speaking of Soph: where is she?" I asked, not seeing her cute face in the window.

Eva glanced over her shoulder. "She's in her crate in the back, probably asleep. She's had a busy couple of days."

"Did she find anything?" Vincent asked, all business as he left our little huddle and began to walk around the vehicle, taking in every detail.

"I'll get to that," Eva said as she shot an eye roll at me. "You investigators are always in a hurry, but you miss things if you rush."

I glared at Vincent with mock ferocity. "Don't rush her."

"Sorry." He held up his hands as if to ward off attack. "I tend to get antsy when a body is involved."

Good point, I thought as I turned to Eva and asked, "What were you able to tell about the body?"

Now I was rushing her too, and Eva laughed at my eager question.

"Not really my department," she said. "You'll have to talk to the Cranford County coroner and state medical examiner about the body. However, we were able to remove most of the remains the first morning, and I understand the body has been transferred to the medical examiner's office."

"Most of the remains were removed?" I repeated. I'd seen the photos, and I knew the body was in poor condition, but there was something disturbing about not being able to sort out body parts from the rest of the fire debris. I looked down at the floor of the LTD and wondered what body parts might still be there.

Eva nodded sadly. "Yes, it's likely there are more human remains in the vehicle, so I've been busy sifting and cataloging. There's still quite a bit to sort through, but already I've uncovered additional fragments—phalanges, that sort of thing—and sent those to the crime lab too. I'm still hoping to find the ignition device in all this mess." She paused and looked us over. "Any more questions before I get on with the story?"

Yup, our interruptions were beginning to annoy her.

"Okay," I said, "message received. Tell us what happened."

"Like I said," she continued deliberately, "I arrived at 5 AM, and Fred, the other local volunteer firemen, and Sheriff Harper had secured the scene and thrown a salvage cover, basically a tarp, over the vehicle. The body was still in the front seat and had not been touched. I began with an examination of the exterior of the vehicle. There were no footprints, but"—she led us toward the back of the cordoned-off area and gestured at the ground—"in the photographs, you'll notice that there seems to have been another vehicle parked here long enough to leave slight depressions in the grass. Of course, you can't tell it now."

Eva pointed at the tires as we followed her to the driver's side. "The LTD appears to have been intact at the time it was burned. The wheels and tires seem to be correct for this make and model, and the lug nuts are all present and tight."

"So they didn't strip the vehicle before it burned?" I asked, wondering if there had been anything on this vehicle worth stripping in the first place.

"It appears not." She nodded toward the center console, which was now a mass of melted plastic. "There's evidence of the radio, and that's usually the first thing removed in those cases."

The hunk of black goop had no resemblance to a radio. I'd have to take her word for it.

"The fire had already popped the windows when the truck arrived, and the doors were unlocked."

I looked at the glass particles on the ground around the LTD. "So you're saying the fire shattered the windows?" I asked skeptically. It sounded so Hollywood.

"Could have, but I can't say for certain."

Vincent and I looked at Eva for further explanation.

"Fire weakens glass by melting it unevenly. In a regular window, it would cause crazing, a complex series of cracks that ultimately results in breakage. You can tell when fire breaks an average window. But tempered glass, which is used in automobiles, fractures into these cubes you see on the ground no matter what breaks it. Hard to tell if it was broken by fire or mechanical means."

"So someone might have broken the windows out?" Vincent asked. "Or at least some of them."

"It's a possibility, but I may not be able to say for sure. As I said, tempered glass can't be reconstructed to discover the reason for breakage," Eva replied as she led us to the front of the LTD. "But I can tell you that the fire did not begin under the hood as a result of any front-end collision."

"We suspected that from the pictures," I said. "Not as much damage in the front as in the passenger area."

"Good eye," Eva responded. "You might make a decent fire investigator someday."

Vincent had been pacing slowly in front of the vehicle, studying every square inch of damage. "How long did the fire burn before it was extinguished?" he asked.

Eva turned to him. "It's impossible to say for certain given all the variables in the fuels present in an automobile, but near as I can tell based on the time of the call and the time the fire was put out, it burned at least twenty minutes."

"Twenty minutes?" I repeated, shocked as I thought back to the pictures. The human remains had been nothing more than a torso, skull, and parts of the left appendages. "That was enough time to cause this much destruction to the vehicle and leave the body in such a condition?"

"Oh, absolutely," Eva said. "With proper ventilation and all this plastic and fabric to burn at high temperatures, the body could have been reduced mostly to bone if it had gone much longer."

I gaped. It was hard to believe a body could be destroyed that fast. If the fireman had arrived much later, we would have had a much more difficult time sorting out what happened.

Vincent did not appear surprised one way or the other as he moved to his next question. "Did the dog find traces of accelerant?"

"Boy, did she!" Eva said with enthusiasm. "Sophie pinpointed several locations, particularly concentrated in the front seat and splashed along the exterior door panels, which accounts for the burned paint. I've already collected some samples to test for specific accelerants, but I'm guessing it'll be good ole gasoline. It's the most common. And I'll most likely find more evidence, such as the source of ignition—a lighter or maybe even part of a matchbook—as I sift."

"So the fire started inside the vehicle," I stated, "and not from a front-end impact as implied by the scene."

"Based on the preliminary evidence, I'd say so." She pointed to the hood. "We investigate from the least burned to the most burned, and here the least burned section is clearly the hood area. The fire spread outward from the passenger area, encountering the firewall at the front and slowing its progress forward, but managing to make it to the gas tank at the rear. Some of the fuel lines failed and leaked gasoline, which ignited under the vehicle."

"So you're confirming arson?" Vincent surmised.

Eva nodded, but her wording was careful. "At this point, I'm going to investigate as though it was an intentional fire."

So if it wasn't an accident, then what were we looking at?

First possibility: Theodore Vanderbilt wanted to commit suicide, but he wanted his wife to receive his life insurance money, and because his policy did not pay out on suicide, he had to make it appear as if he'd died in an accident.

Second possibility: Theodore Vanderbilt had been murdered, and the killer wanted to hide the evidence.

And the obvious corollary: Kathy Vanderbilt had murdered her husband and then burned his body to hide her connection to the crime—and perhaps to make the death appear accidental—so that she could receive a cool million dollars from Americus Mutual.

But could Kathy have pulled that off on her own?

"Has anyone stopped by during the course of your investigation? Any looky-loos?" I asked, wondering if Kathy had an accomplice who couldn't resist a little peek at the carnage he'd caused.

Eva thought back. "We had visits from the claims adjuster from Americus Mutual, who by the way wanted nothing to do with this case once she saw the body and the burn pattern, and a reporter from the *Cranford Gazette*, who was pretty excited to have an actual story to cover. Other than that, we haven't had much traffic."

"When will you remove the vehicle?" Vincent asked, prompting me to look at Sheriff Harper. He'd probably be relieved not to have to send two deputies to guard it all night.

"Soon as I'm done here today, and it'll be a relief to finish sifting and metal detecting in the comfort of my own lab," Eva said with a glance at the two deputies who were watching her as if she were hosting a TV show.

"Keep us apprised of your findings and send us a copy of your final report," Vincent said.

"Certainly," Eva said, "and you keep me updated on what you discover. It could help in my investigation."

We took our leave of Sheriff Harper, Fred, and Eva and returned to my SUV, where we stopped for a moment.

"Nothing about that fire was accidental," I said, realizing that I'd been rubbing my wounded arm unconsciously.

"Agreed," Vincent said.

He was watching me tend my arm, so I dropped it to my side and asked, "But why was it set? And by whom? And what does that mean for Theodore Vanderbilt?" I paused and glanced back at the scene. "We could be looking at a seriously grisly suicide," I said, shuddering at the thought of anyone choosing such a grim way to die.

"Or the cover-up of a suicide so that the double indemnity rider would kick in," Vincent said.

I nodded. "But we could also be looking at murder."

NINE

As the largest town and the county's namesake, Cranford had managed to hang on to some of the amenities necessary to a rural community—grocery store, drugstore, county hospital, and deer processing center. But now its redbrick buildings and quaint architecture stood partially abandoned. The windows that had once displayed the goods that kept the community fed and stocked up on everything from horse feed to pianos were mostly vacant. Strange how this small town was now more of a blank spot in a bustling county.

Fortunately for Vincent and me, there was a restaurant. The food there was pretty darn good, and it was settled fortuitously close to the Eternal Rest Funeral Home, our next destination, where we would meet with the coroner, Morton Ivey.

As we walked together across the street, our appetites satisfied, I mused, "Have you noticed that our investigations seem to take us to the strangest places? Wastewater treatment plant, funeral home…what's next?"

Vincent shrugged. "Maybe one day we'll get lucky enough to be called to some swanky resort on the coast."

"Now that would be nice," I said, picturing Vincent in swim trunks. Quickly I forced myself to think of something else. "Ted would probably take that one for himself."

"Probably." Vincent laughed and then sobered. "But I'd put up a hell of a fight," he added, raking his eyes over me as if he might be thinking of me in a bathing suit too.

Or maybe less than a bathing suit.

Not that it was ever going to happen.

A trip to the coast was a fantasy and nothing more, especially if things panned out as I hoped on the rape investigation. If I had my druthers, I'd learn the name of the rapist quickly, Tripp would arrest him, and he'd be convicted by a jury of his peers and sentenced to rot in prison. Then I'd quit my job at the DOI and do…well…something else.

I didn't exactly know what that might be, but it was damn sure not going to involve visiting funeral homes and wastewater treatment plants on a regular basis.

I turned my mind to the task at hand, pulling open the door of the Eternal Rest Funeral Home and waiting for the musty odor of dust, death, and day-old flowers to assault me.

Why did all funeral homes smell the same?

And why were they always so dimly lit? Death was depressing enough without sucking all the vitamin D from the room.

I squinted into the gloom as Vincent and I headed toward the voices that were coming from somewhere farther inside the building. We discovered three men leaning over a casket in one of the viewing rooms. From the back, the men stood at equal heights and had similar builds, but one had iron gray hair.

"You did a wonderful job on Mr. Perkins," the eldest man said, his voice holding nothing but pride as he clapped one of the younger men on the shoulder. "I couldn't have done it better myself."

"Excuse me," I said softly.

The gray-haired man, whom I assumed was Morton Ivey, turned slowly toward us. If he hadn't been standing in front of a casket, I would have pegged him for a politician or a used-car salesman. His dark pinstriped suit was immaculately pressed, his hair was slicked into a perfect helmet shape, and he offered us an oily smile. But since we had met him over a casket, all I could see when I looked at him was death.

"Ah, are you here for the Perkins viewing?" he asked, striding toward us with a loose-kneed gait.

"No," I said, producing my badge from my belt and holding it out for his perusal. "We're here on behalf of the Georgia Department of Insurance."

"Ah, yes, we have a meeting scheduled." He checked his watch. "I must have lost track of time. I'm Morton Ivey, county coroner and proprietor of this establishment." He paused and then added, "Allow me to introduce my sons. This is Andrew, the acting funeral director here now that I've taken on the coroner duties for the county."

A clean-cut, middle-aged man with a paunch, Andrew reached out to shake my hand.

"Pleasure," I said, but when his hand touched mine I noticed his long, untrimmed fingernails and wanted to recoil.

Not as clean-cut as I'd thought.

"And Calvin," Morton added, "who oversees all the mechanical aspects of the business. He takes care of our machines: hearses, crematory, you name it."

This time, before I offered a shake, I looked at Calvin's hands. The nails were neat but stained with grease. Hardly a surprise if he worked on machinery.

"Pleasure," I said as Calvin looked away shyly.

"Come this way." Morton motioned us forward, leading us deeper into the funeral home. "My own daddy founded Eternal Rest way back in the forties, and I've had the good fortune to turn over many of the duties to my sons." Morton Ivey's pride seemed to shake the hallway.

I didn't know what to say about a successful undertaking business—it just seemed too morbid for someone to be happy over profiting from death—so I kept quiet.

"Andrew followed after his daddy and became an excellent mortician in his own right." Mr. Ivey glanced over his shoulder at me and smiled. "You should see what he can do with a body. We've had more open-casket funerals here since he took over downstairs. He can make a car-wreck victim look like he died peacefully in his sleep."

I acknowledged his words with what I hoped was a smile and not a wince. I don't think Morton intended to sound ghoulish, but that was the result. Apparently, he must have believed my expression because he continued speaking without hesitation. Fortunately for me, he changed topics.

"Calvin has a much more mechanical bent, so his embalming work is not up to our high standards."

"And what do you do here?" Vincent asked as we followed Morton down a narrow hallway to a door marked "private," which opened to the business portion of the funeral home.

"Officially, I'm still the funeral director and will be until I retire, but in actual practice, I'm more of a figurehead now. I've turned the day-to-day operations over to my sons. I keep an office here and only join funeral tasks when the parlor is busy." Morton offered us the guest chairs, and instead of sitting behind his desk, he wheeled his own chair around to join us, making me feel as if he were about to engage in grief counseling.

I had the urge to scoot my chair away from him, but instead I sat up straighter and looked him in the eye.

Vincent was watching him carefully. "You are the county coroner and you own a funeral home in town. Doesn't that constitute a conflict of interests?"

I glanced at Vincent out of the corner of my eye. So much for not putting the witness on the defensive.

And indeed, Morton Ivey appeared slightly taken aback by the question, and though he recovered some of his political pallor, the question seemed to disorder his thoughts just enough. He hesitated, seemed to try to find the right words, and finally managed to say, "It's a perfectly legal arrangement, I assure you." He leaned back and crossed his arms. "We may acquire a large percentage of the county cases, but I always keep my coroner duties completely separate from my work here at Eternal Rest. Unless the family of the deceased chooses to entrust us with the final arrangements for their loved one, I don't even mention county cases to my sons. I'm very discreet."

I wondered how many families didn't choose to use Eternal Rest, given that it was one of the few funeral homes in the county, but I didn't ask because Morton leaned forward and posed his own question. "Now, what's this about? I've never even heard of the Georgia Department of Insurance, much less had a visit from two agents."

"This is in regard to one of your coroner cases," I said and then went on to explain the large life insurance policy, Kathy Vanderbilt's suspiciously fast claim, and our involvement in the case.

Vincent cut right to the heart of the matter. "We're here to find out what you can tell us about the body removed from the LTD."

"Ah," he said. "Unfortunately, I can't tell you much. I'm afraid we don't have the equipment here to perform a full, scientific autopsy. We get so few suspicious death cases here in Cranford County that my role is usually limited to confirming medical death and signing the certificate. Sometimes I take fingerprints to identify a body, but that's rare, and of course, in this case, it wasn't possible."

"Why not?" I asked.

"No fingers, no fingerprints," he said. "In fact, the right side of the body sustained so much damage that the fingers were no longer attached. The remaining digits were reduced almost to bone."

"Were you able to discern any damage that might not have been caused by the fire?" Vincent asked.

Again, Morton leaned back in his chair and crossed his hands over his chest as he thought. "You're concerned that Theodore Vanderbilt was murdered," he realized.

And then he laughed.

"You find murder amusing, Mr. Ivey?" Vincent demanded.

"No, of course not," Morton said, sobering quickly. "It's just that there hasn't been murder on the books in Cranford County in ten years. It seems unlikely that—"

"No one said anything about murder, Mr. Ivey," I interrupted. "This is simply routine. As part of our investigation, we are required to identify cause of death before any insurance monies can be paid. So is there anything you can think of that might serve as evidence that Theodore Vanderbilt did not die in that fire?"

Morton thought again. "Well, the skull did show signs of fractures."

I could see Vincent immediately perk up. I admit that I perked up too. Skull fractures could indicate blunt force trauma and, thus, a potential murder.

"However," Morton continued, "I would bet that those fractures resulted from the exposure to such high temperatures. The ME will have to look at them under a microscope to be sure."

"Was there any other evidence of trauma that might not have been caused by the fire?" I asked, hoping he might be able to tell us something—anything—definitive before we left.

Morton's eyes closed in thought, leaving his face peaceful and serene. "There was some splitting of skin on the torso and neck, but again, that could indicate either trauma or fire damage. In fact, those could have been old surgical scars opening due to the heat." He opened his eyes and looked directly at me. "Without the proper tools, it was impossible for me to tell."

The room fell silent for a moment, and I was mentally ruling this trip as a colossal waste of time when Vincent said, "You've told us exactly nothing. I cannot believe that you, the county coroner and expert in death, would have nothing of use to add to this investigation."

Morton sat up straighter under the attack, and his face went rigid. "I do apologize, sir, but there is no need for rudeness. My role here in Cranford County is largely ceremonial. I'm really more of a politician. That's just the way it is in small towns."

Vincent too sat straighter, and I spoke before he could say another word. "Just tell us this, Mr. Ivey: is there any way for you to rule out foul play?"

Morton turned his gaze from Vincent to me, but it didn't soften. "No, ma'am, I'm afraid I cannot."

He clearly had no pertinent information to impart, so I added, "We can trust you to keep the reasons for this meeting confidential."

Morton gave me a waxy smile. "Of course. I haven't mentioned a word to anyone. Won't start now."

"Good," I said, "then we'll let you get back to work here."

Vincent and I stood to take our leave, and Morton also rose to escort us from the building.

I was fairly sure he wanted to kick us—well, at least Vincent—to the curb.

"Let me know if there's anything else I can do to help with your investigation," Morton said as he led us back past the vacant viewing rooms. As we neared the entrance, I noticed that a small, sedate crowd had begun to gather around Mr. Perkins's body. Morton straightened himself, reapplying his funeral director formality for his guests. "I'm at your service," he said to Vincent and me with a slight smile.

Morton pushed open the front door, and blessed sunlight and fresh air rushed in at me.

I took a deep breath as I stepped outside, and Vincent and I headed silently back toward the square, leaving the Iveys to their morbid business while I pondered the wisdom of mixing the jobs of politician and undertaker.

It was far too creepy.

TEN

We returned to the DOI to do the necessary paperwork, and by the time we'd finished telling Ted what we learned in Cranford County, it was full dark outside, and I was starving.

As if reading my mind, Vincent closed the laptop he'd brought into my office and began stacking files that had been spread out on my desk. Without raising his eyes from his task, he asked, "Want to grab dinner?"

An image of Vincent and me walking to a restaurant in the moonlight invaded my mind. I pushed it away.

"Can't," I said. "My sister had surgery, and I'm spending the night at Mercer Med with her and my mother tonight. I'm bringing takeout."

He looked at me. "Anything I can do?" he asked with a touch of concern. I knew he wasn't worried about my sister. They'd never met.

"No," I replied automatically. "It's only a broken ankle, and I'm just going to give my mother a break."

It sounded normal when I said it that way. Too bad there was nothing normal about Tricia's situation. A normal woman her age would not have ended up on a ventilator for a broken ankle.

Vincent's forehead crinkled.

"But don't worry about me," I added quickly. "I spent years on the night shift at the MPD. I'll be fresh as a daisy tomorrow morning."

Vincent looked at me evenly. "I wasn't worried," he said. "Not about you, anyway. I was trying to figure out what to do with the rest of my night."

I laughed as I slid my own laptop into my work bag. "What about Justin?" I asked.

"He's with his mom tonight."

"Ah," I said. So Vincent's ex-wife was in town. Or lived nearby. I didn't know, and I sure didn't want to ask.

Apparently, he didn't want to elaborate either because he was silent until his phone rang. He pulled it from his belt and checked the caller ID.

His eyes brightened, and he smiled at me before turning to leave the office. "Hey, Justin," I heard him say.

I smiled too. Maybe his night was saved after all.

As for me, instead of having a nice dinner with Vincent, I was going to be sleeping in a hospital recliner.

Lucky me.

As I hauled myself up to Tricia's room in the ICU, I lamented that being the only responsible adult in the Jackson family was a demanding job. I'd already swung by Varnie's, a home-cooking restaurant, and I had a bag of takeout in one hand and my overnight duffel swinging from the other.

When I entered Tricia's room, I found her sleeping and my mother sitting in front of the TV, which was softly playing a daytime rerun on the soap opera channel. I studied the screen and wondered if these were the same actors I'd watched as a child when I'd had to stay home from school.

Probably.

And they were probably still acting out the same storyline too.

I turned to my mother and whispered, "I brought food."

"Oh! Thank goodness you're here," my mother said as she stood and smiled at me gratefully. "I'm starved for real food."

"How's Tricia?" I asked as I leaned over my sister's prone form. She was a bit pale, but I assumed the drugs were keeping her relaxed and out of pain.

"She had an awful day. Just awful. So much pain, and those nurses didn't have any sympathy."

I knew that some doctors disapproved of treating alcoholics in the ICU and wondered if others in the medical field felt the same way. Or if my mother was fabricating the whole thing.

At this point, I couldn't be sure, so I decided to skip the drama. "How long has Tricia been off the ventilator?"

"They finished weaning her yesterday," she said as she paced in front of the bed, looking more lost and agitated than usual. "And those respiratory therapists were so awful, coming in here and making her gag."

"I'm sure they were just doing their jobs," I said as I pressed the Styrofoam container of food into her hands, partially to give her something to do and partially because her blood sugar seemed a quart low. "Here, Mom. Why don't you sit and try to eat something? You're probably hungry."

Obediently, my mother sat, opened the box, and began to pick at her food. "I know you're right. Everyone here is really nice and they're doing the best they can for her, but it's so hard to watch your baby suffer."

I took the other seat, a straight-backed oak chair with a pink padded cushion, and opened my food while listening to my mother recount, more calmly now, what had gone on that day.

God, I was hungry. I tore open the plastic-wrapped fork and knife and shoveled a forkful of stewed yellow squash and onions into my mouth.

After a few ravenous bites, I slowed my pace and considered my sister. It was true. It was difficult to watch her suffer, but by this point, we should have mastered the task because we'd been watching it for years. My reaction had always been different, though. While my mother worried, my sister drank, and my father avoided, I was out playing superhero, trying to right all wrongs and leap tall buildings in a single bound.

I don't know which one of us had coped the best.

We sat together, me eating and my mother watching the soap opera, until someone knocked on the door behind us.

I jumped at the sudden noise, cursed myself, and turned around to find Dr. Janowski standing there in his white lab coat. "I'm here to check on Tricia's progress," he said as he entered the room followed by a nurse with a computer on a rolling cart. She deposited the cart in an out-of-the-way corner and went to the bedside to prepare for the doctor's exam.

Dr. Janowski began scrolling through the charts on the computer, found what he was looking for, and then glanced up at my mother and me. "How does our patient seem today?" he asked.

My mother began to recount the horrors of the ventilator removal, and I listened as the doctor made the appropriate responses and assured her that my sister was breathing well now.

"I'm just going to have a look at her surgical site, Mrs. Jackson," he said.

And though he was already in the process of pulling the curtain around Tricia to begin his examination, my mother said, "Go right ahead. We'll get out of your way."

My mother and I waited quietly in our seats, both pretending to concentrate on the muted TV.

At some point during the exam, my sister awoke, and I heard the sound of her groggy voice and the hushed assurances of the nurse, explaining what was happening.

Soon, Dr. Janowski stepped from behind the curtain and said, "The surgical site looks good and seems to be healing normally. No sign of infection."

"That's great news," my mother said with a hand over her heart and a grateful look on her face. I was afraid she was going to fling herself at Dr. Janowski and hug him until he popped, but thankfully she restrained herself.

Me? I was waiting for the other shoe to drop.

"Can we speak outside for a moment while my nurse redresses the wound?"

And there it was.

Once we moved out into the hall, the doctor spoke to my fears. "Now that Tricia is off the ventilator and awake, her recovery may begin to get more difficult."

"Oh!" my mother said. "Do you mean she'll be in a lot of pain?"

"We'll make sure she's comfortable." He glanced at me. "But alcohol withdrawal is more of a concern at this point."

"Withdrawal?" My mother gasped. "She's not an addict, doctor! She was just a little tipsy when she fell."

Oh, come on. My mother was in big-time denial. It was not an attitude I wanted to share with her.

"Let's just hear him out, Mom."

She crossed her arms in front of her and pressed her lips together in compliance.

Dr. Janowski nodded at my mother and then looked between us. "Based on what she was able to tell us of her history earlier, we've decided to prescribe IV Librium. The dosage has been calculated in ratio to the amount of alcohol she said she consumes, and it should get her through just fine. Still, we'll be watching for symptoms of delirium tremens."

"DTs?" I repeated. "What are the symptoms? Shaking?"

"Yes, shaking, but also confusion, hallucinations, anxiety. If she begins showing any of these symptoms, please tell the nurse immediately. The Librium should prevent them, but the next forty-eight hours are critical, and she may have to be sedated for as many as ten days."

Alcohol was royally screwing up my sister's life. It caused her accident and was now impeding her recovery.

"You said earlier that her bones had also been damaged by her drinking," I said, trying to see the larger picture. "Can the condition of her bones be reversed?"

"Certainly, if Miss Jackson refrains from drinking, her bones may recover rapidly."

That was good news at least. "And if she doesn't? What will her life be like?"

Dr. Janowski looked at me squarely. "I can only speak to her bone health, and if she continues along this path, she is likely to suffer more fractures in the future."

"How long will it take her to heal fully?" my mother asked, ignoring the true problem as usual.

"Well, I always tell patients to give it a year to heal fully," he said, "but in a patient with healthy bones, it takes at least six weeks for the fracture to heal. Most people start driving in nine to twelve weeks and return to normal activities in three to four months. In your daughter's case, it may take longer."

"When can I take her home?"

"I'd like to monitor her recovery until we're sure she's not going to experience DTs, but she will likely be discharged in about a week, depending on how she does."

"Oh, a few days in the hospital, she won't like that. But afterward, I'll bring her to my house," my mother said, her eyes alight at the prospect of taking care of Tricia 24/7.

But the doctor's next words worked magic on me. "It's critical that she not consume any alcohol during her recovery," he said, "especially while she's on this medication."

As I listened, I realized just how much I hoped this accident would turn into a blessing. Tricia would be immobilized during her recovery, and she was already going through a safe detox from alcohol. I had a fresh lead on her rapist, and I knew the bastard would be caught soon. These combined factors could be the impetus for a good change—a real turning point for all of us.

"I'm going to run home," my mother said after Dr. Janowski and the nurse left. "I could really use some sleep, and I need to pack us some overnight bags. I think I have some of Tricia's laundry at home, so I'll bring that. And I need something to read. I'm sick of watching soaps and game shows."

My mother gave me a quick hug and then leaned over Tricia to explain that she'd be back tomorrow, while I went into the hall to call my father.

I assumed he hadn't been updated about Tricia, and to be honest, if we were going to be watching her for signs of DTs, then we needed someone else on the rotation this weekend. It was time to get him here.

My father received the news about the possibility of further complications with his usual stoicism, and he agreed to spend Saturday night with Tricia, which would be a nice relief for my mother.

When I returned to Tricia's room, my mother was gone, but my sister smiled weakly at me. "Hey, Sissy," she said, her voice rough from the ventilator.

"Hey," I said back. "How are you feeling?"

I pulled the recliner beside her bed and leaned close as Tricia turned her wide, unfocused eyes to me. She seemed not to have heard my question. "You'll stay here with me tonight, won't you?" she asked. "You won't leave me, right?"

A feeling of tenderness washed over me, and I brushed her pale blond hair from her face and said, "I'll be here. Don't you worry. Mom will be back tomorrow, and Dad will stay with you this weekend, but you're stuck with me for a while."

"I'm glad you're here." Tricia reached up, and I watched her hand as it wavered a bit in midair before she managed to find my hand and squeeze it weakly.

"They gave you the good drugs, didn't they?" I looked into her glazed eyes and then at the IV bag that hovered above her.

"Yup," she said. "But I'm still glad you're here. You always take care of everything."

You have no idea, I thought. I really wanted to tell her. I wanted her to know that I was about to bring to justice the man who had done this to her. But Tricia wasn't exactly aware of my personal investigation into her rape, and she probably wouldn't approve if she were. She seemed to want to forget what happened by any means necessary, and she certainly didn't have any conception of how close we were to discovering her attacker's identity.

Looking down at her tired face, I wondered how she would take the news when I told her.

Probably not well, given her already chronic alcohol use. I'd known it was bad, but this was the first potentially health-endangering complication I'd witnessed.

Well, except for the DWIs.

No, I'd wait until later to tell her about the investigation. After her ankle had healed and—in an ideal scenario—after she weaned herself from alcohol. Maybe then she would be able to handle the news in a healthy way.

I hoped.

Tricia looked up to find me watching her. "You okay?" she asked, which was a surprise. Usually she was so focused on herself that she didn't notice me.

"Yeah, I just had a tough day. It was only my second back, but it feels like I've worked a month."

"Oh," she said as her eyelids slipped shut momentarily, "tell me about it."

I thought of the charred body and said, "Why don't we watch some TV instead?" Before she could respond, I turned up the sound on the wall-mounted monitor just in time to hear the newscaster announce, "A Cranford County man's body was found last weekend in his car along Highway 403. Local police say the state will investigate for potential car arson."

So much for forgetting work. I flipped the channel to a sitcom. I wasn't in the mood for news reports, even such vague ones, on one of my cases. One of *our* cases, I reminded myself.

I turned to Tricia, pleased that I could tell her something about my day without being too specific. "Did I tell you I have a new partner at work?"

"Nope," she said. "Anyone I know?"

"Nope," I replied in kind. "His name's Mark Vincent. He worked with me on that case a few weeks ago and now he's here to stay."

"Mark Vincent. Is he cute?" she asked, as if we were thirteen years old and suddenly boy crazy.

"I don't know if 'cute' is the word I'd use," I said, thinking of his bulky frame and all-business exterior. "But yeah, he's attractive in a military kind of way."

"Mmmm, I like a man in uniform." Tricia's words were slurred, and I looked over to find her eyelids drooping again. "Is he married?" she managed to ask.

"No," I said as I got out of the recliner to pull the covers higher around her shoulders. "But he has a kid. A son in college."

Tricia wrinkled her nose. "Oh, he's old, then. Probably gray chest hairs. Yuck."

"Not really old." I pushed a stray strand of hair from her face and smiled down at her. "I think he married young, and I've seen his chest. Not a gray hair in sight."

Tricia yawned but still managed to say, "You saw his chest?"

Oops. I hadn't meant to get into all that. "It's a long story," I said, "but I can guarantee that it's not nearly as interesting as you're probably imagining."

Tricia shrugged halfheartedly but didn't let me drop the subject so easily. "You gonna date him?"

"I doubt it," I said as I watched her eyelids fall closed.

I had other things to do besides date cute boys. I had to catch the man responsible for putting Tricia in her current condition.

Eleven

Dumping the first body had been as easy as taking out the trash.

But disposing of the next twenty-five or so had been a hell of a task. First of all, stowing that much waste on one piece of land—no matter how large—requires creative thinking, and second, dead bodies aren't exactly light. Hell, carrying them one by one through the woods had nearly thrown out his back until he'd gotten smart and started using his old wheelbarrow to haul them to their final resting places.

The man grinned at that last thought: final resting places. Ha! It sounded so peaceful and serene, so respectable.

Hardly.

Unless, of course, some of these people had hoped to spend eternity rotting in a septic tank.

Somehow he doubted it.

Still, he whistled as he rolled the old man's remains down the wooded path toward the back of his property. But as his feet crunched through the leaves that littered the forest floor and the wind blew through the narrow pine branches above, he swore he felt the temperature drop, and a sudden chill passed through him, causing him to want to plant this guy as quickly as he could and get back inside his house.

Briefly, he considered throwing the carcass into the pond, but as usual, he ruled out the possibility—he couldn't have bodies floating up if he invited a buddy over to fish. He'd have to take him somewhere else.

He thought he might use the commercial septic tank he'd secretly installed for disposing of the bodies, but it was hidden farther back on his twenty acres, and opening the hatch in the huge concrete lid required so much effort. Usually he only went to that trouble when he had more than one body to dump.

Nah, he thought as he shifted his baseball cap lower over his brow, he'd just use the tried-and-true burial method. Drop the old geezer into the mass grave, toss a bit of lime over him, and he'd be home in time for a nice breakfast. Maybe he'd even put in the effort to make grits to go with his eggs and thick-cut bacon.

As he shoved the wheelbarrow into the small clearing that housed his current dumping ground, he knew grits were going to be out of the question.

Something was wrong.

Bad wrong.

"What the hell?" he said aloud as he parked the old man in the shade of a thick water oak and dashed over to examine the pit he'd dug so carefully with his backhoe. The opening of the hole had definitely been disturbed, evidenced by the pockmarks that had formed in the loose piles of soil around it. He was certain it hadn't looked that way when he'd tossed in the last stiff.

He leaned over the edge of the hole and flinched as he stared down in disbelief.

One of his goddamn bodies was missing.

TWELVE

Bright and early the next morning, I peeled myself off the hospital recliner where I'd slept—or tried to sleep. Between the nurses' constant interruptions and some crazy dreams, I hadn't exactly slumbered peacefully. I looked at Tricia as she lay on the hospital bed. Her skin color was better, and her chest moved up and down regularly under the blanket.

I smiled and gently brushed her bangs from her eyes. She was asleep and seemed serene. After a long night of blood pressure and temperature checks, I wasn't eager to wake her, so I took my bag to the bathroom, changed into a new outfit, and quietly slipped out of the room.

I headed to the office with a quick stop for coffee on the way, and soon Vincent and I were on the road back to Cranford County, with Kathy Vanderbilt as our primary mission.

"What do we know about the widow Vanderbilt, aside from the fact that she stood to gain a crapload of money from her husband's death?" I asked.

"Not a whole hell of a lot," Vincent said from his position in the driver's seat of his GMC.

I leaned down to yank a stack of papers from my work bag, which I'd stowed on the floorboard. I found the printouts from Americus Mutual, Kathy's police record, and the Vanderbilts' financial information and then shuffled them into some sort of order, thinking that I should probably convert to an electronic tablet to keep my work better organized and less coffee stained.

But I was a traditional girl. I liked the feel of paper, which was sometimes the only solid thing in an investigation. I'd made a concession when I'd bought a smart phone and agreed to tote a laptop, but I wasn't ready to go completely digital.

Not yet.

We'd already covered the Americus policy, so after scanning it once more as a refresher, I flipped to Kathy's police record. "Mrs. Vanderbilt has a couple of speeding tickets, and when she was a teenager in the early 1990s, she was arrested twice: once for vandalism and again for disorderly conduct. But here's the interesting one. In 2002, she was arrested for filing a false police report against a neighbor, whom she accused of assault."

Vincent nodded in recollection. "I remember reading that. Weren't the charges dropped for lack of evidence?"

"Yes, the investigation revealed no evidence against the neighbor, and Kathy subsequently admitted that she had fabricated the charge in the hopes of bilking money out of a local battered women's charity."

"Classy," Vincent said.

Yup, Vincent was right. Kathy Vanderbilt was a classy lady.

I flipped to the next page.

"She has one son from a previous relationship: Carter Hashaway, age twenty-one." I completed the narrative as the truck bumped into the parking lot of our destination. "She's been quiet since 2002. Married Theodore Vanderbilt in 2003, and worked alongside her husband here at the U-Strip-Em Auto Salvage."

Raising my eyes from the paper, I took in the U-Strip-Em, which turned out to be an enormous car graveyard conveniently located next to the We-Shred-Em Recycling Center, which the Vanderbilts also owned. Auto mechanics and do-it-yourself repairmen could pay a small entry fee to scavenge the U-Strip-Em for used parts from among the vehicular carnage stored there, and what wasn't used was recycled next door.

I looked between the papers and the building in front of us. "According to their financial records, the Vanderbilts took out a large loan to pay for upgrades to the structure and property, but so far, payments have been on time and in full."

The U-Strip-Em building was, in fact, much nicer than I'd expected to find at a junkyard. The one-story structure appeared newly built and boasted electric sliding doors and industrial metal sheeting accents.

And it seemed to do a good business. The customer parking lot was half full of vehicles of all shapes and sizes, and there appeared to be a steady stream of people pushing large blue wheelbarrows bearing the U-Strip-Em logo.

"So the Vanderbilts weren't necessarily comfortable financially, but they weren't hurting either," Vincent supplied, also watching the foot traffic around us.

"Yeah, but a million bucks is a pretty big temptation for a woman who already has a record of petty crimes topped off with issuing a false police report." I jammed the papers back into my bag. "Let's go see what Mrs. Vanderbilt has to say about it."

We got out of the GMC, crunched across the gravel driveway, and entered the U-Strip-Em through the automatic doors, which spit us into a large open area with two long counters in the center, one to catch customers going into the junkyard and one to catch them going out so that they could pay for the parts they'd acquired.

We approached the in-desk, and a young employee in grease-stained coveralls looked us over with a critical eye.

I glanced down at myself. My black trousers, suit coat, and light blue button-down were immaculate, and Vincent certainly stood out in his gleaming white dress shirt.

Clearly, we were not dressed for a junkyard.

"Can I help you?" the employee asked, leery.

"We're with the Georgia Department of Insurance, and we're here to see Kathy Vanderbilt," I said, gesturing at the badge at my belt line. "Is she in today?"

"Yo, Kathy," the man tossed over his shoulder, and then said to me, "She'll be with you in a sec."

We moved a bit down the counter so he could serve the next customers, and I watched as the thin, blond woman who had been working the out-counter turned to greet us.

The first thing that struck me was Kathy's attire—scrubs that were completely out of place for her environment. Maybe she'd gotten tired of soiling her regular clothes with oil every day.

The second thing that I noticed was her small face. Though her head appeared to be normal sized, all her features were delicate and seemed crowded together.

If my mother had been there, she would have said that Kathy Vanderbilt was suffering from the benefits of her Southern royal lineage. In my mother's lingo, that meant she suspected that her family was a bit inbred.

There was no scientific basis for that assumption as far as I knew.

"Mrs. Vanderbilt?" I asked, just to be sure.

"Yeah, but call me Kathy. We ain't formal around here. You the people from the insurance place?" She rounded the counter and gestured for us to follow her.

"Georgia Department of Insurance," Vincent corrected from beside her. To say that he dwarfed Kathy was an understatement. Next to him, she looked like a child.

"Yeah, that's it," she said. "We can talk in Theo's office."

We followed her toward a small room off the main area, which held only a desk, some chairs, and an old desktop computer that had been shoved aside, probably inoperable. But the window unit air conditioner sure worked. Going through the door was like entering a portal to the polar ice caps.

Vincent and I took the seats across from the desk. I buttoned my suit coat and tried to scoot the chair out of the direct arctic blast from the window unit.

For all the good that did.

Vincent pulled out his notepad and pen, and, trying to ignore the goose bumps that rose on my flesh, I addressed Kathy. "We're here about your husband's death and your subsequent life insurance claim."

"Yeah, I figured," Kathy said, nodding as she sank into the chair behind the desk. Only she began fanning herself with a file folder.

I eyed her. How could she possibly be warm?

And how could she possibly be so calm less than a week after her husband supposedly died in a horrific accident?

"We're very sorry for your loss, Mrs. Vanderbilt," Vincent said, causing me to wonder if he might have been thinking the same thing.

"I think I'm still in shock," she said quickly. Her fan picked up speed. "I mean, it just don't seem real. Every morning since the accident, I keep expecting Theo to show up here with that fast-food coffee he always bought."

I watched her little face carefully, looking for signs of distress or deception, but other than her rapid fanning and a few downward quirks of her lips as she spoke, I saw none.

"I know it probably seems strange that I've got the place open already, but this is our"—she paused and then corrected herself—"my main source of income. I'm left to deal with it now, and if I show any signs of weakness, that pack of jackals out there won't give me the respects I deserve. I had to come in and keep things running."

Kathy's voice had become high and forceful, and in a strange way, it helped convince me that she was not as unaffected by her husband's death as I'd originally thought. Her emotions seemed to be manifesting themselves as defiance. That was not unusual.

And her use of the word "respects" was particularly telling. Often accompanied in conversation by "don't you go disrespectin' me," that word was reserved for a particular branch of Southern society: the angry redneck. We were dealing here with an upwardly mobile, angry redneck, and now that I had a deeper glimpse into her psyche, I'd learned something: Kathy Vanderbilt needed her respects, and that probably meant she'd never felt worthy of anyone's respect in the first place.

I had to admit I kind of admired women like Kathy. She might not have the highest self-esteem, but she fought for what she wanted. She didn't roll over and let life wash over her. No, Kathy Vanderbilt was a fighter.

But just how far was she willing to go to get what she wanted?

"Tell us about Friday night and early Saturday morning," Vincent said, interrupting my thoughts on the finer points of the redneck mentality. "Where was Mr. Vanderbilt headed?"

A short burst of laughter erupted from Kathy. "You might as well call him Theo. Everybody else does." She winced. "Did."

"Okay, where was Theo headed?" Vincent repeated as he took out his notepad and positioned himself to write.

"Home, I expect."

"Where had he been?" I asked. "It was 3 AM when the call came in. That's pretty late to be driving around."

"They was having a drivers' meeting over at the dirt track." She pointed in a vaguely southwestern direction. "At the speedway. It's only a few miles from here, and he's always got some car or other running there. Plus, we get a lot of business from the other drivers."

With the number of wrecks that probably happened in dirt-track racing, I could well imagine.

"Why didn't you go with him?" I asked.

"I get enough car talk on a normal day. I didn't need to go to the track too."

"Was anyone with him?"

Kathy stopped fanning herself for a moment. "Carter went to the meeting. He's a driver too, but they didn't ride together or anything."

"Your son Carter?" I asked.

Kathy nodded.

"Then we'll need to speak with him too," Vincent said.

"What for?" Her tone had become defensive.

Trying to convey calm, I said, "To confirm that Theo did make the meeting and ask if he knows what his stepfather might have done for the rest of the night." Kathy didn't look any more cooperative, so I added, "It'll make the claim go faster."

With obvious reluctance, Kathy gestured over her shoulder. "He works out in the lot, running one of the forklifts."

I looked out the large plate-glass window behind her as two huge forklifts moved cars from place to place, taking out the remains of the scavenged vehicles and bringing in fresh ones for customers to pick over.

My eyes returned to Kathy. "When did their meeting end?"

"Dunno," Kathy said. "Probably late. Once they get to talking, they like to never shut up. I'd guess the thing went on 'til about 11."

"So he didn't come straight home afterward?" I asked.

Kathy shrugged. "Obviously not."

"Do you know where he went?"

"Knowing Theo, probably the Alley Cat Bar."

"Did he go there often?" Vincent asked.

"Well," Kathy began and then paused. "He wasn't there every time the doors were open, but almost."

I hesitated, trying to find a way to ask the next question politely. Then, thinking of Tricia and the way I hated watching people dance around the topic, I figured I'd just be blunt.

"Did Theo have a drinking problem?"

"No!" Kathy said loudly, causing even Vincent to look up from his copious note-taking. "I mean, he drank some, yeah. But he weren't no alcoholic if that's what you're getting at."

"Was he ever arrested for DWI?" Vincent asked, even though we both knew Theo's police record was clean.

"No, not that I know of."

"Should he have been?" I asked, before I thought to stop myself.

Kathy paused again and then laughed slightly. "Yeah, probably a time or two. Is that why you think he ended up wrapping his car around that tree?"

"We're not sure yet, Mrs. Vanderbilt," I lied.

Of course, this wasn't a drunk driving accident, and besides, the description "wrapped around a tree" didn't really apply. Yeah, the car had hit the tree, but the impact had done little damage to the front end. A tree-sized dent and that was all.

But did Kathy know that Theo's death was no accident?

At this point I wasn't sure, so I decided to switch topics and shake things up a bit. "You understand that we're with the Department of Insurance, so our questions will also pertain to the death benefits claim you made Saturday morning at Americus Mutual Insurance," I explained. In my experience, no one really knew that the Department of Insurance existed, much less understood what we did.

"Sure, but I don't get why. I'm entitled to that money," she said, and her voice began to take on a bit of the give-me-my-respects tone again.

"Why make the call so soon?" I asked.

"Why wait?" she responded. "Theo isn't going to get any deader."

I blinked at her harshness. "Most people wait until all the paperwork—death certificates and such—are in order before filing a claim. The majority at least have the funeral first."

"Well, I ain't got that kind of time."

"What do you mean by that exactly?" Vincent asked, eyeing her intently while his pen remained at the ready.

Kathy gestured around. "Look at this place. We just remodeled, and the bank ain't gonna wait around for no funeral before they start demanding payments, and without Theo to keep this place running, I had to give up my part-time job."

"Part-time job?" Vincent's eyes narrowed. We didn't have any record of her outside employment.

"X-ray tech. I just finished school a few months ago and got the job offer last month."

I glanced at her, now comprehending the scrubs. I didn't picture Kathy working in the healthcare field any more than I pictured her working here. She seemed to exist in between. Like I said, upwardly mobile redneck. Hard to pigeonhole.

But there was no way I would want to meet her on the other side of an x-ray machine. I didn't imagine she'd offer a lot of pity as she forced people's bones into the necessary positions.

"I'm not going to lie. I want that insurance money. That's what it was there for. I paid the premiums all these years. It's my money." Kathy dropped her makeshift fan onto the desk. "I want to pay off that loan, sell this place for a nice profit, and between that and Theo's life insurance, I'll never have to work again. So yeah, I made the call." Kathy's hands landed on her hips in a gesture that clearly demanded to know if I had a problem with her explanation.

I did have a problem with it, but her agitation told me that now was not the time to quibble. I didn't want her to shut down completely. But I would definitely be checking her financial records later.

She continued, "When do I get my money?"

Vincent slid his notebook closed, obviously also aware that the interview was rapidly unraveling. "You understand, Mrs. Vanderbilt, that before any monies can be issued, the state's investigation must reach a satisfactory conclusion."

Her eyes turned sharply to him. "Meaning?"

"Meaning we have to be certain of what happened to Theo and why," he said calmly.

"Well, I would think it was fairly obvious what happened to him."

"Still," I said, "we have to wait for the autopsy and fire investigation. Standard procedure."

"Yeah, you follow your standard procedure," Kathy snapped. "But be quick about it."

We thanked Kathy for her time, but we didn't make any promises to be quick. "We'll need to talk to Carter," I said instead.

"Like I said, he's out back." Kathy didn't offer to call him in to the office. She just jerked her thumb over her shoulder. "You can talk to him outside."

Leaving the main building, we waded deep into the bowels of the junkyard, skirting junker cars of all makes and models.

We passed a long row of trucks, and I spied a GMC like Vincent's and was about to point it out when Vincent said softly, "Something just doesn't add up here."

I looked over my shoulder to find Kathy watching us out one of the building's back windows.

"Yeah," I agreed. "I've seen people whose grief comes out in anger, but this seemed different."

"Very cold," Vincent said as we passed another long row of vehicles. "And I don't just mean the temperature of the room."

"Yeah," I said as I took one more look at Kathy's little face in the window and then turned to Vincent. "I wonder if she killed her husband."

"Where there's smoke, there's fire," Vincent said. "She had motive, means, and opportunity."

"She did," I agreed. Then, still realizing that things aren't always what they seem, I added, "But sometimes where there's smoke, you find some other guy rubbing two sticks together."

Thirteen

Carter Hashaway drove the enormous yellow forklift as if it were an Indy car. Vincent and I stood on the periphery of the U-Strip-Em and watched for a moment as he wielded the machine through the rows of vehicles, removing a picked-over car and replacing it with a fresh one.

"Doesn't look like he's taking a break any time soon," I said, as I watched the forklift motor down another row.

"Maybe you should approach him," Vincent suggested. "He'll stop for a pretty little lady like you."

I shot him a hard stare. "Pretty little lady?" I repeated with a major eye roll.

"Thought you'd like that," Vincent said with a laugh. He was jerking my chain, so I slugged him in the shoulder. Hard.

He winced and rubbed the injured area. "Hey, I'm just predicting Carter's reaction. So technically, those are his words, not mine," he said seriously, but there was a hint of amusement in his eyes.

I thought about slugging him again, but we did have to get Carter out of the forklift to ask him some questions.

I considered trying a direct approach by walking up and showing him my badge, but he was wielding a piece of heavy machinery. He could drive right over me.

Vincent was always being pegged as a cop, and I almost never was. I just didn't have the look, and even I had to admit that it was something I often used to my advantage with people I was interviewing.

Why not use my non-cop looks again now?

"Fine, you wait here and let this 'little lady' take care of the hard work," I said over my shoulder as I sauntered toward the row where Carter was using the forklift to scoop up another vehicle. Shielding my eyes from the glare of the sun, I waved at the young man, who did a quick double take, probably surprised to see a woman in the junkyard, and then promptly shut down the machine.

Damn Vincent for being right.

Carter hopped to the ground and lifted his hat in greeting. His dirty blond hair resembled his mother's, but that was where the similarity ended. His face, though covered in a light goatee, was much more to scale than Kathy's, and he seemed to have a little less of the angry redneck mentality.

Or so I hoped.

I smiled at him in greeting, and he seemed to take that as an invitation to look me up and down.

"What's a pretty little thing like you doing at the U-Strip-Em?" Carter asked when he'd gotten close enough for me to hear him.

I grimaced. Double damn Vincent.

Instead of answering, I simply unbuttoned my coat to reveal my badge.

And that's when I realized I'd made an error in judgment.

Carter's face transformed from mild flirtation to utter panic in one second flat.

Before I could even form the words, "Don't run," Carter bolted between a Chevelle and a Nova.

I cursed inwardly as I took off after him.

"Stop," I shouted. "Police!"

He wasn't going to stop, I knew. His legs kept right on churning as he wove a path between vehicles toward the back of the property. Cars blurred in my vision as I flew past them in pursuit of a young man who was rapidly increasing the distance between us.

I was never going to catch this kid on foot.

Then, Vincent appeared in our path, and Carter stopped abruptly.

Hell, I knew Vincent, and if I'd been a criminal, I would have stopped too. He stood, legs spread, hand on the butt of his holstered Sig, in the middle of Carter's path. It was like an old western duel. I half expected someone to yell "draw."

I kept running toward my prey, hoping his moment of shock would last until I could cuff him.

I came within a few strides of Carter when he careened suddenly to the right and made off down an aisle of trucks and vans.

By the time I turned the corner down the aisle, I'd lost sight of him among the taller vehicles. Vincent jogged up beside me and asked, "You see where he went?"

"No," I panted, "but he can't have gotten far."

"He's probably in one of these vehicles."

I looked down the depressingly long aisle. "I'll take the left side," I said, fully prepared to draw down on the kid if I had to.

And with that we divided up and began looking inside each vehicle. I'd made it about halfway down the row when I came to a white panel van. Just the sort of vehicle that killers and child abductors drive in movies.

It would be suitably ironic if he were in there, I thought, as I came carefully to the passenger door, which hung ajar on uneven hinges. I jerked at the handle, and the door screeched open.

In the darkened van, I saw nothing, but he could be hiding somewhere in the inner sanctum.

"Hashaway, come out now," I ordered, my hand on my weapon. "It'll go easier."

Apparently, my order had an authoritative note. Carter leapt out of the side door of the minivan behind me and shoved me hard into the open panel-van door.

He actually hit me!

He seemed as shocked by his actions as I was because he paused briefly as I surged to my knees and whirled toward him.

Just as I reached out for him, Carter took off again, but I managed to grab a fistful of his shirt.

I held on as Carter dragged me a few yards, and then, realizing I wasn't letting go, he spun, his fist flying wildly at my face and his body lunging toward me, leaving him slightly off balance.

My rage exploded, and I grabbed the back of Carter's skull with my left hand and pummeled him under the chin with my right palm. His head snapped backward, and I took the opportunity to twist him to the left, rolling his whole body like a ball over my extended leg and swiftly to the ground.

With Carter off balance, taking him down hadn't required much effort at all, and now he lay blinking up at me in surprise.

My hand on my M&P, I shouted, "On your belly. Now!"

Miracle of miracles, Carter complied.

I cuffed him just as Vincent arrived beside us, looking suitably impressed.

I glanced up at him over Carter's prone form. "Pretty little lady, my ass."

"Why did you run?" I demanded as Vincent pulled the cuffed man into a sitting position and began to pat him down.

"I'm holding," he admitted, head hanging dejectedly. "I thought I was going to get arrested."

"Where is it?" Vincent asked.

"Left jeans pocket."

"Any needles? Knives? Anything that will piss me off when I reach in there to take it?"

"No, nothing like that. Just a baggie."

"Of what?" I asked.

"Glass."

I clucked my tongue at him as if I were ashamed. "Meth? You know that stuff will mess you up."

"I know, I know," Carter said, watching with desperate eyes as Vincent extracted a bag of crystals from his jeans and waved it in front of him. "But I'm hooked. Can't do nothing without it."

"You got any warrants?" I asked as I whipped out my phone to check his police record.

"No, no warrants, man," he said to me.

I raised an eyebrow and glanced at him over my phone. "Man?"

"Ma'am," he corrected himself quickly.

We were silent for a moment as I scanned the twenty-one-year-old's record. Then I glared at him, happy I'd taken him down as hard as I had.

He'd been busted for possession twice and was suspected of cooking meth—or having knowledge of a lab at least—somewhere in Cranford County.

I showed the phone to Vincent.

"You selling this stuff?" Vincent asked Carter, whose gaze went from compliant to defiant.

"No, I'm not selling. I swear!"

"Well, here's the irony, kid," Vincent said. "We're from the Georgia Department of Insurance and had no interest in what drugs you enjoy injecting, snorting, or otherwise inserting into various orifices. But now...." He let his voice trail off, giving Carter the opportunity to spill his guts.

And that's just what he did.

"I'll talk. I'll tell you whatever you want to know." He paused and looked between us. "Insurance cops? This is about Theo's life insurance, right?"

"Yes," I affirmed. At the sound of my voice, Carter's focus shifted from Vincent to me. His eyes had grown wide, fearful. "Were you with him the night he died?"

"Hell, no." Carter's face pulled into a sneer. "I don't go nowhere with that asshole."

I frowned in confusion. "You weren't with him at the dirt-track driver's meeting?"

"I was at the meeting, but not with him."

I groaned inwardly. Leave it to a meth head to sit around and argue semantics with the police.

"When did the meeting end?" I asked, electing not to ask him about his evident hatred of his stepfather until the end of the interview. Or to mention that fact that he shouldn't be allowed to drive anything—not a dirt-track car or a forklift—if he was on methamphetamines.

"A little before 11."

"Did you leave with Theo?" Vincent asked.

"I done told you," Carter snapped. "I don't go nowhere with that guy."

"Did you see him leave?" I asked. "Was he alone?"

Carter shook his head. "No, I didn't see him leave. I got better things to do than keep tabs on him."

"Well, do you know if he was driving his Ford LTD that night?" I asked. Kathy had already said that Theo had been driving the car when he'd left their house, but it never hurt to confirm.

"Man, I don't know. Theo owns hundreds of cars." He gestured with his chin at the surrounding junkyard. "Not all of these have been totaled and had their titles revoked. Some of them are sold to us outright, and we get the titles. He could have been driving any damn one of them."

"You're not telling us much of anything, kid," Vincent said.

"Look," Carter squeaked, "I don't know what he was driving that night, but I do know he sometimes did drive an LTD. God knows why."

"Do you know where he went after the meeting?"

"I only know where he didn't go: the Alley Cat. Me and some other drivers met up for a few beers, and he wasn't there."

I made a mental note to ensure that's truly where Carter had been. He certainly seemed to be building a nice motive for killing Theo himself.

"You didn't like Theo much, did you?" I asked.

"That sure ain't no secret," Carter said. "The guy was a low-rent piece of white trash. He treated my mom like shit. He thought a good day's work lasted ten minutes and always took the easy way out."

"So how did this place become so successful?" Vincent asked, looking toward the newly renovated building and the rows of cars around us.

Carter's chin rose. "Me and Momma. We worked our asses off here, and now that we got the renovations done, we was trying to talk Theo into selling."

"How'd he take that suggestion?" I asked.

"He flipped out, started yelling at Momma, said it wasn't gonna happen."

"Did he say why?" Vincent pressed.

"No, but I figure he just didn't want to give up his easy life. With me and Momma doing all the work here, why would he ever want to sell?"

Unless, of course, he could find a way to make even more money. Say, by faking his own death?

I cut my eyes to Vincent. The picture of the Vanderbilt family was rapidly deteriorating. His meth-head stepson despised him, and neither Carter nor Kathy mourned his death. And why would they? According to them, he was a drunk with the work ethic of a slug, things we couldn't have seen on our financial printouts.

Earlier, when we arrived, I'd pondered the possibility that Kathy had murdered her husband and that she'd acted alone in setting the fire that covered up her crime. But that scenario was fraught with problems. Would little Kathy have been able to muscle Theo's body into the driver's seat by herself?

Now I was wondering if mother and son might not be in this together. That made plenty of sense to me. Kathy would have had a difficult time staging the accident, but with the help of her son, it would have been possible.

"Where was your mother that night?" I asked, trying to sound as if the question had just occurred to me.

Carter was no longer buying my act. "Why?" he asked defensively.

"Doesn't matter why," Vincent snarled. "Answer the nice law enforcement officer, or she'll make things difficult for you."

"At home, I guess," he said. "I don't live in that house anymore. Couldn't stand it there."

"Anything else you want to tell us about that night?"

Carter squinted up at me. "What else is there?"

"I don't know. You tell me."

He shrugged.

Vincent nudged me. "Seems he's done talking, so I'm calling the Cranford sheriff's department to pick him up."

"What?" Carter wailed as Vincent began to dial his phone. "I cooperated! I told you what I knew!" He turned to me. "Make him quit. This will be my third strike! I'll go to prison."

Over Carter's wailing, Vincent managed to identify himself and request a car.

Carter was staring at me now, his eyes begging me to do something.

I only shrugged.

"I'm afraid I can't ask him to stop," I said. "You've got to pay for that little baggie in your pocket, and this will teach you not to run from the cops next time."

And it will keep you off the streets until we figure out what happened to Theo, I added silently.

Carter turned away, shaking his head. "Momma ain't gonna like this."

As it turns out, Carter was underestimating his mother's reaction. Kathy went ballistic the moment the Cranford County sheriff's cruiser rolled up to the U-Strip-Em.

She rushed out of the building with her blond ponytail flying behind her and ambushed the vehicle before its occupants could exit. Vincent and I stood at the edge of the parking lot with Carter still in handcuffs and watched as Sheriff Harper himself emerged from the passenger seat. This was a surprise.

Why send the sheriff to arrest a two-bit druggie?

But even more surprising was Kathy's reaction to seeing him. She went toe to toe and belly to belly with him almost immediately.

"Just what in the hell is going on here?" she shouted in the sheriff's face. "You can't arrest Carter. My boy ain't done nothing!"

Sheriff Harper didn't step back, but he didn't bow up at her either. His hands clenched into fists at his sides, and he said, "Mrs. Vanderbilt, please calm down."

Kathy's back stiffened, clearly relaying the fact that she wasn't going to calm down any time soon. Actually, I half expected Kathy to begin kicking dirt on the man's shoes like a baseball coach disputing an umpire's call.

"No! I will not calm down! You're arresting my baby!"

I couldn't see her face from my angle, but I had a pretty good idea of what it looked like: scrunched up with rage. Kathy sounded pissed.

She leaned even closer and said something I couldn't hear, but it caused Sheriff Harper's calm façade to crack momentarily, and I wondered what that was all about.

The sheriff calmly responded, "I said no such thing," and then he sidestepped Kathy and walked in our direction.

Suddenly seeing fresh prey, Kathy launched herself at Vincent and me.

"And you two assholes! You claimed you wanted to ask Carter about Theo's whereabouts the other night, not get him arrested."

"Ma'am," I said, stepping forward to block her view as Vincent handed Carter into the sheriff's custody, "you need to calm down and let the sheriff and his deputy do their jobs. Your son had a good quantity of meth on him, but you can go to the jail and bail him out as soon as he's arraigned."

I watched as every muscle in Kathy's body seemed to tense, and for a moment, I thought she might try to slap me, but instead she turned her wrath on Carter.

She tried to step around me to get to her son, but I blocked her, effectively keeping myself between her and Carter. Still, she peeked around me and yelled, "What were you thinking? We talked about this."

"I dunno, Momma," Carter said, looking ashamed. "I just wasn't thinking, I guess."

"No, you weren't, and this time you're really going to jail," Kathy shouted, "because I ain't bailing your butt out. You're on your own."

The deputy led Carter toward the prisoner containment section of the cruiser, and with every step the young man pleaded with his mother. "I'm sorry, Momma. Please bail me out," he repeated like a litany. "I don't wanna go to jail again."

I tried to keep a bit of distance between mother and son, but Kathy kept launching herself at Sheriff Harper and Carter as they marched to the car.

"Ma'am," I said, finally sick of the drama. I grabbed her by the arm, twisting it behind her back as gently as I could yet still using enough force to let her know I meant business. "You're not doing yourself any favors."

I led her a few paces away from the car, but despite my physical involvement, she kept screaming at Sheriff Harper.

Finally, Carter went into the back of the cruiser, and frankly, I was a little surprised that Kathy hadn't been invited to join him.

I would have been happy to be rid of her at this point, but instead, I held her still until the car disappeared from the lot.

I pushed Kathy forward and released her, making sure she was just a little off balance and I was out of striking distance if she decided to come after me. She did turn, and she did seem to be contemplating her next move, but Vincent appeared beside me.

"Take it inside," he said. "Now."

And Kathy obeyed.

Maybe she wasn't actually grieving, but she was at least experiencing a great deal of stress over her husband's death, and now we were sending her son to jail. Still, her reaction had been completely over the top. And what had she said to Sheriff Harper?

Once in the relative quiet of the GMC, I looked at Vincent as he put the key in the ignition. "That was more action-packed than I expected."

"Yeah," he agreed as the truck rumbled to life and carried us back onto Highway 403. "Something isn't right between the widow Vanderbilt and Sheriff Harper," he said.

I nodded. "We'll need to check up on that and verify Carter's alibi for the night of Theo's death. But if Kathy holds true to her word, at least Carter will be in jail for a while. One variable out of the way."

Fourteen

He picked up his weekly copy of the *Cranford Gazette* on his way home from work. Reading the paper usually helped clear the bad thoughts from his mind, but today he was hoping for so much more. He needed information.

One of his bodies was out there—somewhere—and he knew it would show up sooner or later.

Oh, he had sources he could ask, but he couldn't risk it. He had to stay invisible. He had to watch from the sidelines and wait and listen. If he asked questions of the wrong people, he could risk turning attention on himself.

And he couldn't have that.

So he flipped to the front page of the paper, and his insides leapt at the headline, which read, "Charred Body Discovered in Vehicle Fire."

Beneath the headline was an enormous picture of a burned sedan surrounded by yellow police tape. He sat back for a moment and smiled. Yes, he knew just how the scene would have looked as the fire took hold.

The body would have gone up like kindling. As flames licked around it, the head and appendages would have been the first to take real damage. The skull would have split under the force of the steam from the person's own frying brain, and the arms and legs would have clenched as the muscles and tendons shrank.

Soon pieces would have begun to fall off, one by one, as the fire did its job. If enough time passed, there would be nothing left but ash and bone chunks.

Fire like that always excited him, and he could feel the tingle of glee run through him now as he sat over the newspaper. But he could not indulge himself. He shook his head violently to force the images from his mind.

He must think logically and not let himself get carried away.

He had to be practical. Ask practical questions.

Could this possibly be his body? Or was it just some drunk driving accident?

And if it was his body, how well had the fire done its job? Was it still identifiable? Could it be connected to him?

And who had taken the body in the first place?

He picked up the paper, and with one last look at the photo, he forced himself to read the attached article, which took up little real estate on the rest of the front page. For such a large headline, it didn't say much specific:

> A blaze that consumed a 1986 Ford LTD early Saturday morning on Highway 403 may have been set purposefully, law enforcement sources say. The fire, which was extinguished by the Cranford County Volunteer Fire Department, left behind the scorched body of an unidentified driver. "The call came in around 3 AM," says Fred Thomas, owner of the Bait and Tackle and one of the first volunteer responders on the scene, "and Mike Symmes and I risked our lives to put it out. It was unfortunate that the victim couldn't be saved." Sheriff Bart "Tiny" Harper says that the case has been handed over to the state for further investigation, and though he cannot reveal the identity of the victim during an ongoing investigation, the body has been transferred to the state medical examiner, and he added, "Foul play is suspected."

"Holy shit!" he said aloud, shattering the silence of his kitchen.

This was his missing body. It had to be.

First of all, foul play was suspected. And torched bodies didn't often show up in Cranford County. Murders never happened either.

He sneered at the thought. At least no murders that anyone knew of.

Second, it would be too big of a coincidence for him to be missing a body and one to show up burned all to hell to obscure the identity.

And third, the fire had taken place on 403, which just happened to be the road he lived on. It was too coincidental. The body had to be one and the same. And now it might be at the medical examiner's office.

His hands were shaking so hard that he had to lay aside the paper to keep from tearing it in half as another realization struck him full force: he had a much bigger problem than just one person—probably a lost hunter—stumbling onto his land and, worse, onto his secret.

The authorities had their hands on the body. What if, even though it had been burned, they could still identify the carcass? After that, it wouldn't be difficult for them to connect him to it, and that was very, very bad for him.

But it had been burned, right? Maybe they wouldn't be able to tell who it was. Maybe they couldn't track it back to him.

The man jammed his hands together in front of him in an effort to stop the damn quivering. He didn't have time to sit around shaking like a coward. He had to figure out how to erase the connection between himself and the body or he would be totally screwed.

What did he need to do?

He needed to find out for sure if the body was indeed one of his. With the stiff already at the medical examiner's office, he had no idea how he could possibly go about it. He couldn't exactly head over to the lab and demand entrance, and he sure as hell couldn't just go up and ask Sheriff Tiny for info.

So that meant he had to find the jackass who had robbed his pit. And thanks to the *Cranford Gazette*, he now had a place to start. He knew the carcass thief owned a Ford LTD. He knew that Fred Thomas had more information, and he knew where ole Fred worked.

He stood, sending the wooden chair skittering behind him at the sudden sense of urgency that overcame him. He had to do something, even if it meant coming out into the open.

Stalking to his back door, he paused to yank a baseball cap from the pegboard and jammed it onto his head as he shoved the screen door open, enjoying the sharp crack as it slammed shut behind him.

He threw himself into his old blue pickup and started the engine.

Fred Thomas knew all about whatever the hell had happened out on 403, so he needed to get him talking. That shouldn't be difficult. Fred was a hunter, and hunters were worse than both fishermen and women in general for telling tall tales, so he'd probably have to listen to a lot of BS before he got the info he needed.

And if that didn't work out, well, he had alternative methods for extracting information.

He'd use them if necessary.

The parking lot was only sparsely populated when he pulled in, which was good. Usually, it was easy for him to stay invisible. People didn't notice him. He didn't know why, but he sure couldn't risk anyone noticing him now. Not with so much on the line.

As he entered the store, the bell on the door tinkled above his head, and in his ears, it sounded sharp and loud. He let the door fall back into place as he slouched toward the far side of the building, ending up in the shotgun shell aisle.

He lowered his baseball cap and picked up a box of twelve-gauge deer slugs. He pretended to read the back of the packaging, but he didn't care for shotguns. It was cheating. Well, maybe not with the deer slugs, but 00 buckshot was definitely an unfair advantage. Anybody could kill a deer with seven to nine balls in one shot.

It required no accuracy or finesse.

"Can I help you?" a voice asked from behind him.

Startled, the man in the baseball cap spun to face Fred Thomas, a short, stocky man with an honest face. "Oh, uh," he said as he turned to replace the box of shotgun shells on the display. "You got any .243 Winchesters in stock?"

"Nice cartridge," Fred said as he motioned for him to follow him back to the counter where the rifle ammo was stocked. "Good for deer."

"Yeah," the man agreed as he bellied up to the glass display counter. He glanced around as Fred pulled three boxes of ammo from behind the counter and laid them out for his perusal. No one seemed to be in earshot, so instead of reaching for the ammo, he pretended to study Fred and let recognition appear on his face. "Hey, aren't you the guy mentioned in the paper today? Didn't you put out that car fire?"

"Sure did." Fred beamed.

"I live off 403 and didn't even see smoke. Must not have been a big fire," the man said.

"Hell, boy, you kiddin' me?" And with that, Fred Thomas launched into a detailed account of the night. "The car was fully involved when we pulled up. Flames shooting out of the engine compartment and the passenger area. That fire was truly impressive." He leaned further over the counter and whispered, "And there was a person sitting right there in the front seat. I never seen anything like it."

"Yeah? That so?" he asked, trying to sound encouraging but skeptical. "I heard all kinds of rumors, but I don't believe any of them. That kind of stuff doesn't happen here."

"Well, buddy, it sure did happen," Fred said, rising to his toes and then lowering his weight back to his heels, "and we had to try to save that guy. Mike kept the flames off so I could work on extracting him."

"Sounds like a damn dangerous thing to do," he said, hoping to keep Fred boasting.

"Definitely dangerous." Fred leaned further onto the glass case, and the man in the baseball cap wondered if it might crack beneath him, sending shards of glass all over. That would be a pretty picture.

He shook the image from his mind and listened as Fred continued, "A bumper strut could have blown off and took out one of my knees, but I went in there anyway. Unfortunately, it was too late." Fred crooked a finger at the man across the counter, urging him to lean forward. Fred whispered in a conspiratorial tone, "I shouldn't say this because the name hasn't been released officially yet, but Theodore Vanderbilt got himself cooked good."

The man almost smiled at how easy it had been. Instead, he shrugged. "Don't know any Theodore Vanderbilt."

But he would get to know him very soon.

"You ever see a burned body, son?" Fred asked.

"No, sir," he responded.

"Well, it ain't pretty, and this whole thing has dragged in more cops than you've ever heard of. And I don't know nothing official, but I'm starting to think it wasn't even Theo in the car." Fred shook his head, not realizing how dangerously close to the truth he had come.

"But who else could it be?" the man asked, enjoying the irony. "Nobody ever gets killed in Cranford County."

"You mark my words," Fred said. "It ain't Theo. Next time I see you, I'll be proven right. You'll see."

"Yeah, we'll see," he said.

"So," Fred said, gesturing to the boxes of .243 ammo, "you want target, varmint, or big game?"

He only had to consider a moment. Even if a rifle wasn't his favorite weapon, he was clearly going to need it soon. And he wanted to be sure he could drop someone big in one shot if he needed to.

He looked the shop owner square in the eye and said, "Big game."

Fifteen

After the fiasco at the U-Strip-Em, Vincent and I returned to the DOI to take care of some miscellaneous tasks. I settled into my office to call the Alley Cat bar and confirm Carter Hashaway's alibi for the night of the car fire. The bar owner—a man who identified himself as Skippy—confirmed that the young man had been drinking with a group from the track until closing time at 2 AM. So Carter had most likely not had time to be involved in the staged accident. Plus, he'd probably been far too drunk, high, or both.

No matter what, I was glad he was safely tucked away in jail. He was one factor we didn't have to worry about, and after a few days without booze and meth in his system, maybe he would end up getting clean.

Ah, my dreams of sobriety for my sister were running rampant if I thought a few nights in county lockup would do anything for someone like Carter.

Just before the end of the workday, Ted dropped by to get a status report on Cranford County. He told me to keep up the good work and report back when we had something concrete.

What a motivator.

Soon the DOI building emptied for the day, leaving Vincent and me alone in our separate offices, so I took the opportunity to pull out my cell phone and make a quick call to Tripp Carver.

"Hey Tripp," I said, spinning around in my office chair so I could look out the window at Mercer in the gathering dimness of evening.

Before I even asked about my sister's case, Tripp waded right into it. "I've had shit for luck with Atkins. My buddies in Orr County have been pushing him to name his associate, but so far, he's mute. I contacted the DA's office, and the prosecutor has offered a plea deal—info in exchange for reduced charges—to Atkins's defense attorney, but they don't seem amenable so far. He's not giving up the name easily."

Damn, I thought.

"That's okay," I said, wishing that something in this case would actually be easy and thinking of poor Tricia in the ICU. She just couldn't catch a break. "At least you tried."

"Well, take heart, Jules," Tripp said. "It's not over yet."

"Oh?" I asked. Tripp's upbeat tone gave me hope.

"I ran into your friend Helena downtown today. We had lunch, and she gave me some ideas about where to go from here. I'm pursuing those now. That girl sure knows how to work the system."

"Hels?" I repeated, feeling a jolt of panic hit my spine. I hadn't told Helena anything about Atkins or my investigation. I wanted to keep that part of my life separate. I wanted to be me without the baggage when it came to my best friend.

"Yeah," Tripp affirmed. "I guess you hadn't had time to fill her in on Atkins, so I told her. Hope that's okay."

"Sure," I said, though I wished he hadn't. I wanted as few people as possible involved in my investigation. There was no need for my actions to hurt anyone else.

Fortunately, there was little Helena could do to get herself implicated in my dishonest dealings.

"Oh," I said, suddenly remembering that I hadn't told Tripp about my sister's current status. "Tricia's in the ICU right now."

"You're kidding!" Tripp said. "What's wrong?"

"She fell and broke her ankle. It required surgery, and now they're worried about her detoxing." I paused and tried to make my next words sound light, but they came out kind of bitter. "You know, the usual."

"That's too bad, Jules. But, you know, this won't last forever."

It wouldn't? It had lasted seventeen years already, and we were getting nowhere with Atkins. I was beginning to despair of ever finding Tricia's rapist. I sighed.

"Don't sound so down. I'll come by the hospital to visit," Tripp promised. We said our goodbyes, and I sighed again.

If only a visit from Tripp could solve all my ills.

By the time I got off the phone, the sky had completed its transformation from bright blue to light purple, and the lights of the city were blinking on, giving the streets a magical glow. This was a moment when the small Southern city resembled an image from a fairytale, all purple and perfect.

The ideal evening for romance. Maybe an intimate dinner for two and a stroll down a moonlit street.

Too bad I was stuck digging through the financial information of a potential fraudster and checking the alibis of meth heads.

A room away, Vincent's presence was palpable. In the quiet of the building, I could hear him tapping at his keyboard, and occasionally a printer would whir to life.

The shrill ring of his cell phone sliced into the pleasant quiet, and I heard Vincent answer, followed by a few grunts of assent, and then the words "hold on."

He appeared in my door.

"Medical examiner," he said to me as he turned on the phone's speaker and set it on my desk.

"Dr. Greene, you're on speaker with me and Special Agent Julia Jackson, who is also working the Cranford fire case," Vincent said. "You have something for us already?"

"Believe it or not, I do," Dr. Greene said in a voice that managed to be deep and rich even through the tinny speaker.

"No offense intended, Dr. Greene. It's just that we usually don't hear from the ME this soon." Vincent's voice was rough and uncivilized compared to Dr. Greene's smooth tone, but as always he was all business, the consummate professional.

He was right about MEs. Even when we did hear back, it was usually via reports, not personal phone calls.

If Dr. Greene were calling us and so quickly, this had to be a major find.

At that thought, anxiety flooded from my toes to my fingertips, and I began tapping my pen on the desk blotter to release nervous energy.

"Well," the ME said, "ordinarily we like to linger over a body and ferret out all its secrets before we call in the cops—you know, because you LEOs are so patient and all—but I found something you might think is interesting."

Dr. Greene paused, obviously a bit of a showman. Unable to stand the suspense for more than a few nanoseconds, I prompted him with unconcealed eagerness. "What did you find?"

"Before I give you any information, I need you to understand that I am still in the beginning phases of the autopsy, and given the condition of the body, I anticipate needing a little extra time. Already I've run across several anomalies, including a distinct lack of blood and some lacerations, that may or may not be explainable by the fire. So I'll need more time to run a bigger panel of tests."

"What have you got now?" Vincent demanded.

Dr. Greene's words came through the speaker bluntly. "I can tell you for certain that the body recovered from the car fire is not that of Theodore Vanderbilt."

Everything went silent for a moment as Vincent and I absorbed this news.

His fingers tightened on the edge of my desk, and I feared that the wood might splinter under the pressure. "Not Theodore Vanderbilt? How do you know?"

Given what Morton Ivey had told us about the inviability of normal visual or fingerprint identification, how could Dr. Greene possibly be sure if he had only begun his autopsy?

"Because," the doctor's voice said through the speaker, "the body on my table is that of a woman."

"What?" Vincent and I asked in unison.

My pen stopped tapping as I listened to Dr. Greene explain. "Bone structure of the pelvis and the internal organs—the uterus was a pretty sure sign—revealed that this was an elderly woman."

Holy crap, I thought, unable to take my eyes off the phone as the news sunk in. The identity of the body had always been in question, but I hadn't expected the victim to be an elderly woman.

Questions entered my mind rapidly: Who was this older woman? Why was she in the LTD? How had she come to be there?

What in the hell were we dealing with?

"I thought that would make an impression," Dr. Greene said into the quiet, and I could practically hear him smiling, pleased to have silenced two LEOs with his news. "I've already x-rayed the victim's teeth and will also run a DNA test to see if either method might help us identify the body. Of course, she'd have to be in our database for DNA to prove effective, which seems unlikely. Our best bet is dental records."

"How long will those tests take?" Vincent asked, echoing my thoughts.

"The DNA test will take at least two weeks," Dr. Greene said.

"Two weeks is too long to wait on a test that may prove fruitless," I said, interrupting Dr. Greene in my eagerness.

"But I've already got my staff working on the dental x-rays. We compiled a list of elderly women reported missing in Cranford and the surrounding counties, and we're working through them one by one. If those prove unhelpful, we'll expand the search statewide. As the autopsy progresses, we'll have more details—approximate height, weight, and age; race; and medical conditions—that should help us narrow the field."

I looked at Vincent, and his expression reflected my feeling of discouragement. Even with the details from the autopsy, compiling the dental x-rays of all missing elderly women in the state of Georgia would take forever, and we needed to identify the victim as quickly as possible so that we could notify the family and reconstruct the crime.

Because we were clearly dealing with a crime.

Insurance fraud was becoming more certain with each new detail we learned. An unidentified woman's body had burned in Theodore Vanderbilt's car, the coroner couldn't rule out foul play, and the fire investigator strongly suspected arson. Eva had discovered some of Vanderbilt's personal effects—his wedding ring and watch so far—in the debris, and now it was looking as if they had been planted on the body to try to hide the true victim's identity. And if that weren't enough to make us suspect fraud, Kathy Vanderbilt was already demanding money from her supposedly deceased husband's life insurance policy.

I was pretty sure we were looking at fraud, but what else was going on?

Someone was trying to pass off an elderly woman for Theodore Vanderbilt. But who? Theodore himself? Kathy? Both of them?

Had they burned an elderly woman alive? Had they murdered her and used her body in their fraud?

We ended the call with Dr. Greene, and Vincent and I looked at each other.

"Who was that poor old woman?" I asked, thinking back to the pictures of the desecrated body and hating every scenario I kept coming up with to explain the presence of a woman's body in Theodore Vanderbilt's car.

Vincent's eyebrows lowered as he considered my question and then added one of his own. "And where is Theo Vanderbilt now?"

Vincent and I stared at each other in silent thought while we digested Dr. Greene's news.

Vincent blinked first. "Theodore Vanderbilt is not dead," he said.

I ran a hand down the back of my neck, trying to relieve the tension that suddenly knotted there. "It seems not."

This information told us a great deal, but it also left us with more questions.

If Theo were alive, then that meant he was hiding somewhere.

But where? We'd been watching the Vanderbilts' financial records and credit card activity, but so far, no suspicious charges had shown up. Their statement included no record of payment to hotels, campgrounds, airports, bus lines, or gas stations, so it was likely that he was hiding out on one of his Cranford County properties.

We also now knew that the Vanderbilts had attempted to defraud Americus Mutual by faking Theo's death. That kind of fraud required two people—one to "die" and the other to collect the money—so Kathy had to be involved.

And the female body in the LTD? Well, that left me with nothing but the questions I'd been asking for the past ten minutes.

Who was she?

How had she come to be in the LTD?

Had the Vanderbilts murdered her in order to fake Theo's death?

A million dollars was a lot of money, but was it enough to induce someone to murder?

The Vanderbilts would certainly be charged with insurance fraud and second-degree arson, but we were now dealing with a potential homicide as well.

And a ten-year jail stretch was nothing compared to the sentence these two could receive if they had committed murder.

Georgia was a death penalty state.

And then Vincent and I were moving with sudden energy, both focused on the same mission: to find Theodore Vanderbilt and bring him and Kathy in as quickly as possible.

"I'll get on the warrants," Vincent said as he turned and bolted for the door. "And download plats of the Vanderbilts' properties."

My hand was already on the receiver of my office phone. "I'll call my contacts at the MPD. If we're going to have any chance of finding Theo without tipping off him or Kathy, we've got to hit all three of his properties simultaneously. And that means we need Mercer SWAT."

I called Captain Morey Sobanski of the first precinct to arrange for his SWAT team to carry out the search of the Cranford County properties ASAP. Those SWAT guys loved their jobs and didn't mind hauling everything across county lines, even in the pre-dawn hours, because it meant a little excitement. I made arrangements to email our entry plans and then follow up with a conference call with the team.

Next, I called Cranford County Sheriff Bart "Tiny" Harper to alert him to our plans and to explain why we'd issued an all-points bulletin for Theodore Vanderbilt.

After going through the sheriff's department switchboard, I was transferred to Sheriff Harper's home line, and I caught him in the middle of dinner. He didn't sound very excited to speak with me. After I identified myself, the sheriff said, "I've got to admit I was anxious to talk to the DOI joker who put an APB out on a dead guy, but it could have waited until after I've finished my chicken."

Ignoring the fact that I'd just been called a joker, I explained, "We have reason to believe that Theodore Vanderbilt is still alive and hiding somewhere nearby until his wife can collect the insurance money."

"How can that be?" he demanded. "I saw his body myself right after the fire was extinguished. He sure looked dead to me."

Thinking back to the pictures of the body, I was pretty sure that was the understatement of the year.

"According to the medical examiner, the body in the Ford LTD was not Theodore Vanderbilt," I said, "but an unidentified elderly woman."

The line went silent for a moment, and then Sheriff Harper asked, "You're saying someone burned an elderly woman to death? In my county?" He sounded ashamed of the whole human race.

"We don't know the cause of death yet," I said. "We're waiting on the full autopsy, but at this point, we're considering murder as a possibility."

A strong possibility.

"Who was the victim?" he demanded.

"She hasn't yet been identified, so we're running searches of GBI and NCIC databases, but you are closer to the situation. You might have a line on something we don't. Have you received any reports of missing elderly women?"

I was hoping we'd get lucky and someone had called in a missing persons report in the past week that had not been entered into the state system yet. "Any concerned relatives calling?"

Sheriff Harper thought for a moment. "Sorry, but I don't believe we've had a missing persons report in recent history. Definitely nothing in the past week."

"What about Theodore Vanderbilt?" I asked. "We know he owns three properties in Cranford County—the U-Strip-Em, the We-Shred-Em, and his home—but can you think of anywhere else he may be hiding?"

"Well, now," Sheriff Harper said, "lots of people here know Theo, but he doesn't exactly have a lot of friends, if you know what I mean."

"So you can't think of anyone he'd hide out with?"

"Hell, no," the sheriff said. "I can think of at least ten people who would turn him in on sight, though."

"So you're saying he's most likely to be hiding on private property where no one will see him," I translated.

"That's right." Harper reconsidered. "Or maybe hiding in the woods somewhere. Like a lot of Cranford's citizens, he's an outdoorsman."

The jackass was probably sitting in front of his TV right now. I quickly explained our plans to use Mercer SWAT to search the properties early the next morning.

"I'll send a car to each property with you," he said. "My guys need to be there. Since they're familiar with the area, they might see something you miss."

"Thank you, Sheriff. Any extra manpower is a benefit. We'll keep you informed of our plans as they develop."

Pleased to have the local LEOs on board, I made a quick call to Helena and asked her to stop by my place to check on Maxwell because, unless I missed my guess, it was going to be a long night at the DOI.

By 11 PM, Vincent and I had taken over the conference room, and the table was covered in property plats, partially finished water bottles and Coke cans, and an empty pizza box. We'd planned the entry of the Vanderbilts' properties and finished the conference call with Mercer SWAT. We were due to start the raid at 5 AM.

Now that the planning was over, I was suddenly exhausted, but it was pointless to drive all the way home. We had to meet with the MPD team at the ungodly hour of 4 AM, and that left me precious little time to sleep, especially if I wasted part of it driving.

"I'm going to catch a few hours sleep on the couch downstairs in the lobby," I said as I pulled my hair from the loose ponytail I'd forced it into a few hours earlier. I massaged my scalp and looked up to find Vincent watching me, his face blank.

"Yeah, good decision. I'll rack in my office," he said as he looked away from me and began stacking papers.

I studied him for a moment, trying to imagine where he thought he was going to find room to sleep in his tiny office, and then trekked to my own, where I would ostensibly be getting ready for bed. The fact was that I didn't have much by way of overnight supplies, but I did have a toothbrush and paste in my desk drawer.

At least my breath would be minty tomorrow.

On my way to the bathroom, I peeked in Vincent's office to make sure I hadn't missed the presence of a couch. Nope. Nothing but a desk and some chairs. No sofa. Nothing he could possibly stretch out on. That meant he'd be on the floor.

Poor guy.

Of course, the decorative sofa in the lobby where I'd be sleeping was probably just as hard, but at least I'd be off the ground.

I finished my bedtime preparations and returned the toothbrush to my office. On my desk was a picture of the fire scene. I picked it up and brushed my fingertips across the charred body in the front seat. Once again, I wondered, who was she? How did she get in that LTD?

On a whim, I sat down and initiated a quick search of the NCIC missing persons database and typed in the parameters I knew, which admittedly wasn't much.

The list turned out to be even longer than I expected, but I scanned it anyway. None of the names sent up red flags. Or at least none of them were Vanderbilts or Hashaways, and none lived near enough to the couple to make me suspicious. Given that we had only dental records for comparison at this point, it was useless to expand the search further.

And it was getting really late.

I had just turned off my laptop when I heard Vincent's office door shut, probably for the night, so I followed suit and made my way to the lobby sofa.

When I finally lay down, I expected my mind to linger on the next day's search plans or to focus on the poor old woman who might have been murdered in the Vanderbilts' fraud scheme, but for some reason, I was thinking of Vincent sleeping just upstairs on his office floor.

I shifted on the sofa and rearranged the back couch cushion I was using for a pillow.

I might as well admit how glad I was that Vincent was back. Arranging that SWAT search would have taken all night if I'd been on my own. And with Vincent, there was no nonsense. No debate. We both saw what needed to be done, and we made it happen.

It was nice.

Better than nice, if I were honest.

We were partners now, and that meant something to me. I closed my eyes and turned onto my back as certain facts invaded my mind.

Life hadn't offered me many opportunities to form truly close friendships, and I regretted that.

And now that life was giving me this opportunity with Vincent—whatever it might be—I wasn't sure how to handle it.

Helena, I felt sure, would tell me to run upstairs and jump him. Ditto Tricia.

And Tripp would tell me to be careful and play it cool.

And my mother? Well, I'd stopped considering her opinion long ago. As for my father, he would no doubt approve of my new partner.

But what did I want?

I flung my arm over my eyes as I pictured Vincent upstairs wedged on the floor between his office furniture and dust bunnies, trying to sleep.

It was pretty blatant that there was an attraction between us, and it was equally clear that neither of us had really acted upon it.

Maybe that was good enough for now.

Maybe one day in the future, one of us would do something to change the relationship, but I couldn't do that.

Not yet. Not with the end of my lifelong quest so close at hand. It wouldn't be fair—either to Vincent or to Tricia—to start something now.

I thought of Vincent's "hold fast" tattoo. Maybe that's what we were both doing: just hanging on for the right moment.

But it sure would be nice if the right moment were now.

I sighed aloud. My thoughts made me sound like such a drama queen. I wasn't sure what I wanted out of my partnership with Vincent, but I knew one thing for certain: I couldn't let him sleep on the hard floor without a pillow at least.

Standing quickly before I could change my mind, I grabbed the other back cushion and headed for Vincent's office.

I knocked softly.

"Yeah?" His voice was soft and more gravelly than usual. Had I awoken him?

I cracked the door and peeked in before opening it all the way. The guest chairs had been shoved behind his desk, and Vincent was lying on his back in front of it, his sport coat wadded beneath his head. Light from the street lamps slanted through the windows, illuminating portions of his face.

In the mottled light, his features seemed softer and his eyes more hooded as he looked up at me silently. Somehow the moment became an invitation. I don't know how because all we were doing was staring at each other. But I knew he wouldn't object if I took the opportunity to curl up on the floor beside him.

God, was I tempted.

But that wasn't why I was there.

With his large frame spread out, there was little room for me to enter, so I stood at the door and said, "I thought you could use a pillow."

He propped himself up on one elbow to look back at me, and I wondered what he saw. What did I look like to him? Did he also somehow know that I wouldn't object if he happened to try to wedge himself on the couch with me?

Probably.

But all he said was "thanks."

Neither of us made any movement to transfer ownership of the pillow. We just remained frozen for a moment, watching each other in the half light.

Then I handed the cushion to him and forced myself to return to the sofa in my portion of the DOI office.

But I left his door open between us.

SIXTEEN

Hours before dawn, the man was dressed in camouflage and toting his .243 Winchester rifle and field knife into the woods.

Yes, he was nothing more than a harmless hunter.

He was out hunting. That was all.

Only he wasn't hunting deer.

He was hunting Theodore Vanderbilt. The man who had stolen his body had to be eliminated.

He grinned as he tromped through the underbrush. He had no real plan beyond entering the property and doing what needed to be done. It didn't matter how Theodore Vanderbilt died, only that he died. Besides, the man had dreamed of these moments of death so frequently that he didn't need to have a plan. He knew that his actions would come naturally. He'd know what to do and when.

He was certain of it.

His small flashlight cut its meager beam through the darkness as he stalked through the cold woods, and his whole body felt both numb and tingly at the same time, but he suspected the sensation wasn't due to the temperature. He always felt like this—excited and almost otherworldly—in his fantasies, so it seemed as if he were having a fantasy now and not actually taking real action.

But soon Vanderbilt's house was before him, and he edged around the perimeter of the woods, trying to get a good look around with his light.

The house was dark, quiet, easy to penetrate.

The outbuildings were dark too.

Except for one.

A light coming from a small aluminum shed across the way seemed to be flickering slightly, so he came out of the woods, forgetting himself and walking boldly toward the flickering light, like a moth to a flame.

He couldn't stop now.

Yes, there was light coming from a window on the left side, and he could hear the sound of a TV playing softly within.

Someone was in there.

He felt his body flush with pleasure as he peeked in the window. The light from the TV in the corner exposed everything he needed to know: a man slept on a small cot.

Theo Vanderbilt.

The man didn't even remember opening the shed door and entering the room, but suddenly there he was, above his prey, knife in his hand.

He didn't recall yanking the man from underneath the pile of covers.

Or taking him by the neck and pulling him to the center of the room.

But when he made the cut—just a small line right at the base of the neck—he knew he would remember everything about it.

The man had screamed, jerked, and then went into convulsions as his blood spurted from his body. Watching, the man with the knife felt giddy, and the room began to spin as he inhaled the smell of copper and saw the blood begin to splatter on the wall, felt it land on his hands, his clothes, his face.

For a moment, he was his father, standing over that dead goat. He knew just how his daddy had felt. He knew the exultation of the blood: both the blood on his hands and the blood in his own veins, the family heritage.

He stood still, enjoying the moment.

A scream sounded behind him, and he turned, jerked from his acted-out fantasy.

A small woman stood behind him, still screaming.

Shit! He'd been caught off guard.

Then he smiled.

To kill again so soon.

"Come here, bitch," he said, reaching for the woman.

But the woman spun, and suddenly she vanished into the darkness. For a while, he was able to follow her by listening for her footsteps ahead of him in the woods, but soon those stopped too. He tried to find her hiding place with his little flashlight, but it was useless. He couldn't see anything.

So he moved deeper into the woods. He would have to wait until dawn, but until then, he could enjoy his memories.

Seventeen

The alarm on my phone buzzed at 4 AM, but I woke up feeling like Julie Andrews singing on the Austrian mountaintop.

I don't know why. Maybe it was giddiness from lack of sleep.

Soon Vincent and I were at the MPD precinct so that SWAT Captain Sobanski could brief everyone on the objectives. Vincent and I fielded a few last-minute questions, and then we all piled into black, unmarked vans and rolled out.

I sat on a bench seat in the back of the lead vehicle between two black-clad SWAT members. Captain Sobanski was at the wheel.

Other than the fact that I wore a Kevlar vest too, I stood out among the rest of the team.

I was the only female.

I was in civilian clothes.

And I wasn't holding a semiautomatic rifle.

Even though I knew I would be in the background and out of danger, my adrenaline was pumping. I was going to the Vanderbilt house, which was the most likely place for Theo to be hiding out and where Kathy was probably still sleeping.

Vincent rode in the second van, which was bound for the U-Strip-Em and We-Shred-Em. He'd lead the searches of both properties, and they had a lot of ground to cover quickly.

But I suspected that if anything were going to happen today, it would be at the Vanderbilt house and not one of the business properties. If Theo were hiding, he probably wasn't going to be at a business where customers might see him and turn him in.

So the SWAT team and I were in for the most excitement.

Our plan was to enter the property from four angles, cutting off any potential routes of escape, so as we neared the site, we began to drop teams at the various entry points Vincent and I had plotted using the property plats and aerial shots of the land. One team would cover the house, while three others were charged with checking the surrounding land and outbuildings.

After the first three SWAT teams had deployed, I remained in the vehicle as Sobanski boldly drove straight up the driveway to drop off the primary entry team. The car from the Cranford County Sheriff's Department followed closely behind. Once the house was cleared, I would lead the search for evidence against the Vanderbilts with the assistance of Deputy Marston while SWAT finished searching the rest of the acreage.

When the van doors finally opened and the entry team hit the front door, I leaned forward to watch from the window. Sobanski had turned up the volume on the receiver so I could hear the progress of the team as they communicated by radio, and then I would be called in.

On edge, I listened as the SWAT team communicated with each other in short bursts, and though I knew exactly what was happening, the whole scene seemed totally surreal. The quiet morning landscape was dusted in a gentle fog, giving the scraggly property an ethereal look. It seemed almost magical, as if I should be looking for pixies and fairies and not watching a couple of men in black fatigues move quietly through the underbrush, marring the mystique of the morning.

The front door was dispatched quickly, and the two-man team entered.

All was silent for many minutes as they searched the house. Over the speaker, I heard each room declared clear.

"You ready?" Deputy Marston asked through the open window. "Looks like no one is home."

Odd. He was right. The team had not found any people in the house.

Where was Kathy?

Why wasn't she in her bed?

I watched the entry team pass by the front bay windows and move through the interior of the home.

I checked the Velcro on my Kevlar vest.

Hell, yes, I was wearing a vest. I was no fool.

Deputy Marston appeared to be all of twelve years old, it seemed, and the eager, nervous look in his eyes told me that this was his first year on the job. I'd be breaking in a rookie. Maybe this would be a good experience for him.

"Once we clear the house," I said, "we'll be free to execute the search warrant."

The warrant authorized me to search for evidence that Theo had been on the property or that he was staying somewhere nearby, for evidence of the Vanderbilts' fraud scheme, and for clues as to the identity of the woman found in his LTD.

Meanwhile, the SWAT team would have to clear the outdoor area, and that was a big job in itself. The Vanderbilts' property was composed of ten wooded acres, and that meant plenty of places for a motivated criminal to conceal himself.

I heard someone call "clear" and knew it was time for me to do my part. Snapping on a pair of nitrile gloves, I led Deputy Marston into the house. "You ready for this, Marston?" I asked.

"Yes, ma'am," he said. "Just tell me what to do."

More than willing to accept help, I handed him a spare pair of blue gloves and the photographs of both Theo and Kathy Vanderbilt. "Why don't you look around the main rooms for evidence of where Vanderbilt might be hiding out? Cash receipts, gas purchases. Also anything pertaining to an older woman or about Americus Mutual."

"Yes, ma'am," he said, snapping the gloves into place and marching straight to his appointed station as he studied the pictures in his hand.

He was cute. A bit eager and coltish, but cute.

"Sing out if you find anything," I said as I headed toward Theo and Kathy's bedroom. I figured that if anything were hidden at the house, it would probably be there. People liked to keep valuable items close.

Before I even made it into the hallway, Deputy Marston said, "This lady looks familiar."

I turned and saw him studying her photograph. "Kathy? Maybe you've seen her around town."

He appeared to think for a moment. "No, I've seen her at the station a couple of times. Always with Sheriff Harper. There was a rumor...." He caught himself and looked at me.

"A rumor about her and Sheriff Harper?"

His lips clamped down firmly.

"What? An affair?" I hypothesized.

He frowned.

So yeah, there was a rumor of an affair between the sheriff and Kathy Vanderbilt.

Interesting. It was probably nothing, but now it seemed we might have a new player in the insurance fraud game. I wasn't sure how the connection would play out. Maybe Sheriff Harper and Kathy had concocted some convoluted scheme to get their hands on Theo's life insurance money. Maybe they had planned to keep Theo hidden until they could disappear with the money. Maybe the woman in the car was related to Sheriff Harper and he had wanted her out of the way for some reason. Or maybe the death of the woman in the LTD, and not Theo's life insurance policy, was the motivation behind the whole crazy business.

At this point, of course, it was all conjecture. What we needed was evidence.

"Thanks, Deputy," I said and then returned to my previous course.

The bedroom was cool, but still warmer than Theo's office at the junkyard, and one side of the bed was unmade. On the other side, the covers were still tucked neatly under the mattress. On a whim, I touched the sheets on the unmade side and found them cool.

One person had slept in the bed, but she—he?—hadn't been here recently.

Where was Kathy?

I moved on to rummage for information in the obvious hiding places: drawers, closets, under the bed. Then I tried between the mattress and box springs and even searched the bathroom.

Still, I found no evidence that Theo had been there that morning.

The next bedroom had been converted into an office, and I spent a long time looking through drawers and files and scanning the computer.

Other than a particularly nasty email from Kathy to Americus Mutual demanding her money, I found nothing. There was no record of hotel receipts or anything to help identify the old woman whose body had been burned in Theodore Vanderbilt's car. Maybe the IT guys would have better luck.

I glanced out the window into the yard, but I saw no one. MPD SWAT had obviously started searching the woods and outbuildings, and I wondered how Vincent was doing at the U-Strip-Em.

Finally, I stood and walked into the main section of the house.

"Find anything out here?" I asked Deputy Marston, who was looking through the drawers in the kitchen.

"No, ma'am, not unless you count beer and beef jerky as something," he said holding up an empty bag.

I shook my head. Those definitely did not count.

His radio crackled to life, and I heard one word distinctly: "body."

My eyes widened.

Who was it?

Where?

I hurried over to Deputy Marston to better hear his radio: "Southeast corner. Shed."

That was all I needed to hear.

Dashing from the house, I turned southeast and saw the shed immediately. Two SWAT members stood at the door, probably awaiting further instructions.

"Body?" I panted as I got within earshot.

One of the SWAT guys gave me a curt nod.

"Who?"

"Theodore Vanderbilt."

I pushed past them, and I smelled the blood even before my eyes adjusted. The coppery tinge filled my nose and mouth, making my throat close violently.

I clenched my teeth to stop the gag reflex and began to suck air through my mouth. I've been told you can't smell things that way, but I swore I could still detect the sickly sweet odor.

The room came into focus, and despite the fact that I knew there would be blood, I was still taken aback.

Every wall was painted with great spurts of red.

And in the middle of it all in a pool of blood was Theodore Vanderbilt.

On the floor.

Throat cut.

Very dead.

I stepped back out of the shed and looked at the two SWAT members.

"Jesus." It was all I could think to say.

"Yes, ma'am," one of the SWAT guys said, his tone serious.

"Has the ME been called?"

"No, ma'am," the other SWAT said, "Cranford sheriff called the county coroner."

My gut told me that Morton Ivey was going to be of little use to us and that the body would have to be sent to the state lab, but I waited outside the crime scene for him to arrive.

In the meantime, I called Vincent to apprise him of our findings, and then I began to pace.

I don't know how much time passed as I walked back and forth across the dusty ground, trying to figure out how the horrific scene in the shed came to be, but soon Morton Ivey ambled across the yard on loose legs.

"I understand there's a body for me to look at," he said to me once he was close enough.

"Yes, in the shed." I gestured with my thumb, and he continued in that direction with me close behind.

Even though I was not eager to view the body again, I followed Morton as far as the edge of the crime scene tape.

He paused in the door, apparently taking in the whole scene from a distance. But he stood there for a long time, saying nothing, and I began to get anxious.

What was he looking at?

I sidled up next to him and looked at the scene over his shoulder.

Was I missing something? Did he see something I didn't?

I turned to ask, but as I took in his face, all the words left my brain.

He was smiling.

A slight grin, just ghoulish enough to make my skin crawl.

"Mr. Ivey," I said, wondering if this man hadn't been around death just a tad too long. Or maybe far too long. Was he one of those sick people who got off on death?

God, I hoped not.

"Sorry," Morton said. "It's the blood. It always reminds me...." Then he cut off his words and seemed to shake himself back into reality. "All right. Let's see what we can tell from a cursory inspection of the body."

I watched him carefully, still wondering at that twisted little smile, as he walked as close to the body as he could without coming into contact with the blood on the floor. He looked quietly at the corpse for several minutes.

He walked around it as best he could. He squatted down and stared at it.

More silence.

Finally, I spoke. "I've called the state lab, and they're sending a team to process the scene, but I'd like to hear your impressions."

Morton continued to look at the body, walking around the periphery and nodding occasionally.

"Interesting," he said.

"What?" I demanded, feeling far too creeped out by the coroner to be polite.

"I only see one wound on the neck," he said. "Of course, there could be others hidden under all that blood and on the front of the body, but I'm guessing the victim's carotid artery was slashed while he was still alive. That's about all I can tell without actually disturbing the scene." He turned around and looked at me then. "This was a terrible way to die."

I left instructions for the SWAT team to keep the scene secure until the state team arrived and began walking back toward the Vanderbilt house. I couldn't think with the smell of blood still assaulting my nostrils.

Theodore Vanderbilt was well and truly dead now.

But who had killed him?

Back at the house, I began to pace the front porch. Kathy leapt to mind as our primary suspect, and that meant we needed to find her pronto. Not only was she still going to be charged with insurance fraud and arson, but now she was also wanted for questioning in Theo's murder.

Try as I might, though, I couldn't imagine Kathy Vanderbilt killing her husband in such a bloody way and leaving him there for us to find, and the only other suspects I could think of were Carter Hashaway, who was still in jail, and Sheriff Harper, but that was based on nothing more concrete than a rumor at this point.

The kill was fresh, so Carter couldn't have done it.

But what about Sheriff Harper? Was he connected? Was Deputy Marston's rumor true? It could be. After all, I'd witnessed that strange exchange between him and Kathy the day Carter was arrested for possession. But I seriously doubted that a LEO would have slaughtered Theo and left so much evidence for us to collect.

I paced back and forth again.

No, we were probably looking for someone else.

But who? Was it someone connected with the body in the LTD?

Those questions had barely registered in my mind when I heard Deputy Marston's voice from within the house. "Special Agent Jackson, I've got a problem."

Expecting to find out that he'd discovered some piece of evidence or maybe heard something on his radio from the teams at the U-Strip-Em, I rushed into the main room of the house to find Deputy Marston being used as a human shield by Kathy Vanderbilt.

For a moment, all I could do was stare. The scene was utterly unfathomable. We were within shouting distance of nine SWAT team members, and here was a young, strong, seemingly competent sheriff's deputy being held neatly at gunpoint by a short, albeit determined, woman.

And this woman looked like her day had gone to hell the moment she'd gotten out of bed. Kathy's blond hair stuck out in all directions, and she wore tennis shoes with a set of plaid flannel pajamas. I could see a swipe of blood on one arm.

But that was all.

One streak of blood on her left arm.

I looked back at Deputy Marston, whose wide brown eyes begged me to do something, and his bloodless cheeks told me that he was probably too shocked to do anything but comply with his captor's every demand. My eyes dropped to his duty belt. The holster was empty, and I spotted his service weapon on the floor a few yards away.

How in the hell had this happened?

Those moments of frozen contemplation and assessment proved to be a mistake. As soon as my brain awoke and told my hand to reach for my weapon, I knew I was already too late.

"Stop," Kathy ordered, "or I'll drop this guy right here. I've got a revolver in his back that could blow a hole clean through him."

Though I couldn't see the weapon clearly from my angle, I heard the definite click of a hammer being pulled back, and I knew Kathy was telling the truth.

I also knew that I'd better keep her calm.

Once a revolver was cocked, it became a hair trigger. One wrong finger twitch, and Kathy could very well kill poor Marston.

I lowered my gun hand slowly, willing my mind to come up with a method for taking control of the situation without getting Deputy Marston shot.

Once my hand hung uselessly by my side, the three of us became a tableau. No one moved. No one spoke. I think Deputy Marston may have even stopped breathing for a moment.

Finally, I recovered myself and asked coolly, "How did this happen, Marston?" I spoke as if I were doing a performance review and not hoping to talk us out of this mess.

"She just appeared out of nowhere behind me," Deputy Marston said in a shaky voice. He cleared his throat and added, "I don't know."

"Ah," I said as if that cleared things up. I turned my focus to Kathy.

"Kathy, what brought you here today?"

God, I sounded like I was welcoming folks to a garden party. And what brings you here today? Can I refill your tea? What a lovely revolver you have there. It matches your eyes.

Ugh. The MPD had trained us on proper hostage negotiation. I knew I should try to put Kathy at ease, and given her current state, that wouldn't be easy.

"This is my goddamn house, so you know goddamn well what brings me here," Kathy said.

There was a beat of silence.

What did she know? That blood on her arm told me that she knew Theo was truly dead now. Had she killed him herself?

I searched her face, trying to read the truth there, but I saw only fear in her eyes and defiance in the set of her jaw. Clearly she was already on edge, and I didn't want to say anything that might make her even more unstable.

"I'm afraid I don't know for sure unless you tell me," I hedged, trying to leave the conversation opened ended, so Kathy could tell me herself what had happened.

"Whatever," Kathy hissed from beside Marston. "Why don't *you* tell *me* what in the hell you're doing here on my property? In my house."

"We're executing a search warrant." I decided not to tell her that we had an arrest warrant for her too. No need to up the stakes. Not with Marston still quivering like a nervous Chihuahua in her grasp. "I can get a copy out of my pocket and show it to you, if you'd like."

"No," she sneered. "Don't you move a damn muscle."

We stared at each other, neither of us moving until Kathy asked, "What are you searching for? If you asked, maybe I'd have told you where you can find it."

I highly doubted that she would have been so cooperative, but at this point, I might as well tell her the truth. Otherwise, we'd be talking in circles until she disappeared with Marston.

"We were looking for your husband."

She stopped and eyed me, and it was probably the first crack I'd seen in her rock-like determination. "Yeah, well, you already know he's dead," she said as she began pulling Marston toward the back door of the house. "He was in the LTD." Kathy's tone sounded uncertain, but her face had hardened further, as if she were now set on some predetermined course.

I couldn't read her mind, but her body language wasn't encouraging. Her posture looked stiff, and her eyes were distant. She was cut off from reality. If she exited through that door, she would be out of view of the SWAT team, which I'd just left behind in the southeast corner of the yard. No one would be able to stop her from taking Marston as a hostage and maybe killing him.

I studied her expression and decided to proceed as if I were just here about the car fire.

"But that wasn't Theo in the car, was it, Kathy?" I asked, trying not to sound judgmental as I followed carefully while she backed Marston onto the rear porch. "He didn't die in a car accident."

Kathy stopped and stared at me. "But Theo *is* dead," Kathy said. "I saw his body myself."

"The body in the car wasn't Theo," I repeated.

She huffed audibly, and if she hadn't been holding Marston and dragging him awkwardly down the stairs, she probably would have stomped a foot in frustration. "I know that," she snapped. "Theo's in the shed"—her voice broke—"dead."

I stared at her, trying to decide what to say next. I decided to go with honesty. "I'm sorry about what happened to Theo," I said, meaning it, all the while wondering if she had killed him and was doing anything to cover that fact. "Why don't you let Marston go, and we can work together to find out what happened to him? We'll figure out who did this to him."

"Hell, no!" Kathy's little face began to contort and twist, and I knew she wouldn't walk away from this. She jerked Marston along faster now that she was off the stairs, and I continued to follow her progress toward the tree line.

I looked around, hoping to see a black-clad SWAT member in the vicinity. But I saw no one. Sheltered here in the backyard, we were completely out of sight of the SWAT team, which was no doubt still dealing with Theo's body. I could expect no backup. Still, I kept going.

Kathy's eyebrows dropped further at my persistence. She was preparing herself in case she needed to do something desperate to get rid of me.

"Just stop right there," she hissed at me. "Don't come no closer. I've had enough today."

"What do you mean? Had enough?" I asked.

"I ain't a fool. I know you're here to arrest me. But I ain't going to jail. Everything's changed. Somebody killed Theo and now he's after me!"

"Who?" I asked, adding calmly. "If you tell us who did this to your husband, we can find him and make sure he's punished."

Frankly, I wasn't sure that Kathy hadn't killed Theo herself, and she wasn't making any sense at all, but my first priority was freeing Marston. Then we'd figure out what had actually happened on the Vanderbilt property that morning.

But Kathy ignored my question. "I heard Theo screaming and I ran to the shed. There was a guy with a big-ass knife. And I'll tell you two things: I wasn't going to let him cut me up, and I ain't going to let you take me to prison."

"Who? Who threatened you with a knife?"

"I have no idea!" Kathy shrieked, causing Marston to stiffen visibly in her arms. "His face was all covered in my Theo's blood...."

Kathy's words ended in a strangled cry, and I decided not to push her. "It's okay, Kathy. You don't have to talk about it anymore. Just let Marston go, and we don't have to say another word about it."

I watched Kathy's bottom lip wobble. "I...I...found him like that...dead...bloody." A sob burst from her throat, and I knew I had to change the subject quickly to keep her from becoming too emotional.

"Did you see the police show up?" I asked.

"Yeah, but I didn't know you were cops. I didn't know who you were! I just heard a ruckus and saw a black van come up the drive. I didn't know what the hell was going on, so I stayed hid in the attic and y'all didn't find me up there. The knife guy didn't either. I was safe there."

"Well, now that you know we are police, why don't we sit down somewhere and figure out what happened to Theo?" I repeated myself in order to help Kathy see that there was still a nonviolent way to try to solve this.

But Kathy was beyond the point of listening to me and seemed to be talking to herself. "I know what happened to Theo, and if that psycho comes back, he'll do the same to me. All we were trying to do was get a little money. I don't know what the hell is going on now." Her eyes went wide and panicky, and my hand dropped automatically to my M&P. "But he's dead! Dead! And I ain't sticking around to join him."

I was certain she was about to go off the deep end and take Deputy Marston with her.

"Don't you think about it, lady," Kathy warned as she noticed my hand on my sidearm. "I got a revolver right here on this guy that says you're going to obey me. Now, put that gun down and we won't have no trouble."

I took a deep breath, willing my mind to function. I nodded at Deputy Marston as if I knew what I was doing and then laid my weapon on the ground.

"Look," I said. "Let's just talk. What can I do to help you out of this mess, Kathy?" She appeared to contemplate my offer even though I'd made the same one several times already, so I added, "If we work together, we can figure out what happened. We can find justice for Theo."

She squinted at me as if she just now recognized me. "You're the chick who interviewed me about the insurance policy, right? You're some big-shot state investigator."

I did not want to confirm that fact. I didn't want her to set her sights on me as a more valuable hostage. Maybe now was the time to take a risk, I thought, but one look at Deputy Marston told me that he was too frozen to attempt anything in his own defense, so talking was still the safest course. "Yes, we spoke a few days ago."

"Well," Kathy drew out the word. "I'll tell you what. You come with me, and we'll talk it out."

That didn't go well at all, I thought. Now she wanted me to become her hostage.

"I don't think that's a good idea. I can do more for you if we just forget the guns and talk."

"No!" Kathy said. "I am not going to jail, and as long as I've got this kid, you've got no choice but to let me go or I'll shoot him, I swear!"

"Okay, okay," I said with my hands raised in front of me. I wasn't sure if they were there as a defense or as a ploy of submission. Maybe both.

By this point, Deputy Marston looked like he was about to vomit. There was no doubt in my mind that he was well past the point of acting and would just go along with Kathy while she had the gun in his back.

I could not let that happen. I could not let an innocent suffer if I had a means of preventing it.

"Get over here," she said.

"Let him go first," I said, hands still in front of me.

"Oh, I'll let him go," Kathy spat, "but I'll be aiming at his head the whole time. You hear me?" she asked Marston. "I'll blow your brains out."

Time stopped for a moment, and then Kathy shoved Marston forward, her gun still trained on him.

"Get over here," she said to me. "Now."

Suddenly, she was beside me, pushing a revolver into my lower back just under the Kevlar.

With the gun shoved into my flesh, I had no opportunity to disobey, and for a moment, I was just as frozen as Marston had been.

A gun to the kidney will do that to most people, but this was my worst fear coming to fruition. I'd been too frozen to take advantage of Kathy's moment of vulnerability, and now I was a hostage.

"You're going to walk with me, and then we'll talk somewhere safe." Kathy's grip tightened and the gun pressed harder into my lower back, bruising me I was sure, as she pushed me into the woods. "And don't you try anything. I'll shoot you right here."

Everything seemed to solidify when I felt her shove the muzzle hard against my body one more time, pushing me in the direction she wanted me to go.

Here is where I should have gone back to Hostage Negotiation 101 and given her the same spiel about helping her out of this mess. About it being us against the world. But honestly, I was fed up with the situation, with Kathy, with myself.

I couldn't believe a tiny woman had appeared from nowhere with a gun and managed to gain an advantage on a sheriff's deputy. And now me.

Of course, I knew this sort of thing happens with alarming frequency. Police officers make mistakes.

Still, statistics didn't stop me from feeling like the biggest idiot on the planet, and that made me angry. Really angry.

I had done everything right, dammit.

I had called in the SWAT team.

I made sure the place was clear before entering.

I had a police escort.

I had my own damn weapon and wore Kevlar.

And still.

When the moment had come, I'd frozen.

Kathy's hand grasped my left arm, and she dug the gun harder into my side, using it to angle me deeper into the woods, but I have this crazy rule that I don't go anywhere with whackos wielding guns.

Adrenaline began to race through my body, and my mind seemed to unlock. Hell, no, I thought. I was not going to let her drag me to the woods and kill me. I took a deep breath, preparing to pivot and try to take her down, when Kathy suddenly stiffened and went down like a ton of bricks.

And a millisecond later, so did I.

My world stopped.

Every muscle in my body went rigid, like one giant, full-body cramp.

I couldn't move. I couldn't call out for help. I couldn't do a damn thing except feel pain pulsating through me. I somehow felt numb and itchy at the same time.

Then the sensation ended.

Just like that.

I blinked and a little bit of the world around me came into focus. I became conscious of a pounding in my head, and I struggled to see where Kathy was.

Every movement was like a knife to my skull, but I looked anyway. I had to know if she was going to shoot me. It turns out Kathy was lying partially underneath me. We had somehow ended up in a heap on the ground.

I struggled to move off her, but I couldn't get far under my own power.

Then I heard the sound of metal clinking and a voice from above saying, "Shit, shit, shit. I'm sorry, ma'am. I was aiming for her."

"What?" I asked, totally confused, as I looked up and saw Deputy Marston kneeling above us. "What happened?"

"I watched her lead you farther from the house and into the woods. I stayed close. She didn't even notice me. After what you did for me, I had to at least try. You saved my life," he said. "So when I got close enough, I figured I'd subdue the suspect with my Taser. Only I guess she was touching you at the time."

Ah. I'd been tased. That explained the blinding pain and nausea. I'd probably hit my head on something—a rock or tree root—when I fell.

Deputy Marston paused for a moment to haul Kathy's legs out from under me.

I pulled myself into a sitting position to look at her, but I regretted it almost immediately and lay back down, clutching my forehead in my palms. My head pounded, and I suddenly felt woozy.

"Is she conscious?" I asked as I gritted my teeth and closed my eyes against the pain.

"Don't worry. She's cuffed," Deputy Marston said, "and her weapon is secured. I've notified SWAT and an ambulance is on the way."

Well, in the grand scheme of things, being tased and sent to the hospital was a hell of a lot better than being dragged into the woods and then shot.

Or cut up and left to bleed to death.

"I can't believe that happened," Marston rambled. "I mean, we did everything right and this place is crawling with LEOs. And this was my first takedown. How'd I do?"

I squinted up at him, but it made me dizzy so I squeezed my eyes shut again. "You got disarmed by a ninety-pound woman."

"She caught me unprepared," Marston said.

"Then you tased me," I pointed out.

"But I cuffed the suspect," he said.

"Yeah, you did." Thank God he'd at least done that right because I was feeling a blackness wash over me, and then I was gone.

The next time I tried to open my eyes, I caught sight of a crowd of SWAT team guys and deputies gathered, and a team of paramedics was working around me.

Kathy had apparently already been taken to an ambulance or to a sheriff's car—I didn't know which—and now they were in the process of shifting me onto the transfer board en route to the stretcher.

"No," I said, trying to lift a hand. "Wait. Where are you taking me?"

"Cranford General."

"A few tests, or is this an overnight?" I managed to ask.

One of the paramedics leaned closer to me. "Ma'am, I can't say for certain, but sometimes head trauma symptoms don't show up for hours. The doctors might want to observe you overnight."

Well, that was a yes to the overnight stay.

"No," I said again, trying to sound forceful.

"I strongly recommend you go now and have a CT scan."

"Where's Vincent?" I asked. Something in me knew this was random, but my mind was foggy.

"Who?" the paramedic asked.

"My partner. Vincent."

From somewhere behind me, I heard someone say, "He's still at the U-Strip-Em with the other team."

Damn, I thought. I'd been hoping he'd take me to Mercer Med. If I was going to be in the hospital overnight, I at least wanted to be in the same one as my sister.

"Get me off this thing, and let me sit up," I said, even though I wasn't sure I was capable of sitting without vomiting. "I'll ask one of the Cranford deputies to take me to Mercer Med."

"Yes, ma'am," said the paramedic, "but again, I strongly caution you against it. You hit your head pretty hard when you fell, and you're risking subdural hematoma or subarachnoid hemorrhage even now."

I blinked at him.

"In short, this is serious. If you'll just let us take you—"

I waved a hand at him. "My decision is made."

"Okay," the paramedic relented, "but you're doing this against medical advice."

I gritted my teeth and allowed him to help me to a waiting Cranford County cruiser, and somehow my personal effects, purse and ID, had appeared beside me. A deputy I didn't know was at the wheel. I sighed, partially from the pain I was suffering and partially from knowing that every LEO in the Middle Georgia area would hear about this.

"My weapon?" I asked the deputy as he began to pull out of the Vanderbilts' driveway.

"Don't worry," he said. "I left instructions to give it to your partner."

I admit I zoned in and out as we made the trip back to Mercer, and my hours in the hospital getting carted from room to room and test to test were not much more than a vague blur. I saw ER doctors, a neurosurgeon, and a neurologist. I had a CT scan.

Apparently, I had no bleeding on the brain.

So that was good.

And my cervical spine was okay.

But I was still in too much pain to celebrate these victories.

Eventually, I was admitted to the ICU, which was probably overkill, but I was okay with that too because I was finally settled in a room with a reasonably comfortable bed. And I was near Tricia but apparently in another wing.

That's when I asked for the good drugs.

"Sorry, Special Agent Jackson," an evil nurse told me. "Acetaminophen only tonight."

"Can I have a dozen, then?"

She laughed and handed me two pills and a cup of water.

I pretty much hated her, and that feeling only grew as the night progressed and nurses came in every hour to evaluate my mental status.

Well, I could tell you what my mental status was: not good. I was in pain and tired, and no one would let me sleep.

At some point, Vincent appeared in the room. I don't know how he got there, but after one of my wonderful hourly tests, I looked over to find him sprawled out on the recliner beside the bed.

If he'd looked out of scale at the dainty iron café table at Hugo's, he looked ridiculous now. His head hung off the top of the chair, and his calves were barely supported by the footrest.

I would have laughed but my head hurt too much.

"Hey," I said to him softly. "You looked more comfortable on the floor last night than you do in that chair."

In the dim light, I saw him turn his head and smile. He looked tired, but the relief and care that showed on his features caused an unnameable feeling to wash over me.

Suddenly, I was a lot less annoyed at being in the hospital.

"You're here," I said.

His gruff voice came back soft, almost gentle. "Of course I am."

"You're not going to mock me for getting tased, are you?"

"Maybe later," he said. "And only a little. But I'll definitely congratulate you on saving that deputy's life."

By now, I'd figured Marston would have told the story so that he'd saved me and not the other way around. "He told you what happened?"

"Yeah, I forced him."

I laughed a bit and then regretted it.

"Figures," I said as I watched Vincent shift in the recliner. "You don't have to stay here, you know. You had a long day too, I understand."

"Yeah, we moved Theo's body to the state lab. We're waiting for the full autopsy, but so far, we've found no other apparent injuries. He bled out in less than two minutes."

"Kathy?"

"She's in here too under lock and key and in much better condition than you."

"Yeah, lucky her." Then I recalled what Deputy Marston had told me earlier. "The deputy who assisted me, Marston, mentioned a rumored affair between Sheriff Harper and Kathy Vanderbilt. Said he'd seen her around the station often."

"Interesting," Vincent said as he scrubbed a hand through his hair.

I faced forward, looking at the ceiling in thought. "Who killed Theo? And who burned the body in the car? And where did it come from?"

"Kathy claims she has no idea who killed Theo. She claims they were in the death benefits fraud together, but that was it. He found the body they put in the car—she says she doesn't know where—and they set up the whole thing together."

"So we still don't know where the body came from? Or who she was."

"No."

"And we have no idea who the killer is."

"Unfortunately, no. But we'll grill Kathy again Monday. Somewhere intimidating and official, not in a hospital. Maybe she'll talk then."

"Hmmm," I said. It was all I could think to say because my head was hurting and I was suddenly tired again. "You don't have to stay," I added as sleep began to overtake me.

The last thing I heard before falling into my hour's sleep was Vincent saying, "I'm staying."

Eighteen

The man paced in front of his fireplace, rubbing his hands together convulsively.

Things had not gone well for him that day.

Theo Vanderbilt was dead; that much of his plan had been successful.

But he had not anticipated the arrival of a SWAT team. He'd been lurking on a local high point on the ten-acre property, watching, waiting for the little woman to reappear, when he saw the black van pull into the driveway followed by a sheriff's cruiser. Picking up his binoculars, he'd watched as two black-clad men burst out of the van and into the Vanderbilts' house.

He'd known then that he was not safe.

If one group hit the house, there might be others searching the property. Without another thought, he'd turned and fled.

Now that he was home, he could think again.

How had they heard about Theo's murder so fast?

That bitch who'd seen him in the shed must have managed to get to a phone.

Could she identify him?

Feeling his nerves begin to jump at the idea of being picked out as the killer, he looked in the mirror above the mantel, trying to see what the woman had seen. He hadn't yet washed the blood from his face, and it had crusted over, hard and dark, giving him an organic mask. He smiled at himself and felt the blood crack as his skin moved beneath it.

In the dark and covered in Theo Vanderbilt's blood, he wouldn't have been recognizable to the woman.

For now, his secret was still safe, but he had to be careful who saw him. He stared into his own eyes as he considered this. Who had seen him?

Only one man.

Fred Thomas.

And now he had to die too.

Nineteen

I wish I could say that I awoke the next morning to a peaceful moment with Vincent when I was able to thank him for staying and tell him I was glad he was my partner, but that's not the way it happened.

I awoke to the shrill echo of my mother's voice.

"My baby!" she screeched—or at least that's how it seemed inside my fragile head—as she rushed to the bedside. "Both my babies in the hospital at the same time." I'm not sure if her voice was as loud as it sounded to me, but with my concussion, it sure felt like an ice pick to the brain.

I opened my eyes just wide enough to find her leaning over me and to see Vincent pulling himself out of the recliner.

"Hi, Mom," I said, rushing to reassure her that I was okay. "Don't worry. This is just a formality. I'm fine."

"You don't look fine to me!" she said, her concern evident in her features. "I got worried when you didn't check on Tricia last night, so I called Tripp this morning."

"You called Tripp? Why didn't you just call me?" I asked as I rearranged my hospital gown.

"I did," my mother explained, "but you weren't answering. It's not like you to turn your phone off, so I figured something must be wrong."

Oh. I reached for my phone, which was lying on the rollaway table beside me. Dead. I guess the battery ran down during my electrocution and my night of exciting medical tests.

"And then Tripp wouldn't tell me anything useful. He just said you'd been hurt on the job and were in the hospital for observation. I practically had to beat the information out of that duty nurse downstairs! Now, tell me what happened to my girl."

"Tripp told you pretty much how it went," I hedged.

"He hardly said a word. What happened? Why are you here?" my mother demanded, glancing at Vincent for the first time since she'd entered the room, maybe hoping he'd pony up the information.

I looked quickly between them, feeling more than a bit awkward to have Vincent and my mother together, and because the right moment had not arisen for me to introduce them, I decided now was as good a time as any.

"I'll tell you all about it, but first, I want you to meet my partner at the DOI." I gestured toward Vincent. "Mom, this is Mark Vincent."

My mother studied him from top to bottom, assessing him boldly, and then extended her hand, palm down, across the hospital bed as if she were the queen of England and he was required to kiss her ring. "It's a pleasure to make your acquaintance, Mark."

Vincent appeared totally unfazed by my mother's superior airs, and I watched as he took her hand and nodded a curt greeting.

"I'm Celia Jackson," my mother continued, "and if you don't mind my asking, where were you—her partner—when my daughter was hurt 'on the job'?"

"Mom—" I reprimanded, but before I could continue, Vincent spoke.

"Your daughter saved another officer's life, ma'am. She's a hero, not a victim."

I looked up at Vincent and wanted to hug him. Just hug him. Of all the replies he could have made to my mother's blame-laden remark, that was the best one.

And it seemed to settle the tension in the room enough for me to explain that I'd been inadvertently tased and had hit my head hard when I'd fallen.

The doctor, who arrived shortly thereafter, confirmed what I'd told my mother and also said I would be able to go home later that morning with the proviso that I take it easy and not operate heavy machinery for a few days.

No forklift driving for me. Unfortunately, no driving my SUV either.

When the doctor left, my mother leaned over me and kissed my forehead. "Oh, honey," she said, "I'm so glad you're going to be okay. You'll stop by and see your sister before you leave, won't you?"

"Of course," I said, and, hoping to remind her that I didn't have transportation home and could really use a ride, I added, "I just don't know how I'm going to get home. My Explorer is still in the MPD lot, and I probably shouldn't be driving."

The words had barely left my mouth when my mother's cell phone rang, and she pulled it from her pocketbook, fiddled with the buttons for a moment, and finally answered.

"ICU," she mouthed to me as she listened. Panic darted onto her face. Her eyes went wide and teary, and the phone shook in her hands.

She had barely ended the call when she began to explain. "Those DTs started."

"What?" I asked. "How? Tricia was on the meds."

"She keeps ripping out the IV," my mother said as she raked a hand through her bangs. "She must have done it again."

And long enough this time to allow her withdrawal symptoms to escalate. My mother looked frantically around the room as if one of us might provide some sort of explanation as to why Tricia might have done that. "I need to go," she said, but she looked at me regretfully. "But what about you? What will you do?"

"Don't worry about me, Mom," I said. "Vincent will take me to my car later. I'll be fine."

We both looked at him for confirmation, and he nodded.

My mom went back up to my sister's room, and I sent Vincent out so I could change and he could check in with Ted at the DOI. I had to wear my clothes from the previous day—actually from the two previous days—and that was highly unpleasant. I left the Kevlar I'd worn in the search of the Vanderbilts' property in the plastic hospital bag and slung it over my arm. After doing the checkout paperwork, I managed to talk the nurses out of forcing me to leave the hospital in a wheelchair since I was heading right upstairs to check on my sister.

That was a difficult task. Liability, I understood, and the duty nurses only let up when I showed them my badge.

I stepped into the hallway to find Vincent just finishing his phone conversation with Ted.

He watched me from the moment I stepped into the hall, his face blank. When he ended the call, he said, "Well, all hell's broken loose over Theo Vanderbilt, and Kathy's not being cooperative at all."

"Naturally," I said as I led Vincent toward the bank of elevators. "She admitted to being complicit in the fraud yesterday before I got zapped. Why won't she tell everything she knows about the body? She should know where it came from. She helped light it on fire."

"She claims that Theo found it—"

"Found it?" I interrupted. "Found it where?"

He shrugged. "She also says he staged the accident and lit the fire by himself, but she's lying. Someone had to pick up Theo at the fire scene. There was another set of tire impressions there in the grass."

Vincent followed me into the elevator, and I debated asking him to wait in the lobby instead.

Did I really want him to meet my sister? Moreover, did I want him to meet her while she was experiencing DTs?

I pressed the button for the fifth floor.

In that moment I had decided two things: one, I was going to let Vincent meet my sister, and two, I was going back to the DOI as soon as possible. I had to know what was going on out there in Cranford County.

The scene in Tricia's room was worse than I'd feared. My sister was crying and talking incoherently while a nurse I didn't recognize stood on one side of the bed, presumably to watch her until whatever drugs she'd been prescribed finally took effect and she stopped thrashing.

I looked at my mother, who stood on the other side of the bed, stroking Tricia's hair. Though she had only been up here for about twenty minutes, she already looked stricken. Her blazer had been laid aside, and her hair showed evidence of her running her fingers through it repeatedly.

"Julia, thank God," my mom began, her hand resting on Tricia's blond head as she looked at me. Then she noticed Vincent, and her face fell a bit. Clearly, she thought he was intruding. Still she said, "Well, hello again." Her voice was heavy with Southern charm, as if a strong dose of etiquette might cause Vincent not to notice the insanity of the scene before him. "How kind of you to come up and visit with us."

Vincent gave a quick nod at my mother's welcoming words, but he understood her tone and didn't further insert himself into the situation. Instead, he retreated to the doorway and leaned casually against it.

Tricia focused her wild eyes on me. "Sissy, help," she begged. "They're holding me hostage here! You're a cop. Arrest them!"

Yeah, Southern charm wasn't going to help out here.

"Mom," I said as I approached Tricia's bedside and tried to take hold of her left hand where the IV should have been. "Has the doctor been here?"

"Yes, they gave her a shot and it calmed her down."

Tricia rolled from one side of the bed to the other, and though the room was cool, an anxious sweat had broken out on her forehead.

Calmed her down? My sister looked like she could launch herself to the moon.

The nurse supplied, "The doctor ordered a change in her medication, and your sister's nurse will reinsert the IV with the new medicine in a few moments."

"Well, I wish she'd hurry," my mother said. "At least Tricia's not trying to get up anymore." She looked at Vincent, who remained silent but observant. "But she's obviously still in pain."

Though I didn't look his way, I was sure Vincent wasn't buying it. He knew this wasn't pain. He might not know exactly what he was witnessing, but he would probably figure it out shortly.

"I don't want medicine," Tricia said in a loud, clear voice. "I want to leave. I don't know why I'm in here. And why it's so itchy."

"Itchy?" I took her arm in my hand, looking for signs of a rash. Nothing.

"Yes, I itch all over, like bugs crawling on me. And I don't know what's happening."

"You hurt your ankle, remember," I said, trying to be gentle. "You can't leave until you're healed."

"Then bring me something to drink." She looked around wildly. "I'll even take some of that hand sanitizer over there. I've got to have something to make the room stop spinning."

"I can't do that, Tricia. It will make you sicker."

Tricia began to rock back and forth, jiggling her injured foot where it rested in front of her. That had to hurt, but she didn't seem to notice. I tried to still her.

When my sister spoke again, her loud voice was hysterical. "No one ever listens to me. I tell you what to do, what I need to feel better, and you always refuse!"

"That's not true," I said. "I'm only trying to help."

"Well, you're not helping!" she shouted again.

I cringed and stepped back. My head was killing me, and I literally could not bear her volume.

"You won't let me forget!" she accused. "You won't ever let me forget what that man did to me. I just want to forget."

Here Tricia's words descended into incoherence, and she sank more deeply into the bed, shaking. My mother had stopped trying to stroke her head and now held her shoulders to restrain her, but it didn't seem either to stabilize her or bring her any measure of comfort.

Finally, mercifully, Tricia's regular nurse returned, hooked a new IV to the pole, and reinserted the needle into her hand, covering it with what must have been about a pound of tape.

Almost instantly, Tricia began to calm down.

"Valium," the nurse explained, looking none too pleased at my mother and me. Obviously, we had not been watching Tricia properly. "We'll keep a close watch on her. As long as we can keep that IV in her over the next few days, she should be fine. And then she'll be out of here."

If the nurse seemed a bit pleased at the idea of Tricia's departure, well, I couldn't blame her. My sister created drama wherever she went, and this woman's job was probably stressful enough already.

My mother smiled and patted Tricia's arm as it began to go limp beside her. "Yes, I'll be glad to bring you home."

Soon Tricia was asleep, and I finally ventured a quick look at Vincent. He was still leaning calmly against the wall. Our eyes met, and I knew that this one incident had allowed Vincent a good look into my psyche. That part of me was no longer secret.

Fall had happened overnight, it seemed. While I was in the hospital, the trees had shed their leaves, and this morning a cold rain fell from the sky in cords. The windshield wipers on Vincent's old truck shrieked as they flew across the glass, providing brief glimpses at the world beyond as he drove me to my house. I'd been planning to try to convince him to take me to the MPD to pick up my SUV, but the foul weather and my lingering headache made me reconsider.

I was supposed to be taking it easy, so for once, I'd follow doctor's orders. At least for the weekend. On Monday, all bets were off.

I glanced at Vincent. He had been silent since we left Tricia's room, and now he was focused on the drive, his large hands wrapped firmly around the steering wheel. The open buttons on his cuffs had allowed his sleeves to fall back and expose his forearms. Occasionally, I got a peek at his "hold fast" tattoo.

I looked forward again as the truck rolled to a stop. Between strokes of the windshield wipers, I caught quick flashes of my house, and then Vincent shut off the engine, stilling the wipers mid-swipe.

My house became completely obscured, and the clatter of the rain on the metal roof drowned out all other sound.

Suddenly, nothing else existed.

Not Tricia, not Theo and Kathy Vanderbilt, not my family. Nothing.

There was only Vincent and me.

It was an awful and intimate feeling, and I didn't know whether to stay in the cab or throw myself from the truck and try to make it into my house without getting soaked and chilled through.

Vincent hadn't moved since he'd parked the truck. His hands still gripped the steering wheel even though we were now safely in my driveway, but instead of focusing on the road, he was studying me intently.

I swallowed.

This was not good at all. His time at the hospital with my family had been a mistake. I could not allow this false intimacy to build between us as it had between Tripp and me all those years ago.

After Tricia's rape had set off the downward spiral of my family, I had turned to Tripp for comfort. Only later did I realize I'd sought from him all the love my family had begun to withhold.

It became clear, too, that Tripp, for his part, had fallen in love with his role as my savior more than he had with me. That's why our romance hadn't lasted.

He loved me in spite of my weakness rather than for my strengths, and the difference was detrimental. When the dust settled and I began to recover, it was obvious that we had never truly known each other at all. I could not accept the idea of Tricia's rape remaining unsolved and was willing to do anything to keep her case alive. Tripp was against my quest, and I couldn't blame him.

If I learned anything from my doomed relationship with Tripp, it's that I don't want someone to fall in love with me because I need a savior. I don't need a savior. I don't need to be fixed.

Sitting there in Vincent's truck, I adamantly told myself that if were going to be with any man—especially Vincent—it would not be out of my weakness.

Vincent's hands fell from the steering wheel to his lap, and it occurred to me that he wasn't looking much like a savior at the moment.

"You okay?" I asked, though he ought to have been asking me that question after what he'd witnessed less than an hour ago in Tricia's hospital room.

His left hand came up to scrub along his jaw line, and he looked as if he were going to balk, but he didn't. "When I transferred to Mercer," he said, "I was hoping Justin would decide to move out of the dorm and bunk with me permanently."

"He didn't?" I asked, surprised. I'd watched the two of them interact with each other, and it had seemed like Justin was amenable to rebuilding their father-son relationship. "I thought everything was working out well."

Vincent spoke, now staring straight ahead. "Things were going well at first, and I thought...."

He trailed off, but I didn't let the silence linger. Instead, I took pity on him. "Something went wrong?"

"Yes, my ex found out."

I didn't say a word. I only looked at Vincent as his hands clenched into fists.

He muttered a curse. "I thought this was over. He's a goddamned adult now, and still, she's trying to keep me from him."

He paused for a moment, and even though I was dying to know something of his past, I figured I'd let him decide whether or not to continue with his story.

"I made a lot of mistakes," Vincent said. He hesitated, took a deep breath, and continued. "But after our second child died, everything just went to hell. My wife blamed me, and to tell you the truth, I blamed myself too for a lot of years."

I nodded, unwilling to say anything that might prevent me from learning a little more about the stoic man beside me.

"I'm sure Justin told you I abandoned him, and I did leave. But I never abandoned him. Ever."

Vincent's voice had become tight, and I couldn't retain my distance any longer. I slid across the bench seat and took his clenched fist in both of my hands. Slowly, he loosened his grip so that I could entwine my fingers with his.

He stared at our joined hands.

"His mother got sole custody, and after several failed attempts to see my own son, I couldn't take it anymore. I couldn't bear to think of what Justin would endure if I kept trying to make contact.

What his mother might do. So I joined the Navy. I thought once he was an adult, her power over him would cease."

"But it didn't?" I asked softly, and I wondered that he could hear me through the rain pounding on the roof.

"No. She's paying his college tuition and gave him an ultimatum. Her money or my house. I lost again." Vincent's free hand curved around the back of his neck as if he were trying to massage away the tension knotted there. "Justin's a good kid, but he's hardly motivated enough to get up before noon. He's not going to work his way through school, and I can't afford to pay for it, so he's leaving and she wins again."

Now Vincent turned his blue eyes on me, and all the breath suddenly left my lungs. I felt his fingers tighten on mine as his thumb began to stroke the back of my hand.

"Today at the hospital with your sister," Vincent said, "I understood you. I understood everything about you. I know why you do what you do. I know what made you who you are. There always seems to be that one event that sets the course of a life, and you let me see yours."

I nodded, watching as his eyes searched mine. "You don't even know the half of it," I said, though I hadn't planned to. "I've been investigating my sister's rape for seventeen years. Still am."

"Of course, you are," he said without taking his eyes from mine, "and you should be. Even before I understood where it came from, I admired your dogged pursuit of justice."

Feeling overwhelmed by the intensity of his gaze and mesmerized by the brush of his skin against mine, I didn't say anything in response. He was the first person who understood and didn't secretly think I was being obsessive.

At length, he looked down again at our joined hands. I looked too. My fingers peeked out from between his larger ones, but it was me who was giving comfort now. The small and weak comforting the big and strong.

"I wanted you to understand the same things about me. I don't know why," he said, "but it seemed important that you know."

And it was true. I did understand Vincent a little more now. His insistence on justice, like mine, came from suffering injustice his whole life. And his need to protect came from the lack of protection he'd been able to provide his own children.

We were the same, Vincent and me. A moment of powerlessness had borne in us the desire never to experience that feeling again, and we ordered our lives around avoiding it. And we fought on behalf of others.

But as I'd learned countless times with Tricia and my parents, we cannot will others to make the right decisions, no matter how badly we want them to. And Vincent could not force his son to stay with him when an easier path was available. It had to be Justin's choice, and it was one he might never make.

I don't know how long we sat in the warm cocoon of the truck and looked at each other, our hands clasped tightly as the rain eased. But before I ended up doing something I'd regret, like leaning against his shoulder or tracing my fingers along his tattoo, I leapt from the truck.

When I got inside my house, I was damp and chilled, but I didn't feel anything other than the warmth of Vincent's hand on mine.

TWENTY

The first part of my weekend was a wash thanks to the concussion. After Vincent dropped me off Friday morning, I alternated between sleeping, taking copious amounts of acetaminophen, sitting in a daze on my sofa, and impotently cursing Deputy Marston for tasing me.

Maxwell, at least, was appreciative of my slower pace. He kept a silent vigil beside me, getting up only to eat and make use of his indoor kitty facilities.

Occasionally, I attempted to get some work done, but all I managed to do between bouts of sleep was to check my email and read Eva Sinclair's final fire report. She had tested the fluid she'd collected from the LTD and confirmed her suspicion that the vehicle had been doused in gasoline. In the remaining debris, she'd discovered the metal springs and tube from a butane grill lighter, which was the likely source of ignition.

So according to our expert, we were, in fact, looking at arson as we'd suspected.

And given the fact that the body in the car was not Theo Vanderbilt and that the real Theo had definitely been murdered, we were looking at quite a bit more.

But what it was, exactly, we weren't quite sure.

I wracked my brain all weekend, trying to make sense of it all, and eventually I gave up.

I had an excuse. I had a concussion.

At noon on Sunday, my phone rang, and because I was pretty sure it was my mother calling to check up on me again or to tell me something awful about Tricia's condition, I wasn't keen on answering it. But I couldn't shed myself from the curse of a good, responsible daughter, so I picked up my cell phone without bothering to look at the caller ID and said hello.

I was overjoyed to hear Helena St. John's voice instead. "Oh!" she said. "Did I wake you?"

Might as well admit it. "Yeah," I said as I reached down to pet Maxwell's black and white fur. "I've had a lot on my plate lately."

And a slight concussion.

"And that's why you have no choice but to come to lunch with me and go shopping like we planned. It'll be fun."

I shifted Maxwell out of my way, slid my legs over the edge of the bed, and slowly sat up. My head didn't spin off its axis, so that was a good sign. "Sounds great," I said, and, realizing how hungry I was, I added, "I could demolish an entire buffet."

"And then shopping!" Helena added with a bit too much glee.

I didn't really want to spend my Sunday at the Mercer Mall, which seemed to stock only clothes suitable for sixty-year-olds who were trying to appear thirty or fourteen-year-olds who were trying to look twenty—both were pretty scary—but I'd promised.

Besides, Helena was probably right. It would be a good distraction from, well, everything. And now was as good a time as any to go.

Kathy Vanderbilt was safely in police custody with insurance fraud charges pending, and she would keep until Monday when Vincent and I would question her more thoroughly about Theo's murder. Supposedly, Vincent and I would receive the final autopsy report on the unidentified woman and the preliminary findings on Theodore Vanderbilt himself. But until we knew more, there was little we could do to move the death benefits case forward.

Tricia was tucked in the hospital under my father's watchful eye, and that meant there would be no more nonsense with her IV. If I knew my father, he would be checking that sucker every five minutes to make sure she hadn't pulled another removal trick. Now that her withdrawal symptoms were back under control, it was likely that she would be released as soon as the danger period for DTs had officially passed.

However, if I were perfectly honest with myself, I wanted Tricia to remain at Mercer Med—and away from access to alcohol—for as long as possible.

This was the longest she had remained sober in years, and now that she had been through a safe, medical detox, I did not want to see her go right back to drinking again.

And if anything was going to drive her to drink, it would be the news that I was pursuing her rapist.

Yeah, it was best for her to stay where she was.

But of course, the rape case was stalled at the moment too while we waited for the lawyers to go through the motions of the plea agreement in order to find out the name of Atkins's accomplice.

And as for Vincent himself, well, I pushed away thoughts of him with every effort I could muster.

So there was nothing for me to do but say yes when Helena protested, "Oh, come on! I know you're not a girly girl, but you're also not a fashion dud. Besides, I need to freshen up my wardrobe, and I don't want to do it alone."

She was right. I wasn't a girly girl. As a LEO, I couldn't wear skirts or sexy heels on a daily basis, especially if I knew I was going to be mucking about crime scenes or staking out a suspect. And now that I was required to be armed at all times, skirts were out completely for work.

Gun belts and skirts do not work well together on any level.

So unfortunately, my options were limited mostly to trousers, serviceable boots, and jackets. When I wasn't in the field, I did spice it up in the shoe department, but still, my wardrobe was not particularly exciting.

I sighed. It couldn't hurt to step it up in the LEO fashion department. My supply of jackets and tops that concealed my M&P was pretty slim. "I guess I could use a few new things," I admitted.

"Oh? And why would that be?" Helena asked with a lilt in her voice, obviously teasing me for my unenthusiastic response. "You wouldn't have your eye on a new gentleman, would you?"

I rolled my eyes. Ever since Vincent had shown up to help on my last case, Helena had become inordinately interested in my nonexistent love life. But as far as she knew, Mark Vincent had gone back to Atlanta. And after our incident in the truck Friday morning, I was inclined to let her keep thinking that.

But I could still torture her a bit.

"Didn't I tell you?" I asked slyly as I made my way to the closet to find something to wear on our excursion. "I've decided to hit the Mercer singles scene."

Honestly, I didn't even know if there was a Mercer singles scene. Where did unmarried people go to meet each other in this town anyway? I had no idea.

"Seriously?" she asked, sounding skeptical and yet also hopeful at the same time.

I let her question linger for a moment before letting her down. "No, not seriously. I've got more important things to do, but I do need to upgrade my work wardrobe to accommodate the...equipment I need."

"Oh," Helena said, and I could hear her disappointment. "Well, that could be fun too. Come across the street when you're ready. I'll drive."

A half hour later, I was showered and dressed in jeans, a crewneck sweater, and a pair of comfy shoes. I secured my M&P in the gun safe, checked Maxwell's food and water bowls, locked up the house, and headed across the street for my day of shopping bliss.

Helena must have been watching out the window because she met me in the driveway looking like a well-dressed wood nymph. I'd always envied her short hair, mocha-colored skin, and almond-shaped eyes, but mostly, I envied her ability to know what she wanted out of life and to go after it.

Right now, she wanted to shop, and nothing short of nuclear war was going to stop her from giving me a fashion makeover.

"Hey, girl," she said as she looked over my attire. "Lord, you should be thanking me for dragging you to the mall. You really do need some new clothes!" She motioned me toward her waiting BMW.

I lowered myself inside, enjoying the new-car smell and the buttery leather seats and wondering how she managed to keep it so clean with a baby in the mix.

"What are Tim and Violet up to today?" I asked.

"Oh, you know, father-daughter stuff. Probably a few Disney princess videos. Maybe a tea party."

I smiled, thinking of Helena's husband, the grilling king, sipping pretend tea from a little pink plastic cup.

"I ran into Tripp Carver downtown the other day," Helena said.

"Oh, yeah?" As my two closest friends, Helena and Tripp knew each other, of course, but they were from different parts of my life, so they didn't often socialize together.

"We talked about your sister," Helena said, her voice hesitant.

"Right," I said, suddenly remembering my conversation with Tripp. I turned to her as guilt overtook me. "I'm sorry I didn't tell you."

"About your investigation?" Helena said with a small wave of her hand. "Anyone with half a brain knew you were still looking for the man who hurt your sister. I mean, you became a cop."

"It's just that...." I hesitated. Here is where I should have told Helena the whole story: how I'd copied my sister's file and stolen bits of evidence. But how do you explain that? How do you explain that you don't want to pollute the best friendship you have developed as an adult by dragging your past into it? So I said, "Tripp told me that you gave him some direction on how to proceed with Atkins. Thank you."

"It was nothing," Helena said.

And then I changed to topic to work.

Her work. Not mine.

She was so excited about her new job at the US attorney's office that the topic carried us all the way through lunch, which ended with her announcement that it was time for us to hit the shops. "You're gonna be the hottest chick at the DOI when I'm done with you," she proclaimed. "Maybe I'll even get you to show a little leg."

"Can't do skirts with a sidearm," I reminded her, only briefly wondering what Vincent might say if I did show up in a skirt. I dismissed that thought almost immediately.

"Well, a little cleavage then." She tilted her head sideways and shook a finger at me. "You can't tell me a gun can stop you from wearing a nice, deep v-neck."

I groaned.

The sad truth was that I was already the best-dressed chick at the DOI. Our office assistant Matilda recycled the same slacks and boxy blouses every week, and she was the only other woman employed there at the moment. Besides, the last thing I needed was to show a little cleavage, especially with Vincent around.

But on the other hand, I didn't want to end up like my mother, who wore the same outfits she had ten years ago. I looked at my own attire. It wasn't so bad, was it?

"Come on," Helena said as she pulled a small menu from the side of the table. "Let's have dessert. You're going to need your strength, girl."

Helena wasn't lying. It was a good thing I'd eaten the whole order of lasagna and a piece of tiramisu at lunch because we spent the next four hours hitting every department store and women's clothing boutique in the mall.

Fortunately, I managed to hold the line and purchase mostly items that I could wear to work, and that meant blazers, trousers with belt loops, and tops that could be tucked in.

But I admit that I did get into the shopping spirit and give in a bit to Helena's suggestions. I got talked into a blouse with small ruffles around the neckline and a few empire waist tops that could conceal my M&P without a coat.

Those would be excellent in the summer.

I also ended up purchasing two lower-cut v-neck sweaters and some lacy camisoles to go underneath. Helena insisted I didn't need the camisoles, but even though I occasionally used my feminine wiles to manipulate a suspect, I couldn't get my head around the idea of flaunting my wares with my colleagues on a daily basis. Not in a business dominated by men.

Helena bought so many suits and coordinating pieces that I lost count. In a way, I envied her. She didn't have to think about weapons and handcuff cases. She bought what she liked, pure and simple. But the more I considered it, the more I realized I was thankful for my wardrobe limitations. Sure, I often wore sexy shoes, and I owned a few cute skirts, but when it came right down to it, I was a practical girl. I liked having a good excuse for wearing comfortable attire and shoes that didn't crush my toes.

And I could still ratchet up the sexiness factor when I needed to.

Yeah, I was fine with my wardrobe.

And even though I hadn't expected to find much solace in a shopping excursion, by the time we were finished, I was feeling rather peaceful, and that was when I made the mistake of talking about my work.

We were settled at a small table outside a bookshop with our bags—mostly Helena's, actually—piled around us like a barricade.

"You would not believe the crazy case I'm working right now in Cranford County."

"Oh, yeah?" Helena asked as she sipped a latte.

I explained about the death benefits case, the suspicious car fire, and even the craziness with Kathy Vanderbilt. I omitted the part about being in the hospital, but then I added, "I don't know what's going on around here lately, but I keep getting the oddest cases."

Helena sat up straighter. "You aren't in danger again are you?"

"Oh, no," I assured her, "they've made changes at the DOI."

She nodded eagerly, obviously sensing some delectable tidbit I was withholding. "You already explained about the gun. Is there something else?"

"Yeah." I wondered how in the world she could read me so easily. "We're required to carry at all times, but now we work with partners too," I admitted.

Helena's face lit, and I realized my mistake.

"Who's your partner?" She grinned and studied me. "It's Mark Vincent, right?"

I didn't say anything, trying to decide if it was worth it to lie.

"Oh! It is Vincent," Helena giggled. "I can tell by the look on your face. And that's why you didn't object too much to those low-cut tops."

Great. She was onto me. Might as well come clean.

"Yes," I said. "Vincent is now at the Mercer field office, but I can assure you that he had no influence on any of my clothing choices."

Helena clucked at me. "Oh girl, he's got it bad for you. Why else would he move all the way down here?"

I leaned back. There may have been a spark or two between us, but I wouldn't say he had it bad for me. "He told me he transferred here to be closer to his son."

Helena tilted her head sideways and narrowed her eyes at me. "That may be part of it. But only part."

"No," I said, thinking back to the conversation Vincent and I had on the subject. I didn't want to break any confidences, but I also couldn't have Helena thinking I was on the verge of a great romance. I'd never hear the end of it. "Justin was the main reason. Vincent was forced to break contact with him when he was young."

Helena's eyes narrowed further. "I don't know if I like that."

"Yeah," I admitted. "Well, Vincent didn't like it either, so he moved here in the hopes that Justin would move in with him while taking classes at Central Georgia College."

"That's good, I guess. Shows that he wants a relationship," Helena relented. "So how have things been between you and Vincent?"

"Not as steamy as you'd hope," I said, purposely omitting the rather intimate moment we'd shared of late. That would only provide fodder for Helena's romantic imagination, and I didn't know if I could handle it. "It's been all business."

"Yeah," she said as she considered me over her coffee cup, "we'll see how long that lasts."

I finished my latte and plunked the empty cup on the table. "Don't get your hopes up."

Helena smirked. "Too late."

TWENTY-ONE

The killing had been better than in his fantasies. With one cut of the knife, he had become all-powerful. He had owned and discarded Theodore Vanderbilt at will, and it had been glorious.

His only disappointment was that the woman had gotten away from him, and he felt that loss more than he'd expected.

He needed to do it again.

As he climbed into the truck, his hands shook and sweat poured from his brow. He lifted his cap and mopped beneath it with the sleeve of his camo coat.

He was going to do it again already.

He pulled the truck sideways into a parking space at the Bait and Tackle. The lot was empty, and this pleased him. There would be no waiting around. He could simply walk in and get down to business. And so he entered the building, found Fred Thomas dusting the long glass counter, and pulled his knife from his belt.

Fred was the last connection between himself and the burned body, and he had to be erased. Crossing the showroom in a few swift steps, he found himself right behind the shorter man, and without his realizing he'd even done it, his arm was already around Fred, and the knife was at his neck.

Just one cut, and the job was finished.

The squatty little man hardly made a sound, but he began to thrash wildly in his arms. He released his grip and Fred crashed forward, falling through the display case, sending shards of glass flying. He felt them land on his skin and cut him, and he stood there watching as his own blood mingled with Fred's.

It was over too soon, leaving blood and broken glass everywhere.

It was a mess, but he didn't care.

Fred wouldn't be able to tell anyone that he'd come around asking about that body.

Now to get Fred to his pit.

He looked around quickly, his eyes landing on a display of sleeping bags. He ripped the packaging open and zipped Fred into one, lifted him over his shoulder, and carried him out of the store. He hefted the body into the bed of the pickup, and it landed with a satisfying thump.

And with no witnesses and no trouble, the man disappeared from the Bait and Tackle, leaving only blood and the promise of death behind.

Twenty-two

Monday morning found me anxious to get back to the DOI so that Vincent and I could get on with the business of questioning Kathy Vanderbilt, who had also been released from the hospital and was now being held at the Mercer jail. I checked my bedside clock and found it was already 7:30, so I had to rush to dress, realizing in the process that I hadn't done laundry in days, and with a wardrobe as small as mine, that was a real problem.

I had no clean clothes.

Then I remembered my shopping trip with Helena. I immediately grabbed one of the bags that I had stowed in the guest bedroom and began removing tags.

I ended up wearing a pair of khakis and a v-neck sweater cut low enough that the top of my lace camisole peeked out occasionally. Mentally, I shook my fist at Helena for talking me into this outfit, even if it was only mildly revealing.

I looked at myself in the mirror, trying to decide if I should change, but then I realized I didn't have time to dither. We had work to do.

I refilled Maxwell's food and water bowls and vowed to get him a nice cat toy as soon as the case was over. He'd been a real comfort while I was recovering from my concussion, and he deserved a reward. It wasn't until I walked into the garage, dressed and ready for work, that I remembered my SUV was still at the MPD.

I called Vincent from the middle of my empty garage.

"I need a ride," I said by way of greeting. "Where are you?"

"In your driveway," he said, and I could tell he was smiling.

Well, it was good that at least one of us remembered my lack of a vehicle.

I made my way outside to find Vincent leaning against the bumper of his truck, his legs crossed casually as he waited.

I wondered how long he'd been there, but before I could ask, I spied Helena, who was pretending not to watch us from her front porch. She was already dressed for work in one of her new suits, which I remembered because of its striking deep purple fabric and the fact that it fit her like a glove. I glanced at my own new clothes and knew Helena was congratulating herself. I'd worn a new outfit, and if Vincent's ardent attention were any indicator, I was looking pretty darn good.

And what would Vincent's expression say to Helena?

Had she seen him drive up?

Did she think he'd been at my place all night?

Did it even matter?

No matter what, Helena, romantic soul that she was, would imagine a romantic scenario.

Briefly, I contemplated walking straight up to Vincent and hugging him, just to watch Helena's jaw hit the deck.

But that would send all the wrong signals to Vincent, so instead I sauntered over and said "good morning" before making my way to the passenger seat.

There, that should be appropriately boring. My thought was interrupted as I felt Vincent's hand land gently on my back.

"How is your head this morning?" he asked as he unlocked the passenger door and took my bag while I climbed inside.

Great day for him to act gentlemanly, I thought. If anything, this would prove beyond a shadow of a doubt that Helena was right. Something was going on between us.

He handed me my bag, but he didn't let me take it from him immediately. I looked up at his face and found that he was watching me intently, as if I should say something.

That's when I realized I hadn't responded to his question.

"Oh, my head!" I said. "It's fine."

He lowered his eyebrows, and I saw his concern. If I couldn't answer a simple question about my health, then he was probably unsure of my mental status.

"Well, the concussion is causing less pain," I added, "but I'll be doing much better after I've had coffee."

"That'll be our first stop then." He let go of my bag and shut the door for me.

As Vincent put the truck in reverse, I shot Helena a glance and found her giving me a subtle thumbs up.

Great. So much for disabusing her of her romantic notions.

I shouldn't be thinking of Helena or romance. I ought to bring my focus to the case right away.

"Are we set with Kathy Vanderbilt?" I asked.

He nodded.

"Given what I learned about the rumors of her and Sheriff Harper, it's good that we held her in Mercer and not at the Cranford jail. Best to keep them separate, just in case."

"And right now Americus Mutual is in a tight place," Vincent said. "Kathy has already confessed to attempting to defraud them—and she'll be prosecuted, of course—but now Theo actually is dead. And if Kathy didn't have a hand in his murder, she could still end up getting a million bucks."

What he said was true. Yes, Kathy had attempted to defraud Americus, but because the life insurance policy had been in effect when Theo actually had been killed, the company would still be required to make good on their policy as long as it was proven that she had nothing to do with his murder.

We needed to untangle the matter of Theo's murder and the origin of the body in the car.

Kathy was brought to a small, square interrogation room in the MPD. Vincent and I watched on the closed-circuit TV monitor as she fidgeted alone for a few minutes.

"Shall we?" Vincent finally asked.

I led the way into the tiny, boxlike room, and though there were two chairs set out for us, I elected to stand behind Vincent. I really wanted to pace, but the room was far too small for it.

I didn't feel like starting off with idle chitchat. I'd spoken with Kathy enough to know how deceitful she could be.

"So tell us, Kathy," I said. "Tell us everything that happened, starting with the day you and Theo came up with this insurance fraud scheme."

Kathy glared up at me and then began to pick at the legs of her orange jumpsuit.

"It'll go easier on you if you talk," Vincent said. He tried to sound nice, but I don't think he quite pulled it off. Forget good cop/bad cop; we were pulling a bad cop/bad cop.

Kathy said nothing.

"We think you killed Theo," I said flatly. "And what about the woman in the LTD? Did you kill her too?"

"I did not kill Theo," she said. Her voice came from her little mouth with great volume.

"Didn't you?" I asked. "Didn't you want the insurance money?"

"I did want the money, but Theo wasn't supposed to die," she said as her fingers left her pants and gripped the edge of the table between us. "I told you that."

"If he wasn't supposed to die," Vincent said, "then how did he end up in the shed?"

Kathy looked at me directly for the first time. "I don't know."

"You don't know?" I asked, my tone oozing skepticism. "It sure looked to me like he'd been in that shed for a while. He had a bed and a TV."

"Like I said, I don't know."

"Well, right now, we have some pretty damning evidence against you. You just admitted to a motive: you wanted the money. You had the means: you own knives. We gathered them as evidence from your kitchen. And you had the opportunity: he was in your shed. Tell me why we shouldn't add murder to the list of charges against you already."

"Because I didn't kill my husband!" Kathy's eyes blazed at me, but behind the anger, I saw fear. And that's probably what loosened her tongue. "If I tell you everything, you'll figure it out. You'll figure out what happened to Theo."

"If you tell us the truth, we'll deal fairly with you," Vincent said.

Kathy's bold expression faltered, and she began to fidget in her chair. "I...," she began and then stopped herself.

No one spoke, and the intensity of the silence became palpable.

Finally, Kathy slumped forward in defeat, and I knew she was going to cave.

With her eyes riveted on the table in front of her, she began to talk. "Theo and me, we were tired of being in debt and working all the time. I still had nursing school to pay for, and I hated my new job. Theo hated the junking business. Carter was doing all the work there anyway."

"But he didn't want to sell it?" I asked, remembering what Carter had told us earlier.

"Carter and I begged him to sell, but Theo kept saying we couldn't afford it. We had taken out that loan to remodel, and we'd only be able to break even on a sale. We wouldn't make any profit. We wouldn't have enough money to live on, so I'd have to keep working at the doctor's office, and Theo would have to find something else to do to earn a living."

"And you didn't want to work?" Vincent asked.

"Hell, no," Kathy said without a hint of shame in her voice. "Who wants to work?"

Ignoring her question, I asked, "So that's when you came up with the car fire idea?"

"No, we had the idea a year back. It was just a dream that we used to talk about, really. One day, we'd fake Theo's death and use the life insurance money to go on vacation permanently in the Caribbean. We had it all planned out—the car accident, the fire—but we never could figure out how it would work without a body.

"But one day last week, Theo comes home from hunting and says, 'I figured out how we can do it. We can get that money and move to the tropics.' I thought he was crazy, but then he tells me he found a body."

"Found it?" Vincent repeated. "Where?"

"Yeah, found it, but he didn't say where," Kathy said, leaning forward to explain. "I didn't believe him either, so I told him to prove it, and he brings me outside and opens the trunk of the LTD and there she is."

"He just walked you outside and showed you a dead body, and you didn't think of calling the police?" Vincent demanded. "At the very least, he's stolen a body. Or killed someone."

"I was shocked," Kathy admitted, "but there was this old woman in the trunk of Theo's car. He'd already gotten us into this whole thing. I had to go along with it."

"And he never told you where the body came from," I said, crossing my arms in front of me and narrowing my eyes at her.

Kathy gave me a level stare. "He never told me," she said, enunciating each word.

"Who was the woman? Did you recognize her?"

"No," Kathy said.

I studied her face. She kept looking between Vincent and me and that spot on her pants she'd been picking. She seemed nervous, but was she lying now? I wasn't sure.

"And you didn't suspect that Theo killed her?" Vincent asked.

"Hell, no. Theo wasn't that way. He wasn't a killer. He was just a nice, normal guy."

A nice, normal guy who thought it was okay to desecrate and burn a body so he could fake his own death in order to collect his life insurance money and move to a tropical island.

Nice and normal.

"Right," I said.

"So you helped Theo set up the accident," Vincent prompted.

Kathy's gaze shifted between us as if she were considering the merits of denying it. "Yeah," she said. "I drove him out to 403 and helped him get the lady in the car. We dumped gas all over and tried to light the car on fire. It was harder to light than I thought it would be, and I had to get one of those grill lighters to do it.

"We got the fire going and left. Theo decided to hide out in the shed because we knew police would be coming to the house eventually. And that was the whole plan. I'd call the insurance company and get the money. That's it."

"That's all? Theo would just hide in the shed until you got paid?"

"Yeah," Kathy said.

"Then why is Theo dead?" Vincent asked.

"I don't know."

"What happened the morning we came to arrest you and search your home?" Even though I'd asked her these questions while she'd held Marston hostage, I wanted to hear her answers again. "You weren't in bed when we arrived. Where were you?"

"I heard Theo screaming around 4 AM, so I ran outside to see what was the matter. And that's...that's when I saw what I saw."

"What did you see?" asked Vincent in a more restrained tone.

"Theo dead, and a man covered in blood holding a knife." Kathy stopped. She seemed to need to gather herself to tell the rest of her tale. "We stared at each other, and then he reached out and grabbed my arm. 'Come here, bitch,' he said."

Kathy's hands were back on the table, but now, instead of gripping the edge, they shook. Her pinched facial expression told me that she was experiencing the true trauma of her husband's murder. And if she were telling the truth, she had come face to face with his killer, which could explain how Theo's blood came to be on the arm of her pajamas.

"Could you see who it was?" Vincent asked.

"I don't know who it was." Kathy sniffled, and a tear landed on the metal table between us. "I couldn't tell. His face was all covered in blood, and I couldn't tell."

"What happened then?" I asked.

"I ran into the woods to hide, and he followed me, but I got away from him in the dark. I had just sneaked back into the house when I saw the black van pull up. At first, I thought it was the knife guy back to get me, but then I realized it was the cops. Either way, I hid in the attic." She paused and looked at me. "The rest you know."

"When you saw the van in your driveway, you knew it was the police? How?" I asked. The vans had been unmarked.

"I know a police van. Plus, there was a sheriff's car behind it."

"And no one called to warn you we were coming?" I pressed.

Kathy met my gaze, and I could see she was surprised by my accusation. "No. Who would have done that?" she asked.

"Sheriff Harper," I said.

Kathy's brow furrowed. "Sheriff Harper?"

"Do you know him?"

"No," Kathy said. "Not really."

"What does that mean?"

"It means I don't know him."

"You're not having an affair with him?"

Kathy's jaw dropped slightly. "No! With Sheriff Harper? No way."

"Then how do you explain your frequent presence at the sheriff's office?" I bluffed. All we had were rumors, but it never hurt to test them with a good lie.

Kathy looked down at her pants again, but this time her eyes didn't return to Vincent or me. "I can't tell you."

And she stuck to that story until we finally left the interrogation room.

TWENTY-THREE

After we finished questioning Kathy Vanderbilt, Vincent left for the DOI. Because we were still largely stalled in our investigation, he seemed ready to call the medical examiner and force the autopsy results out of him.

And I was no less anxious to be about my own tasks, but since I was at the MPD, I checked Tripp's office, intending to say hello. When I saw he wasn't there, I collected my SUV from the MPD parking lot where it had been waiting since the SWAT raid and returned to the DOI.

Now that we'd spoken to Kathy, we were simply waiting on the ME's information, and since I had a few questions for Sheriff Harper that needed to be cleared up, my next task was to give him a call. There was something between Harper and Kathy Vanderbilt, but I had a difficult time suspecting the sheriff of slaughtering Theo Vanderbilt and leaving his body for us to find. It didn't make sense.

Still, Kathy was hiding something about the sheriff, so I had to follow up. Instead of carting myself all the way to Cranford and insulting Sheriff Harper by interrogating him in his own department, I thought I'd give him the courtesy of a phone call instead.

The call was answered by none other than Deputy Marston.

I identified myself and then asked, "Desk duty, huh?"

"Oh, hi, Special Agent Jackson," Marston said, sounding both happy to hear from me and slightly ashamed. "How are you feeling?"

"I'm fine," I said. "How long are you trapped as receptionist?"

"Well, Sheriff Harper didn't look too kindly on me being disarmed and then tasing another LEO, so it'll be at least a month. Maybe more, depending on his mood, I guess." I heard papers rustling in the background. "But it's okay because I love filing."

I laughed.

In a quieter voice, he asked, "Got any more info on who killed Theodore Vanderbilt?"

"No, nothing yet," I said, not interested in starting any rumors. We already had enough to deal with.

"Three murders in one week in Cranford," Marston said, clearly speaking as softly as he possibly could. "Everyone's saying we've got a serial killer on our hands. Is that true?"

I raised an eyebrow at this new information. "Three murders?"

"You haven't heard?" he asked. "Fred Thomas went missing this weekend, and when we searched the Bait and Tackle, we found blood all over, just like the scene of Theo Vanderbilt's murder. Only there was no body at the Bait and Tackle."

"What?"

"Yeah," he said. "Everyone's saying we've got a serial killer on our hands."

Even though I had no more idea of what was going on in Cranford County than Deputy Marston did, my gut told me he was overreacting.

"Three suspicious deaths does not a serial killer make," I said. "We may not know the full story yet, but the body in the car is different. She was burned, not knifed. And we found Theo's body at the scene, remember?"

All true.

Still, while the MO was different in the fire case, I did not add that I strongly believed that the body in the car was the key to Theo Vanderbilt's death and, now, to Fred Thomas's disappearance and likely murder. Theo had procured the woman's body from somewhere. Perhaps he had killed her himself. If one of the woman's relatives were bent on revenge, Theo's death made a kind of twisted sense.

But Fred's connection? He had been the first on the fire scene. Had he seen something or someone and not realized it? Did the killer suspect he might be able to identify him? Or did Fred have some connection to the body? Had he helped Theo and Kathy set the fire? I knew some firemen enjoyed lighting a good blaze almost as much as they liked putting one out.

I wasn't sure about Fred.

"So it's not a serial killer?" Marston asked, sounding slightly disappointed.

Though annoyed that I hadn't been told about Fred Thomas's disappearance, I had to laugh. "Cheer up. This is not necessarily a bad thing. But why didn't anyone inform the DOI of Fred's disappearance?"

"I don't know, ma'am," Deputy Marston said. He was speaking normally now that we were off the serial killer topic. "I guess no one thought to call. All hell has truly broken loose, Special Agent Jackson."

I would definitely be speaking to Sheriff Harper about that, but first I needed to verify his whereabouts the morning of the SWAT raid, just to be sure he wasn't covering anything up.

I asked in a purposefully offhand tone, "For our report, we need to verify the locations of all the officers involved in the raid on Thursday morning. Can you work on that for me?"

"Oh, yes, ma'am," he said, sounding grateful that I'd offered him a task other than filing. "It won't take long. There weren't many people involved that morning." He began to tick off a list of officers, including the sheriff.

Once I heard Harper's name, I stopped him.

"All those people, what time did they arrive at the sheriff's department?"

"Sheriff Harper had us here at 4 AM."

"And everyone was here?"

"More or less. Some people drifted in a bit late."

"Including the sheriff?"

"No, we pulled into the parking lot at the same time, a little before four, and he commended my promptness." Marston paused. "Too bad I screwed it up later."

"Everyone makes mistakes," I said. "You'll learn from it."

"Oh, yes, ma'am. I already have," he said. "I learned it's never a good idea to tase another cop."

"Indeed," I said. "Now, is Sheriff Harper available?"

"I'll transfer you." He paused again. "And I'm sorry about tasing you."

As I waited, I pondered Deputy Marston's words. Given the tight timetable, Sheriff Harper would not have had time to murder Theo Vanderbilt, clean himself up, and arrive at the precinct in order to oversee the SWAT raid.

But there was also Kathy's mysterious connection with the sheriff and her story about the bloody-faced man in the shed to sort out. Was the killer in the shed a concoction to protect her lover Sheriff Harper? If so, how had she gotten Theo's blood on her arm? We had to know for certain whether or not the sheriff had anything to do with the death benefits fraud or Theo's murder.

When I'd made the phone call, I hadn't decided exactly what technique I was going to use with Sheriff Harper, but after hearing his honest voice over the phone line, I knew that the straightforward approach would be best.

Plus, it would catch him off guard.

"How well are you acquainted with Kathy Vanderbilt?" I asked after we'd exchanged brief pleasantries.

"Her son's in my jail," he replied. "So I'm acquainted just enough to incarcerate her firstborn."

I didn't smile at his blithe response. "Do you know her personally?"

"Personally?" he repeated, his voice level and even. "Yes, I know her, but not personally. Not really."

"How well do you know her then?" I asked.

There was a long pause, and for a moment, I thought he was going to confess to an affair, but he said, "I know her through her son Carter Hashaway. I busted him a few times for possession, but I think he's a good kid. I've been trying to save his ass—you know, show him some tough love—but seeing as how he's sitting in my jail again for possession, I don't think it's working out so well."

"You're trying to rehab Carter?" I asked in an incredulous tone. I had nothing against the kid aside from the fact that he'd tried to hit me, but I sure wouldn't have picked him as a charity case.

"Yeah," the sheriff said with a sigh, "but frankly I think he's a lost cause, and his momma is just mortified about the whole thing."

"So you do know her?"

"Yes," he admitted. "She came to my office after both of his arrests."

"What have you done so far for him?" I asked.

"I let a few things slide is all," he said, his voice laced with shame. "I know he has information on who's cooking meth in this county. I thought if I could turn him—and save him—I could do some good here in Cranford."

I lowered my eyebrows in thought. "So you're not having an affair with Kathy? You're trying to take out meth dealers?"

"An affair with that little witch?" Sheriff Harper sounded totally appalled. "Hell, no. I'm a happily married man."

"And you didn't call to tip her off about the raid on Thursday?"

I heard a loud thump, and I imagined Sheriff Harper standing up to yell at me. "Just what the hell are you accusing me of?" he demanded. He didn't sound calm or kind now. "You use my department resources and then insinuate I'm perverting justice in my own county? I won't have it."

"Look," I said, rising too, even though he couldn't see me. I leaned forward as I pressed my palm into the cool, flat surface of my desk. "We had information that you were possibly involved in an affair with her, and that might have given you a reason to help her fake Theo Vanderbilt's death. Did you?"

"I'm trying to save Carter for her," he said firmly. "That's all."

"Where were you just prior to the raid?"

"Here," he said. "Right here in the department waiting to meet you and the MPD SWAT."

"Can anyone corroborate that?" I asked, knowing that Deputy Marston already had but pressing anyway just in case.

Sheriff Harper growled, "Any damn person in the department will tell you where I was."

Convinced that he was telling the truth about everything, I sat down, crossed my legs, and said, "I believe you."

"What?" he asked, sounding confused at my sudden shift.

"I said I believe you, but I had to check. The timing of Theo Vanderbilt's murder was awfully close to our raid, and if you were having an affair with Kathy, then maybe you were involved in the fraud, and knowing that we were going to figure out the crime, you might have wanted to get rid of Theo for real."

"I would never kill a man that way," he said. "Whoever did that was a monster, and I'm no monster."

"Speaking of monsters, Deputy Marston said Fred Thomas was missing."

"Yeah," the sheriff confirmed. He seemed relieved to have the attention off himself. "His wife called yesterday and said there was blood all over the Bait and Tackle. I've been up all night trying to find him."

"Apparently, there has been some concern about a serial killer. Why? Were there similarities to Theo Vanderbilt's murder?"

"I'll send you the information we have," he said. I heard him tapping at his keyboard and assumed he was emailing me the reports. "There were a lot of similarities in the blood spatter and amount, but we don't have a body yet. Frankly, I'm still hoping Fred's alive, but the coroner doesn't think so. There was a lot of blood."

Twenty-Four

We already had the fraud charge locked down. Kathy had confessed, but there were still the issues of Theo's actual murder, the body in the car, and now Fred Thomas's disappearance. My suspicion that the three were connected and somehow hinged on the old woman in the car meant we needed to find out the victim's identity pronto. It was certainly important that we figure out what the hell was going on in Cranford County, but we also needed to inform the woman's family of her death and lay her to rest properly.

So when Vincent came into my office with his phone in hand and said, "The ME wants us at the lab ASAP," I leapt from my chair and grabbed my bag, and we were off.

On the way, I told Vincent of the news from Cranford, beginning with Sheriff Harper's alibi for the time of Theo's murder.

"And I now understand that little interchange between him and Kathy when we arrested Carter," I said. "He'd been trying to keep the kid out of jail in hopes of convincing him to give up information on the local meth dealers."

"So they weren't having an affair," Vincent said.

"No," I confirmed.

"Well, that's one more possibility ruled out, and that means we're running pretty short on theories right now. Let's hope the ME has something big for us."

One of the newest facilities in the country, the state crime lab for the central part of Georgia is located about twenty minutes from Mercer. This particular building houses the region's medical examiner as well as labs that test everything from firearms involved in murders to blood alcohol levels of average drunks.

All the scientists at the lab are civilians charged with the task of impartial testing of evidence from around the area, and there isn't a lot of interaction between lab workers and police officers. In fact, the lab is largely inaccessible to officers. This ensures that the scientists don't receive any information about the cases associated with the tests they're running, so their findings are as unbiased as possible.

I'd dropped off evidence for processing before, but I'd never had reason to go into the lab. This would be my first visit to autopsy, and if I hadn't felt so sure the information we received there would break our case wide open, I would have dreaded the trip.

I was at the point where I was ready to endure almost anything to unravel the case.

Vincent and I entered the rotunda and informed the front desk attendant, a young man with a blond crew cut, that we were there to see Dr. Kelly Greene.

"You can wait over there." He gestured at a bench across the room. "He'll be with you shortly."

Within five minutes, Dr. Greene, a rather large dark-skinned gentleman with a pleasant expression and a heavy step, appeared before us.

"Special Agents?" he asked, and I recognized his deep, velvety voice from our previous phone conversations.

Vincent and I stood and introduced ourselves.

"Pleasure to meet you in the flesh," Dr. Greene said. "Come on back."

He led us down a long, plain hallway and stopped at a door with a large, orange sign alarmingly marked "biohazard." I willfully hid my unease as he used his security badge to open it.

Here we go.

Vincent and I signed in at the administrative desk, and then Dr. Greene escorted us into a room so large it encompassed one full wing of the building. It was bordered by dozens of sturdy metal- and glass-framed cubicles, which seemed to be filled exclusively with young, attractive women.

I don't know what I was expecting to find in a medical examiner's office, but it wasn't a bevy of hot babes. I guess the career path had increased in popularity since the advent of forensics-focused TV shows. Probably, they all thought they were going to meet some hot male cop-scientist and solve crimes together in blissful happiness for the rest of their lives.

Or maybe they were like me. Maybe they had come to the forensics world because of something that had happened in their past. Were all these women as damaged as I was? Now that was a scary thought.

Or maybe they had taken this job because they liked science and it actually paid a decent salary.

"This way," Dr. Greene said, handing us nitrile gloves and surgical masks. "We'll head into the lab and discuss the bodies. You're in luck," he added with a smile. "It hardly smells in there today."

Dr. Greene used his swipe card to gain access to a lab marked "autopsy." As I walked inside, I sniffed cautiously.

Not so bad.

Not nearly as bad as the wastewater treatment plant Vincent and I had visited on our last case together.

Cleaner too. I took a look around at the autopsy suite, which was all nonporous surfaces and stainless steel. Plain and functional, the decor was more like that of a high school science lab than a set for a TV series. Not one fancy neon light or touch-screen computer in sight.

What it lacked in visual appeal, it more than made up for in top-of-the-line ventilation. Though there was no breeze, the air in the room was constantly moving, and the cooler temperature seemed to give the area a more sterile feel. I was glad I'd worn my wool blazer to cover my M&P. I buttoned it as Dr. Greene led us to two stainless steel tables whose subjects were draped in white sheets.

I wondered which body we would see first, and I almost expected Dr. Greene to whip one of the sheets off, like a magician doing a trick, but he ignored both bodies for the moment. Instead, he leaned his hip against a counter and crossed his arms in front of him.

"I know you're probably most curious about the female victim, but I'd like to begin with Theodore Vanderbilt. The real Theodore Vanderbilt." He looked between us, and hearing no objections, he continued. "This autopsy was much more straightforward since we already know that he was the victim of foul play, but it did reveal something rather unusual."

Dr. Greene walked toward the victim's head, pulling back the sheet to reveal only a portion of Theo's throat. I could see a neat cut on the right side of his neck, much smaller than I'd anticipated given the amount of blood in the shed. I was expecting to find the throat slashed from ear to ear, but this slice was only about three inches long and was positioned an inch above the clavicle.

"See this?" he asked, pointing to the cut. "This is the cause of death."

"All that blood came from one cut that size?" I asked, still vividly remembering the sight and smell of Theo's blood in the shed, the pool beneath the victim's chair, the spurts on the walls.

"Yes, ma'am," Dr. Greene affirmed. "The key isn't the size of the cut but the placement. This incision severed the carotid artery and jugular vein, which led to massive blood loss, cardiac arrest, and finally death."

Vincent leaned slightly closer to the body. "It's extremely precise," he said with a quick glance over his shoulder at Dr. Greene.

"Indeed," he said. "The killer knew exactly what he was doing. There were no hesitation marks or misses. The victim exsanguinated in less than two minutes."

I stared at the cut. Of all the people we'd spoken to in conjunction with this case, who had the knowledge to make such a precise incision?

My first thought was Kathy Vanderbilt. After feeling her revolver in my back and knowing she wouldn't have hesitated to kill Marston or me in order to escape, I had not only lost my respect for the feisty redneck but would also have no problem believing she had killed Theo herself. She had the biggest motive and might have had the knowledge to cut the jugular and carotid artery so precisely. After all, she had recently received medical training.

Still, there were problems with that idea. Kathy and Theo had been in the fraud scheme together and planned to disappear to the Caribbean. If she had wanted to kill him, why choose such a messy method? Why not poison or gunshot? And would she have been able to overpower Theo in order to cut him so neatly?

It didn't seem likely. Besides, Theo's killer would have been covered in blood. Kathy only had one swipe of blood on a sleeve when she tried to abduct Deputy Marston and me.

And I believed Kathy when she said she didn't intend for Theo to die. I believed she loved him.

Vincent straightened and faced me. Obviously, he'd been thinking of suspects too. "Hunters might kill this way," he said. "It's not recommended practice today, but old-timers would slit an animal's throat to bleed it out right away."

Hunters.

Hell, that could be almost anyone we'd spoken to, but Fred Thomas leapt immediately to mind. He owned a hunting store. Of course, now Fred was missing, and, given the amount of blood at the Bait and Tackle, he might have been attacked in the same way.

"LEOs would also be familiar with the anatomy needed for this sort of death," I said, thinking of Sheriff Harper, "but I can't fathom a cop killing that way. Too messy." And Harper had been at the SWAT meeting, also clean.

"Before you go on compiling your suspect list," Dr. Greene said, "let me add another monkey wrench to this. Come over here."

Dr. Greene led us to the other table and pulled the sheet to one side, revealing the head and neck of the charred female body. He didn't say a word, but amid the burned flesh, I saw it.

A cut nearly identical to the one on Theo, only this one was slightly more open.

"What the hell?" Vincent said. "The same person killed both victims?"

"Well, not really," Dr. Greene said. "The female victim did not die as a result of exsanguination."

"How did she die then? Smoke inhalation?" I asked.

Dr. Greene shook his head. "Despite the length of this body's exposure to the fire, we were still able to collect fluid samples, and we dissected and retrieved samples from several organs to view under the microscope. Based on the condition of the body, one would assume that the victim had burned to death and that we would find signs of smoke inhalation, particularly in the moist areas of the nose and throat and also in the lungs. We did not."

"Blunt force trauma to the skull?" I asked, thinking of the damage to the victim's head visible in the fire scene photos.

Dr. Greene shook his head. "The fire caused the damage present in the skull." He pointed to the fracture pattern. "Prolonged exposure to fire causes the bone to harden and become brittle, and it can crack in various patterns. Under a microscope, it was clear that this damage was done by thermal insult and not mechanical means."

"Then how did she die?" Vincent demanded. He looked like he wanted to bang a frustrated fist on the autopsy table, but fortunately he restrained himself.

"Ah, always impatient, you investigators," Dr. Greene chided. "It appears that this victim died of a myocardial infarction."

Vincent and I looked at him blankly.

"Heart attack," he explained.

"So this woman died of natural causes?" I asked as I stared down at the body, confused.

Dr. Greene smiled cryptically. "Well, maybe yes and maybe no. The cause of death was certainly a heart attack, but the means of death—the circumstances that led to the cause of death—well, those are less certain. This person did likely die of natural causes, but I've sent fluid and tissue samples to the toxicologist for further testing to rule out poisons. Unfortunately, we won't have the results for at least ten days."

Vincent and I grimaced in unison at the timetable, and Dr. Greene noticed.

"But there's something even more important here," he said. "When I began the internal portion of the autopsy, I noticed a distinct lack of blood."

"Could it have evaporated in the fire?" I asked.

"Yes, but that doesn't explain the presence of formaldehyde and other such preservative chemicals in the body."

"Formaldehyde?" Vincent and I repeated.

"Are you saying that this woman had been prepared for burial?" I asked, frowning.

"That's precisely what I'm saying. Look at this wound here." Dr. Greene pointed to the incision on the woman's neck. "This is where an embalmer likely inserted an arterial drainage tube. I also found evidence of the insertion points of a trocar, the tool used for removing fluids and other debris from the organs after death."

Vincent and I were silent as we absorbed his words.

"Knowing that this victim had previously been embalmed changed our search parameters drastically," Dr. Greene continued. "We stopped looking for missing women and began a search of recently deceased women in Cranford County. Just before I called you, we were able to identify her as Merle Cummings, a retired schoolteacher from Cranford County who died of a heart attack a week ago. Her niece, Charlene Twilley, discovered Mrs. Cummings's body at the decedent's residence last Monday. Her obit was simple, and there was no mention of a service, so I'm not sure who prepared her body for burial or where she was interred."

Questions leapt to my mind.

When and where had she been buried? How had her body shown up early Thursday morning in Theodore Vanderbilt's LTD?

But I asked a different question. "Is Charlene Twilley the victim's next of kin?"

Already I was dreading the idea of paying Mrs. Twilley a call with our news about her aunt's body. Breaking the news of a loved one's death was difficult enough, but this situation was so convoluted that I had no idea how to proceed. How did we even begin to explain to Mrs. Twilley that her loved one's body had been used in an insurance fraud scheme and been burned in the process?

That scenario wasn't covered at the police academy.

"Yes, ma'am," Dr. Greene said. "I've got the information in the report. I guess I could have just emailed it, but to be honest, I've gotten real interested in this case. Particularly given the similarities in the incisions on both these bodies."

"What do the similarities tell you?" I asked, wondering if I were interpreting the information correctly.

"Well, maybe nothing, to be honest. But maybe those incisions were made by the same person."

"Maybe we're looking at someone in the funeral business," Vincent supplied.

"Exactly," Dr. Greene said. "And if you don't mind, I'd like to hear what you learn after talking to Mrs. Twilley. We don't get to do any investigative work here in the ME's office. We usually just run the test and send on the results, but I've got to admit that this one has me curious."

"Yeah, it's got me curious too," I said, anxious to figure out the next step and take it. "I'll let you know what we discover."

As Dr. Greene led us out of the autopsy suite, my mind reeled with the possibilities of what might have happened. But Morton Ivey was now my primary suspect. He'd been on the fire scene. He'd had access to Merle Cummings's body, and he would have been familiar with the anatomy necessary to kill Theo Vanderbilt with one precise cut.

Plus, he'd had that creepy reaction to seeing Theo's body when he'd first arrived at the crime scene. Maybe the sicko was admiring his own work.

Without even realizing we'd done it, Vincent and I had disposed of our masks and gloves, checked out of the lab, and signed for the autopsy report.

As we walked out of the crime lab building and back to the car, he looked at me and said, "I'm willing to bet that the Eternal Rest Funeral Home is somehow involved."

I nodded. "But we should talk to Charlene Twilley and find out the details of her burial arrangements to be certain."

Before we even reached the GMC, I was already looking up Mrs. Twilley's home phone number in the ME's report, and about ten seconds later, I was making the call.

Twenty-Five

The ride from the crime lab to Cranford was quiet. I didn't know about Vincent, but I wasn't sure what to say. This case had been strange from the beginning, but now it had taken an even stranger turn.

"So did Theo exhume Merle Cummings?" Vincent asked at length. Then he paused for a beat and added, "That's far more screwed up than I anticipated."

"At this point, I could believe almost anything of Theo," I said, sadly shaking my head. In the course of proving him guilty of attempted insurance fraud, we'd considered possibilities from suicide to murder and now grave robbery.

What would be next?

A mistaken identity kidnapping?

Perish the thought.

At least we were certain that Theo was not a murderer. He was just an ordinary guy who wanted to get rich quick. Only he clearly chose the wrong way to go about it.

Had he thought we wouldn't realize the body in the car was an elderly woman?

I shook my head again.

Sometimes I was truly amazed at the schemes people concocted to try to get something that didn't belong to them.

And this time, apparently, the scheme had included desecrating a poor old woman's body.

Located in a 1950s tract home community in Cranford County, Charlene Twilley's house fit in with all the others—small, boxy, and clean. As Vincent and I walked to the front door, I looked over my shoulder at his 1970s GMC. Somehow, it seemed to blend in with the vintage flavor of the neighborhood as it sat in the driveway.

I thought of mentioning that fact to dispel some of my nervousness at having to break such horrible news to someone, but Vincent had gone into serious cop mode, marching up the steps and ringing Mrs. Twilley's doorbell with a violent stab of his finger.

After a few minutes, the door opened, but only a crack, and I saw a short, blue-haired woman peeking out from below the security chain.

Vincent looked to me to take the lead, so I smiled at the woman and asked, "Mrs. Twilley?"

"Yeah, who's asking?" she demanded in a shockingly strong voice for someone so tiny.

"Um," I said, trying to conceal my surprise at her harsh tone. "Georgia Department of Insurance, ma'am. We called earlier."

"You got ID?" she asked.

I produced my badge and held it in front of the crack in the door.

Mrs. Twilley squinted at it and then eyed Vincent. "Where's yours?"

He yanked it from his belt and held it through the crack for her inspection.

Then, without warning, the door slammed closed, and Vincent tried to jerk his hand back, but not quickly enough. His badge clattered to the ground as he pulled his fingers from between the door and the frame.

"Ow!" he said, and I felt sure he was holding back a string of curses.

I knelt down to pick up his badge. "You okay?"

He examined his red fingers. "That hurt like hell."

I stood and took his hand, examining it as if I could tell if something were broken. Other than the fact that it was starting to swell, I could tell nothing. I shrugged at him. "You'll live," I said, handing him the badge.

Vincent made a noise like a snarl as he took the badge and turned back to the closed door. He was looking as if he were about to pound it into oblivion and demand that the old lady apologize when the door swung open all the way, revealing Mrs. Twilley in her five-foot-tall glory.

She took in Vincent's red face and watched as he tried to rub the pain out of his fingers. "What's the matter with you?" she asked.

But Mrs. Twilley didn't wait for a response and gestured at us to enter. "Well, let's get this over with. I got things to do today."

Vincent and I followed her quick steps into the house, which was laid out in a typical tract home fashion. The front door opened into the living room with the kitchen beyond, and the opposite side was devoted to bedrooms and bathrooms. A collection of canes stood in an umbrella stand in the front room, but it was clear that Mrs. Twilley did not require one herself.

She moved like an Olympic sprinter, hurled herself into the wingback chair in front of the TV, and sat there staring at us. "All right," she said, "what's this about?"

Vincent and I took seats on the couch, and I found myself disappointed that she hadn't followed typical Southern protocol and offered us a glass of sweet tea. Or water at least. I'll bet Vincent would have liked to hold a nice cold glass in his injured hand to keep the swelling down.

Instead, he seemed to have completely forgotten about the incident.

"Mrs. Twilley," he began, taking the lead this time. Obviously, he was no longer worried about her fragility.

And I was pretty sure Mrs. Twilley could handle herself well enough against an invading hoard.

"We're here about a deceased relative of yours: Merle Cummings," Vincent continued.

"Great-aunt Merle?" Mrs. Twilley asked, pronouncing "aunt" a bit like "ain't."

"Yes, ma'am," I affirmed, wondering just how old this Great-aunt Merle had been when she died. Judging by Mrs. Twilley's blue hair, her niece had to be at least seventy.

"She's been dead about a week now."

"Yes, ma'am, we know that," Vincent said. "We're here to tell you that her body has been discovered."

Mrs. Twilley narrowed her eyes. "What do you mean her body's been discovered?"

"We found her remains in the course of another investigation," Vincent said, and I could tell he was trying to make the strange crime sound logical.

"Her remains?" Mrs. Twilley repeated, looking at him as if she'd like to slam his hand in the door again. She looked abruptly at me and jerked her thumb back toward Vincent. "What's he talking about?"

I glanced at him and shrugged. "We found your great-aunt's deceased body in a burned vehicle."

Mrs. Twilley didn't even pause to think before saying, "That's ridiculous. Great-aunt Merle didn't drive."

I looked at Vincent again. Might as well be as plain as possible. "We believe someone used your aunt's body to attempt to fake their own death," I said.

That seemed to get through to Mrs. Twilley, who looked as if she were considering this new information. "Why are you so sure it was Great-aunt Merle?"

"Dental records confirm it," I answered.

She looked at me blankly. "You got pictures of Great-aunt Merle's teeth?"

"Yes, we compared those taken from the body with dental records of recently deceased women in this area. We're certain it was your great-aunt, I'm afraid."

"But Great-aunt Merle was cremated," she said. "How could her body be used to fake someone's death? It doesn't make sense." Mrs. Twilley stood and walked to the brick fireplace. "We had a small, private service at Eternal Rest, and then Mr. Ivey, the owner, sent me her ashes."

Vincent and I nodded at each other. Now we had confirmation that the Eternal Rest Funeral Home and Morton Ivey were definitely involved in this somehow.

"No, ma'am, it doesn't make sense," Vincent agreed. "That's why we're here to talk to you. To figure out how this could have happened."

We watched as Mrs. Twilley rose to her toes and reached toward the mantel for a wooden box that slightly resembled a hope chest.

She pulled open the lid and looked inside. "Well, if Great-aunt Merle was burned up in that car fire you're talking about," she said as she held up the urn, "who the hell is this?"

Then, before either Vincent or I realized what she intended to do and long before we could think to stop her, she turned the urn completely upside down and gave it a great shake.

"Holy shit," Vincent said.

"Mrs. Twilley, no!" I said.

And then there was a heavy crack as the contents of the wooden urn hit the floor, followed by a cloud of gray dust.

I closed my eyes tightly. I didn't want the remains of Great-aunt Merle—or whoever was in there—to get in my eyes, and when I opened them, the dust had settled and we all stared at the solid chunk of…well…we weren't sure what, sitting on the floor in front of Mrs. Twilley.

Vincent leapt up and gently pushed Mrs. Twilley away from the area. "Please step back, ma'am. This could be evidence."

"Jackson," he tossed at me, "do you have any gloves or bags?"

I raised an eyebrow at him. "No," I said. "I don't carry gloves and evidence bags with me."

But after this case, I'd probably get in the habit.

"The Cranford Sheriff's Department doesn't have a crime scene unit. We're going to have to do this ourselves."

That was true enough. If we wanted to get this sorted out with any speed, we had to collect the evidence on our own.

I turned to Mrs. Twilley. "Do you have any freezer bags?"

"Sure, I got freezer bags. Hang on and I'll get the box." She looked around at the mess on her floor. "And a broom."

Mrs. Twilley hurried from the room, and I approached Vincent, who was still studying the chunk on the floor, and stood behind him.

I leaned closer, resting my hand on his back for support as I looked at the pile of debris. In the center of the mess was a heavy-looking, rock-like mass, surrounded by a covering of debris ranging from pebble-sized pieces to fine powder.

It looked familiar.

"Is that…?" I began.

"Cement," Vincent finished, looking over his shoulder at me.

For what was certainly not the first time on this case, I wondered what the hell was going on.

TWENTY-SIX

Vincent procured the services of Deputy Marston, who was thrilled to be away from the front desk of the Cranford County Sheriff's Department, and sent him across the state with the freezer bag of what seemed to be cement for testing at the crime lab. A surprised Dr. Greene said that a run through the mass spectrometer should reveal exactly what we were dealing with, but Vincent and I did not plan to wait.

Whatever was in that bag was not human remains.

And that meant the Eternal Rest Funeral Home was somehow involved.

"So what do you think?" I asked Vincent, feeling overwhelmed by the possibilities. "Did someone at Eternal Rest sell Theo Vanderbilt a body? Is this some kind of organ harvesting operation gone wrong?"

"I don't know about organ harvesting, but Theo could have bought the body. Maybe he promised to pay out of his insurance money."

"And something happened," I said, continuing that stream of thought. "Something went wrong and caused his contact at Eternal Rest to panic and kill him."

"Or could this be a crime of negligence on the part of Eternal Rest? Did the body get lost in transport?"

I shrugged. "How do you lose a body? Maybe Theo stole it."

"Surely they would have noticed if a body went missing."

"And they would have contacted authorities. They wouldn't be culpable for theft."

"No, you're right. Theft doesn't make sense."

"There's no use in sitting around here hypothesizing. We need to get the facts from Morton Ivey."

When Vincent and I visited Eternal Rest this time, there was no small talk, no tours of the facility, and no family history. We simply entered the funeral home and headed straight to Morton Ivey's private office in the back, passing both his sons en route.

Now we sat facing Morton, whose arms were folded across his chest as he looked down his craggy nose at us and listened to us explain that we needed his help in an insurance fraud case. We didn't provide specifics.

"And you think Eternal Rest is somehow involved in this life insurance fraud?" he asked.

"No, sir," Vincent lied. "We've hit a snag in our case, and we're looking for information about how a body is processed for its final resting place."

No need to get Morton Ivey on the defensive quite yet.

"Oh, well, that I can help you with," he said as he turned his head slowly from Vincent to me. "What specifically do you want to know?"

"How do you acquire bodies?" I asked. "And what method do you use to transport them to your facility?"

"After the bereaved family decides to hold their services at Eternal Rest, we retrieve the body from the hospital morgue in our van. The body is shrouded modestly and then removed with great respect on a stretcher."

"Who normally picks up bodies?" I asked.

"That job is divided between myself and my sons, depending on who has time to make the run. We're on duty twenty-four hours a day, so some of our trips to the hospital happen at odd times. Then we turn the body over to Andrew, who begins the embalming process with utmost respect and consideration."

Morton was beginning to sound like a cross between a sales brochure and the archangel of death.

"Andrew is the embalmer?" Vincent asked, and I knew he was thinking about the incisions on the necks of Merle Cummings, who'd been embalmed, and Theo Vanderbilt, who'd been slaughtered.

"Yes, Andrew does the bulk of the embalming work now that I'm the coroner, but we've all had classes in mortuary science."

"How does your process differ when it comes to preparing a body for cremation?" I asked.

"It's really not much different from preparing a body for burial," Mr. Ivey said.

"You embalm bodies that are set for cremation too?" Vincent asked.

"It depends. If the family desires a viewing or an open-casket funeral, we embalm and prepare the body according to their preferences. Many choose this option, but if they prefer cremation only or if finances prevent embalming, we ship the body directly to our crematory, which is Calvin's domain. As soon as the body enters his property, it becomes his responsibility. Our facility processes bodies from all over the southeast, and so Calvin must be meticulous in his recordkeeping. He takes his job so seriously that he won't let anyone else even bring a body into the holding area for fear that he'll misidentify someone. He handles each body himself from the moment the van enters his driveway to the time it departs that facility in the vessel of the family's choice."

"That facility?" Vincent repeated, his eyebrows raised. "The crematory isn't on this site?"

Mr. Ivey shook his head in a slow, measured rhythm. "Back in my daddy's time, it used to be, but these days, townsfolk are a bit touchier about death. Seems they didn't like driving through town and seeing our chimney going, so in deference to their needs, we moved our facility into the country where it won't disturb anyone. We do not offer to hold memorial services in our crematory like some other funeral homes do, so having the facility off-site is hardly an issue at all. In fact, I've always thought it was a more peaceful end for all involved."

I leaned back and rubbed my injured arm, which I guess had become a bit of a habit because it didn't ache at all anymore. "Who moves the body from the funeral home to the crematory?" I asked, wondering if Great-aunt Merle might have disappeared somewhere in this leg of transport, causing the driver to panic and put cement mix in place of her remains in order to hide what had happened.

Good Lord, what a horrible thought.

"Again, it depends on our weekly schedule. All of us share the transport duties whether it's to and from the hospital morgue or to and from the crematory."

"Where is the crematory located?" I asked.

"We have two twenty-acre tracts out on Highway 403. Calvin lives in the old homestead, and Andrew lives on the hunting property behind it. We moved the crematory to the homestead since Calvin operates it and keeps track of all the accompanying paperwork and taxes." I sat up a bit straighter. Things were beginning to make a little more sense. Great-aunt Merle's body had disappeared near Highway 403, likely when she was in the care of the Eternal Rest Funeral Home staff.

Perhaps Theo Vanderbilt had discovered the crematory and broken in to remove a body, or he had removed it from a hearse while en route.

Or had any or all of the Iveys been complicit in the desecration of the body? Had they sold Theo the body? Had they simply covered up the theft of the body to save their own reputations?

At this point, I wasn't sure, but I could believe either scenario.

And how did the incisions on the necks of both victims fit in?

Our interview so far had revealed that any of the Iveys could have "misplaced" Great-aunt Merle, and all of them had the knowledge to kill by cutting the jugular and carotid artery. So it seemed we knew little more than we did when we'd first arrived.

Apparently, Vincent agreed because he upped the ante. "Did Eternal Rest prepare Merle Cummings for cremation?"

This question actually caused Mr. Ivey to alter his posture. He unfolded his hands and rubbed a finger across his waxy lips. The gesture was at once curious and suspicious. "Merle Cummings?" he repeated. "That name sounds familiar. Let me look her up in the computer."

His fingers reached for his keyboard, and he tapped the keys for a few moments.

"Yes," he said. "We had the honor of working with Merle Cummings and her family just last week. Why?"

I ignored his question and asked one of my own. "Do you have records of how the body was handled once in your care, Mr. Ivey?"

"Of course, but—"

Vincent cut him off, saying, "We need to account for the movements of her body from the morgue to her final resting place."

"Okay," Mr. Ivey said, squinting at Vincent slightly. "But if you are accusing us of somehow mistreating the deceased or defrauding the family, I can assure you that you couldn't be more incorrect."

"We aren't accusing you of anything," I said, mentally adding "at this point."

Mr. Ivey looked at his computer for long moments, and when he finally spoke, I got a strong feeling that he was concealing something.

"The family of Merle Cummings requested cremation, but they did hold a small ceremony here in the chapel, so embalming also took place."

"Tell us where the body was from the moment you received it from the hospital morgue."

Mr. Ivey studied the screen. "I retrieved the body from the morgue, at which time it underwent refrigeration here until Andrew began the embalming process early the next morning. The service was held in the chapel later in the week. Afterward, Andrew prepared the body for transport to the crematory and delivered it to Calvin." He paused. "According to our records, cremation happened on Thursday of last week, and the cremains were returned to Charlene Twilley that Friday."

"We'll need to speak with your sons," Vincent said.

Mr. Ivey leaned forward and folded his hands on the desktop. "Just what is this all about? I demand to know," he said, his voice still monotone despite the threatening words.

"The body of Merle Cummings was discovered last week in conjunction with a death benefits fraud case we have been investigating," Vincent said.

Mr. Ivey shifted slightly in his chair. "What do you mean her body was 'discovered'? Are you referring to her ashes?"

"No, sir," Vincent said. "The body inside Theodore Vanderbilt's LTD, which you declared legally dead in your position as county coroner, was Merle Cummings, whom you also supposedly cremated last week."

Mr. Ivey did not react in horror or revulsion as most people might when faced with such a truth. He only shook his head and said, "But that's impossible. I have a record of her cremation having taken place on Thursday. There is no way the body I examined on Saturday morning was Mrs. Cummings. It's impossible," he repeated.

"But it was Merle Cummings," I said. "Dental records confirm her identity. Can you explain how this might have happened?"

Mr. Ivey went very still. "I cannot."

"Are you sure about that?" Vincent asked. "Because near as we can tell, the body disappeared while in your care. How do you explain that?"

"I cannot explain it," Mr. Ivey repeated, his eyebrows dropping lower on his face.

"Now, about your sons," I said. "Call them in here."

Mr. Ivey picked up his desk phone and dialed a number. While it rang, he said, "Let's clear this up now. Eternal Rest was in no way responsible for whatever it was that happened. I assure you. And there was no way for me to know that the body in the LTD was Mrs. Cummings."

I wasn't so sure about his first assertion, but I supposed I could believe the second. It had taken a skilled ME with a full staff to discover the identity of the body, so it would make sense that he hadn't recognized her.

In short order, Calvin and Andrew Ivey arrived in their father's office.

They nodded at Vincent and me in recognition from our prior introduction.

It was time to lay our cards on the table. Before us were the only three potential suspects in this crazy case.

Or three potentially negligent funeral home workers.

I wasn't sure which yet.

"The medical examiner has been able to identify the body burned in the vehicle fire on 403 as Merle Cummings," I explained, "and we know that her body was entrusted to your care after her death."

"What we need to know," Vincent intoned, "is how a body that was supposedly cremated in your facility ended up being used to fake Theodore Vanderbilt's death."

The room fell silent, and I watched as Andrew crossed and recrossed his arms over his chest and Calvin shifted his weight.

"Can either of you explain that?" I asked, looking from one man to the other. Andrew had turned a putrid shade of green.

"One of our bodies?" he squeaked. "You're sure?"

"Unfortunately, we are. You prepared the body for the funeral and later transported it to the crematory."

"Yes."

I looked to Calvin. "You were tasked with cremating the body, and therefore, you were the last person to be in contact with it. Is there something you want to tell us?"

Calvin shifted again and looked away. "No, ma'am."

"Do you even remember Merle Cummings?"

Calvin looked at the floor. "No, ma'am, I don't."

"I do," Andrew said quickly.

"Now, how is that possible?" I asked, skeptical. "Andrew remembers, but you don't, Calvin. Why not?"

"I deal with a lot of bodies is all. I don't get as personal as Andrew does. And with the number of bodies I get, I just can't remember them."

"How many cremations are there in Cranford County?" I asked skeptically. Not many good ole Southern Baptists were interested in cremation, and that was the predominant religious denomination in the area.

"Not many," Morton said, "but we accept bodies from all over the southeast. Not all funeral homes have crematories. It's not a popular method of preparation. But because we're fortunate enough to have a crematory, it's become a vital part of our business."

"How many bodies do you process per month?" I asked.

"It varies," Morton said, "but it's not unusual to run the crematory eight hours a day."

"And how long does the process take for each body?"

"Two or two and a half hours."

Holy cow. They were processing a lot of bodies per month if the crematory was running up to eight hours a day. The place was much busier than I'd expected.

I could now believe that a body might have been stolen or misplaced.

Still, I studied Calvin carefully. His gaze moved between the floor and his father's back, and I began to wonder if he wasn't covering for his old man or his brother. Had Calvin even received the body for cremation? Had he known about its disappearance and put cement in the urn to cover it up?

Or had it been an honest mistake?

I glanced at Vincent out of the corner of my eye. The tests were still being run on the substance in the urn, so I didn't think it was wise to use partially developed information in this interview. We didn't know what we were dealing with exactly. Had some cement-contaminated human remains been confused with those of Merle Cummings?

We needed to find out before we flung around accusations.

Well, any more accusations than we already had.

"What about you, Andrew?" I asked, deciding to press someone else and give Calvin time to stew. "You prepared Mrs. Cummings for her memorial service. What happened after that?"

"I secured the body for transport and"—he glanced beside him at his father—"took her to Calvin."

"And did the body make it there?" I asked.

"Of course, it did."

"Theodore Vanderbilt didn't make you a better offer, then?" Vincent demanded.

Morton Ivey stood, his bony hands shaking, but he said nothing.

"Because," Vincent continued, "we're beginning to wonder if one of you didn't meet up with Theo and arrange an exchange. The body for a big stack of money after Americus Mutual paid out."

"I didn't even know Theodore Vanderbilt," Morton said. His lips began to move soundlessly before he recovered his voice. "You're accusing Eternal Rest of selling a body?"

"That's preposterous," Andrew said, also rising to defend the family business, causing Calvin to step forward and join them too. "We would never sell a body."

"At any price?" I asked. If the Vanderbilts had gotten their payout, they could easily afford to drop a hundred grand or more on procuring the body.

"At any price," Calvin said, crossing his arms in front of his chest.

I looked carefully between the three Iveys.

Yes, we had certainly shaken them up, and now they were united in the family defense.

Time to play the last card.

"And of course, there's the matter of Theodore Vanderbilt's death. Did you know that he was killed with a very precise cut to the jugular and carotid artery?" I asked. "Just the sort of thing any of the three of you would use in draining fluids from a deceased body."

"In fact, Andrew," Vincent added, turning to the elder son, "didn't you use that same cut on Mrs. Cummings?"

Andrew's lips had pulled back in an expression of horror. "But I use the same incision on all the bodies I see. I didn't kill anyone. I didn't know Theodore Vanderbilt, either."

"We'll see," I said.

"As the owner of Eternal Rest," Vincent said, looking plainly at Morton, "you are responsible for the ultimate care of all the bodies in your charge. Is that correct?"

"Yes, sir. I take full responsibility for Merle Cummings," Morton affirmed.

"Then you'll be willing to come downtown to help us figure out what happened to her," I said. It was not a question.

Morton stood. "I will."

"We'll wait while you get the pertinent files and then take this to a more official location," Vincent said.

"You can't arrest Daddy," Andrew protested. His face began to twitch in agitation. "He's done nothing wrong."

"This isn't an arrest," I assured them. "But we do need to talk to the person in charge and figure out what happened because someone here is lying."

"No!" Andrew cried, but Morton held up an authoritative hand.

"You boys go back to work and keep our business running, and I'll take care of this."

"But Daddy," Calvin said, stepping forward and putting a hand on his father's shoulder. "You haven't done anything wrong."

"No, and that's why I'm going to go with them. I'll prove that we are not engaged in the selling of bodies, murder, or any other illegal venture." Morton looked at us. "If that body was Merle Cummings, we had no part in her desecration. And we did not kill Theodore Vanderbilt."

Vincent ejected the younger men from the office while we waited for Morton to gather his information.

Bringing Morton Ivey to the DOI for questioning had not been our original plan, but maybe this would shake something loose. Either Morton would crack, or one of his sons might.

Vincent left his card on Morton's desk in case the brothers thought of anything they wanted to share.

As if that were going to happen.

And I called the Cranford County Sheriff's Department to request another car. We couldn't all ride to Mercer in the cab of Vincent's truck. At least, I didn't like the idea of being sandwiched between Vincent and Morton.

The three of us walked out of the Eternal Rest Funeral Home, and Vincent shut our charge into the back of the waiting sheriff's department cruiser for transport back to the DOI.

Before getting into the GMC, he pulled me aside and ran a hand along his stubble. "We've got enough for a warrant to search the properties out on 403."

"Yeah," I agreed. "Something is definitely hinky out there."

"Did you get the feeling that they were covering something?"

I nodded. "Maybe it was Morton himself who sold the body. Or he could be covering for Andrew, the golden-child mortician."

"Of course, Calvin runs the crematory," Vincent said, "so he could have been the person who substituted cement powder for the ashes."

"True, but Calvin claims he doesn't even remember Merle Cummings. His father could have done it all himself. After all, he knows how to do all the jobs at the funeral home." I paused. "Do you think they were part of Vanderbilt's fraud? Did they sell him the body of Merle Cummings?" I shuddered. "Was he going to pay them out of the insurance money? Did they kill him?"

Vincent shrugged. "One thing is certain: we need to find out exactly what is going on out there on Highway 403."

TWENTY-SEVEN

Investigators were getting too close now, and he couldn't afford to wait and hope anymore. He had to act, even if it risked revealing himself completely.

He remembered Merle Cummings, just as he remembered them all, and now that he knew it had been her body that went missing, he knew exactly what needed to be done.

There was no choice but for him to clean up as many loose ends as he could, and the loosest of all was Charlene Twilley, the old biddy's next of kin. She had the only evidence that could tie him to the old lady: the "remains."

He had to get those back.

Finding her address in the computer records had been a snap, and now he stood outside her house in a suit and tie, trying to look official and clean cut.

He approached the door and knocked, hoping the right words and actions would come to him as they had with Theo and Fred.

He smiled as the door opened slightly and a woman's face pressed into the gap.

"Who are you?" the woman demanded.

"Mrs. Twilley?" he asked.

Her watery blue eyes narrowed. "No, that's not your name. Who are *you*?"

"I'm from the Eternal Rest Funeral Home, Mrs. Twilley," he said, trying to be smooth. "May I come in?"

The eyes narrowed to slits. "Why?"

"It's about Merle Cummings," he said. "I'm afraid there's been a mix-up—"

"No shit, Sherlock," Mrs. Twilley interjected.

Did she already know?

No matter. He tried to appear ashamed. "Well, ma'am, can I come in and explain what's happened?"

The old woman began to grumble, and he managed to make out some of her words. "Damn right, someone should explain. Everyone's coming here about Great-aunt Merle. It don't make any sense. I'm calling the cops."

No. No goddamn police!

He hunched forward like a linebacker and hit the door as hard as he could. Pain exploded in his shoulder, and he felt the thrill of the agony all the way to his bones.

He wouldn't stop.

He hit the door again and again until finally the chain broke.

Half-crazed by the pain in his shoulder, he paused in the doorway to take in the whole scene.

The old lady had been thrown to the ground when he'd broken the door chain. He stood over her now, enjoying the dazed look on her face.

Good.

He grinned down at her as he closed the door behind him, but he couldn't kill her yet. He might need her to help him find the remains. The files said the urn was made of wood, and while the old woman languished on the floor, he took a quick look around the small house, hoping it was on display.

It wasn't.

"Where is she?" he demanded as he reentered the front room, thinking to find Mrs. Twilley still prone on the ground.

But she was gone.

"Where's the urn, Mrs. Twilley?" he repeated, heading toward the kitchen and fingering the knife tucked at his waist. "I'll just take care of the little mix-up and bring her right back to you."

"The hell you will," Mrs. Twilley said, standing in the kitchen with phone in hand. "I've already dialed 911. They're coming here. That's how it works."

"That ain't how it works," he said, reaching over to cut the cord in one swipe. He pointed the knife at the old lady. "Now, tell me where the urn is."

"I gave it to the big insurance cop," she said, sounding totally unafraid even though he towered over her and had a knife pointed at her throat.

Could she not feel his power? Sense it as it radiated from his fingertips?

He could kill her now, but she'd already called the police. He might not have time. And the big cop had the evidence. This was worse than he'd feared.

Now he'd have to kill both the old lady and the big cop.

"You'll have to come with me, Mrs. Twilley," he said, leaning down to grasp her elbow. He propelled her down the hallway and through the front room toward the door, but suddenly she stopped.

"The hell I will!" she proclaimed. And then, though she was a little thing, she yanked herself free and spun.

As he reached for her again, he felt something crash into his head.

He blinked. Something was dripping on him.

He felt another blow land and saw Mrs. Twilley rearing back with a cane to whack him again.

Whack.

Whack.

She was beating the shit out of him, and he was just standing there like an idiot. Blood was dripping everywhere. There was no chance of making her just disappear. They'd know there was a struggle and find him easy now.

He thought of killing her where she stood, but he couldn't see straight with all the blood in his eyes.

And she had dialed 911.

He had to run now if he had any chance of getting the big cop.

So he turned, his face dripping with blood, and ran.

TWENTY-EIGHT

Back at the DOI, Vincent and I collected Morton Ivey from Deputy Marston, put him in the conference room, and then stepped outside to speak privately. "You take care of Ivey," I said with a nod toward the closed door. "And I'll see if I can get Ted to start the search warrant paperwork for all the funeral home properties, including the crematory."

Vincent leaned against the wall. "This case still doesn't make any sense. If we're right and one of the Iveys sold Merle Cummings's body, why would they kill Theodore Vanderbilt?"

"Maybe he reneged on the deal," I offered.

"But butchering him and leaving him in the middle of a shed seems extreme when they could just make him disappear. They could have run him through the cremator and scattered his ashes."

I shrugged. "Maybe they didn't have time. What bothers me is the idea that the funeral home lost the body. They might be desperate to hide their negligence, but murder?"

"And if Theo just flat-out stole it, why didn't they report it to the police? It wouldn't reflect poorly on them."

"We're still missing something," I said.

"Yeah, hopefully one of the Iveys will crack."

We parted in the hallway. Vincent joined Morton in the conference room, and I went to Ted's office. "I need a favor," I said.

"Name it," Ted said, looking up from his desk.

"I need you to get the paperwork started on a warrant for two pieces of property out on Highway 403 in Cranford County. We've got things in motion, and we'll need to get in there quick to see what's going on."

I relayed the pertinent information, and Ted began tapping away at his keyboard. By the time we were finished, he had promised to expedite the warrant, so I decided to see how Vincent was doing with Morton while I waited.

But as I put my hand on the doorknob, my cell phone rang.

"Special Agent Julia Jackson of the Georgia Department of Insurance?" a voice asked.

"Yes," I confirmed. "Who's this?"

"Denise from 911 dispatch. Do you know a Charlene Twilley?"

"Yes," I said as a feeling of dread descended on me.

"Mrs. Twilley called to report a break-in at her home on Griswold Drive, but when the sheriff's deputies arrived, she wouldn't open the door. She said she was attacked by a young man who was carrying a knife and saying something about a body. She kept demanding to speak to those 'idiots from the Department of Insurance.'"

"Idiots?" I repeated.

"Her words, not mine, ma'am. I finally got your name and called."

I wasn't sure how I felt about my partner and me being identified as "those idiots," but I knew we had to get to the city of Cranford to find out what had happened to Mrs. Twilley.

I burst into the conference room.

"Someone attacked Charlene Twilley," I said. "We've got to go now."

Vincent stood up, but instead of turning for the door, he leaned across the table. Placing his hands wide on its surface, he stared at Morton Ivey.

"If this was one of your sons," he said, "and we find out you even suspected one of them was involved in this mess, we'll charge you as an accessory to murder."

Morton fidgeted.

"And you'll lose everything. Your family business. Hell, even your family."

Morton looked up into Vincent's face. "It had to be Andrew," he said. "Calvin was a terrible embalmer. He couldn't have killed that way."

As Vincent propelled himself to the door, he shot over his shoulder, "Wait here."

With a quick stop in Ted's office, I made sure Morton would be supervised and that we would have all the warrants we needed to wrap up this case as soon as possible. "And put a APB out on Andrew Ivey," I added on my way out the door.

A sheriff's cruiser idled in Mrs. Twilley's driveway when Vincent and I arrived.

"She won't talk to no one but you," the deputy explained.

Her voice rang out just as our feet hit the steps. "Get the hell off my porch!"

Even through the closed door, Mrs. Twilley's tone was loud and clear. Her low-pitched voice was so angry that I almost obeyed her command to leave. There was no telling what kind of weapon she might have in there, and I knew she was capable of using whatever she had, but as I looked at the splintered wood of the door frame, I knew I couldn't just leave her alone.

"Mrs. Twilley," I forced myself to say with calm confidence, "it's Special Agent Julia Jackson with the Georgia Department of Insurance. I'm here to help you."

The door opened a fraction of an inch, and Mrs. Twilley peeped out. "Show me some ID."

We produced our badges, and I angled them so Mrs. Twilley could see them through the crack, thinking of Vincent and making sure to keep my fingers clear in case she slammed the door again.

This time, the door opened wide, and Vincent and I got our first real look at Mrs. Twilley. She stood with a cane clutched in both hands and held aloft like a baseball bat.

"Mrs. Twilley, put the cane down so we can talk," I said.

I walked into the entryway slowly, with Vincent close behind.

"Hell, no, not after what I've been through today," she said. "I'm thinking of keeping this thing with me at all times. It works real good."

I nodded, stopping short of her reach. I glanced over my shoulder at Vincent, who looked like he feared she might unleash on him. "Well, why don't you at least hold it so that the bottom is on the floor? That way we can talk better."

"I can talk just fine like this," she insisted.

I sighed. "Put the cane down, or else the police are going to think you're threatening me."

"I am threatening you," she said, eyes wild.

"Well, now would be a good time to stop," I said softly, "so we don't have to arrest you."

The older woman considered this. "Fine," she said, lowering the cane to the floor with a thunk.

"Okay," I said, still not fully comfortable with the situation. "Why don't you tell me what happened?"

"Some bastard came up in here, ringing my doorbell. I kept the chain on and asked just what in the hell he wanted. He said he was from the Eternal Rest Funeral Home."

"Did you recognize the man?" Vincent asked.

"No."

"What did he look like?"

"Young guy. Dark hair. Wore a suit and tie. Dirty fingernails."

That wasn't Andrew.

"It's Calvin," I said to Vincent, who quickly disappeared out the front door. I figured he was heading to put an APB on Calvin too.

"What happened next?" I prompted Mrs. Twilley.

"Well, I slammed the door in his face." Given that she'd slammed Vincent's hand in the door, I could well believe she'd done the same to Calvin. "And I told him I was calling the cops."

"And then?"

"He didn't like that too much, so he busted down the door, knocked me over, and walked in like he owned the place. He came right up to me and started demanding to know where Great-aunt Merle was."

"He asked for your Great-aunt Merle? By name?"

"Yeah, he wanted the ashes," Mrs. Twilley said as she sat down and put the cane within easy reach. "He said there had been a mix-up at the funeral home."

"What did you say?"

"I said, 'No shit, Sherlock.'"

I almost laughed, but given the seriousness of the situation, funny lines from little old ladies were low priority. "What next?"

"Well, he got real mad and cut the phone line with a great big knife, and then he had the gall to point that thing at me. 'Where is she?' he asked. I told him she wasn't here anymore. That I'd given her to the big guy, your partner."

"You told him that Special Agent Vincent has the remains?"

"Yes, ma'am, I did, and that's when he got real quiet and his eyes got all squished up. He tried to kidnap me, but I knew what he was going to do to me with that knife. If I left with him, I was a dead duck. So I grabbed Great-aunt Merle's old cane from the umbrella stand beside me, and I whacked him good right in the head a few times."

Given what I knew about her deceptively strong body, Mrs. Twilley had enough force to disable a man momentarily.

"He lit outta here after that and then those cops showed up." She shook her fist at the door as if the deputies were her enemy. "You can all go home now," she called. "I got things taken care of."

And by God, Mrs. Twilley had taken care of things.

I didn't let Mrs. Twilley dismiss the Cranford County deputies just yet. Instead, I set them to writing the report and collecting evidence like fingerprints and blood samples while Vincent and I discussed our next move.

"We have probable cause to arrest Calvin Ivey now," I said. "He's running around out there, desperate and careless, and he's putting people in danger. And by now, Ted should have the search warrants finished, so we can have a look at the Iveys' properties."

Vincent nodded. "We need to send a car to the funeral home, but I think we need to have a look around that crematory ourselves."

Twenty-nine

They would come for him now, those two insurance cops. The old lady had called the police, and they would know exactly who he was.

They would be all over his property within the hour, he guessed, and that meant they'd find Fred Thomas's body where he'd shoved it in the crematory building.

They'd find his pit and his septic tank.

They'd figure out that he had killed Theo.

They'd figure it all out, if they hadn't already.

And that meant they had to die.

But this was different. He couldn't knife two cops who were carrying handguns. He knew. He'd seen them tucked into their belts when they'd shown their badges to his father. So he had to be smart. He had to use his every instinct. He had to take every advantage he could, and so he pulled on his camo suit and grabbed the old .243 Winchester rifle, the scope, and the box of big-game ammo Fred had sold him earlier. He knew just where he'd go.

The old deer stand was perfect. Located far enough into the woods on the north side of his house, the stand would give him a good view of everything below and yet keep him concealed in the tree branches. Besides, people always forgot to look up.

So he climbed the rickety, rotted ladder that some relative or other had hammered into the oak tree and took his position. Yes, the house, driveway, and crematory were clearly visible in his scope. Here he would see everything and enjoy the view as the cops died.

He giggled the moment the olive-colored truck pulled into the driveway and angled behind his blue one. As if a little barricade like that would stop him.

Nothing would stop him.

Immediately, he sighted in on the big cop as he walked toward the house with his partner and then disappeared onto the porch. He would be the first to die.

Now all he had to do was wait for the right moment.

THIRTY

We rolled up to Calvin Ivey's driveway and straight into a moment all police officers dread. Here we were—two LEOs without vests, Tasers, helmets, pepper spray, or shields—and yet we were contemplating entering the property of a suspected murderer.

By ourselves.

Of course, we had our sidearms and handcuffs, and the killer used a knife.

Everyone knows you don't bring a knife to a gunfight.

We had the advantage.

Vincent looked at me, making sure I was ready to proceed the rest of the way up the driveway.

I raised an eyebrow at him. "Shall we?" I asked. This was a time to go balls to the wall.

"I'm in if you are," he said.

"All in," I said with a nod.

With that, he nudged the GMC forward along the driveway, which was lined with a charming low stone retaining wall and opened into a clearing just big enough to hold a small, one-story stick-built house and two outbuildings, one of which I knew housed a crematory.

A blue Chevy pickup was abandoned in the driveway.

Vincent angled the GMC perpendicularly behind the blue truck, cutting off Calvin's escape route, and killed the engine.

Ready to get Calvin into custody, I sprang from the truck, my hand already going for my M&P.

Vincent met me at the stairs, and we positioned ourselves at the front door, ready to take down the man who had killed Theo Vanderbilt and probably Fred Thomas. He raised his fist to pound on the door. "Calvin Ivey! Police. We have probable cause for your arrest. Open the door."

We waited but heard nothing. No footsteps in the hall, no voices.

I pounded again.

Still nothing.

Slowly, I reached for the knob, glancing sidelong at Vincent to make sure he was ready to search and clear the house. His blue eyes shone with intensity when they met mine, and he nodded.

The knob turned easily in my hand, and the door squeaked on its hinges as it opened.

Slowly, carefully, quietly, we crept into the house. The entry was clear, and, hugging the wall, we peeked first into the dining room. Vacant. Then we checked the living room. The TV was on and muted, but the room was empty.

Next were the bedrooms and all their hiding spots. Thinking of Kathy Vanderbilt, I even checked the pull-down attic ladder in the upstairs hall. The contraption groaned in protest as I pulled the cord, and bits of insulation and dust fell around me and onto the clean floor.

No, no one was up there.

"He's not here," I said to Vincent as we finished checking the kitchen.

"Let's try the crematory," Vincent said, pointing to the large outbuilding with the stainless-steel chimney poking out of the roof.

I nodded and led the way from the house, across the driveway, and to the building in the side yard. Constructed of painted wood planks, it was not fancy. It had only one door and a window on each long side.

When I opened the door, the odor of death assaulted me.

Something was rotting inside.

In the dim light, I could see little, but Vincent produced a mini flashlight from his pocket. He shined it methodically around the space, revealing the crematory furnace itself, a desk covered in mounds of paper and file folders, and a three-drawer body vault.

Beneath the vault was a sleeping bag.

We approached it slowly, guns drawn in case Calvin was hiding inside.

Vincent reached down and yanked back the top flap.

"Shit!" he said as his light focused on the contents of the sleeping bag.

Fred Thomas.

He was dead. Very dead.

But as Vincent shone his flashlight around the rest of the room, we discovered that poor Fred wasn't the only source of the foul smell in the room.

Three more bodies were piled in the back corner in various stages of decay. Slowly, Vincent directed the beam of light around the perimeter of the room. More bodies were stowed in piles beside baseboards, under tables, everywhere.

"What the hell?" I said, wondering what else we'd find.

I pulled a nitrile glove from my pocket, put it on, and opened one of the drawers of the body vault. Three corpses had been shoved inside.

"Jesus," Vincent said as I slid the drawer shut again, "did he even bother with the crematory at all?"

We turned to investigate the machine in question. The large metal-faced cremator looked like it had seen better days. Evidence of heat warpage and discoloration was visible on the cremation chamber door, and when Vincent opened it, we saw that the brick side walls were crumbling, leaving large gaps where some sections of brick had completely deteriorated.

"This thing isn't functional," Vincent said, crouching to study the base with his flashlight. "It would probably burn down the building if Calvin ran it again."

And that explained the bodies stacked all around.

Why hadn't he repaired the crematory? Or purchased a new one?

But now I was starting to understand how Theo Vanderbilt had gotten access to one of Eternal Rest's bodies. He could have simply taken one from this building or the other outbuilding I'd seen.

And I was also starting to understand Calvin Ivey. Well, as much as a crazed killer could be understood. Calvin had probably been trying to keep his secret by killing Theo Vanderbilt, who might have discovered this cache of bodies.

But why murder Fred Thomas?

That I didn't comprehend.

"I'll call the Cranford Sheriff's Department. Let them know we found Fred's body," I said, already dialing.

"And many more," Vincent said. He'd risen from the crematory and begun opening more drawers, which I assumed were also packed to the brim with bodies.

I spoke with Deputy Marston again, and he informed me that all available cars had been sent to the Eternal Rest Funeral Home and were at least ten minutes out.

I ended the call and took another look at the carnage in the crematory building. "Do you think there are more bodies in the other outbuilding?" I asked.

"Let's find out."

Vincent and I stepped into the orange sunlight of the early fall day, and I'd just taken my first breath of fresh air when the hairs on my arms began to stand on end. Something was wrong.

I saw Vincent fall before I ever heard the gunshot.

The flow of time stopped, and I felt myself turn toward my partner. All at once, I took in the scene. Vincent was sprawled on the ground with a patch of blood beginning to seep through the right shoulder of his white dress shirt.

Without a thought for my own safety, I threw myself on the ground beside him, tucking my body behind the low retaining wall as I felt another bullet land somewhere nearby. I heard the report of the rifle. I had to get Vincent out of the driveway. Even with the cover of the short wall, he was far too exposed.

Another bullet passed, coming from the other side of the house. I unholstered my M&P, thinking to defend our position, but when I peeked quickly from the cover of the wall, I saw that would be a mistake. The house was surrounded by woods on all sides, and I was unable to locate Calvin, though, given the timing of the bullet strikes and the sound of the rifle, he must be nearby. Probably somewhere high where he could see as much of the property as possible. A local highpoint.

I couldn't fire into the woods without clearly identifying the target. I had to wait until he revealed himself, and that might be too late.

Shit. What had we walked into?

Calvin had a clear advantage. He was invisible, and he had height on his side and far better concealment. It was only a matter of time before he adjusted his position and got off two shots that would end us both.

I looked into Vincent's face and was relieved to see his eyes open, focused on me, but his breathing sounded ragged. "Mark!" I said, not bothering to hide the panicked urgency in my voice. "You've got to get up. We've got to move. We're sitting ducks here."

His mouth opened and his eyes followed me, but he said nothing. He didn't move.

Another bullet. Another report of the rifle. Closer.

Calvin was already working on a better angle of attack.

Vincent still hadn't moved—he was probably in shock—and I knew we didn't have much time. If we had any hope at all, I'd have to move all 250 pounds of him myself.

From my prone position, I grasped his left arm and tried to pull him.

Impossible.

I got into a low crouch, hoping to get some leverage, and pulled again.

Vincent's breathing began to sound worse, and I tried once more to drag him out of the line of fire, only to hear another bullet embed itself in the stone wall in front of me.

I looked down to find Vincent staring straight at me. "Julia, go," he said.

All at once, I thought of his desperate desire to reconnect with his son and of the expression in his eyes after he'd met my sister, and everything within me screamed to protect him, to get my partner to safety, but it was only a matter of time before Calvin hit us both. And Vincent was wounded already.

I had to think. How critical was the wound? Could I leave him here unassisted and hope the paramedics would arrive in time to help him?

Quickly, I studied the location of the wound: right shoulder just beneath the clavicle. He was bleeding, but not so much that I feared he might bleed out. However, his breathing concerned me. Every breath came in determined but ragged gulps, though he showed no signs of oxygen deprivation. His lips and the skin under his fingernails had not turned blue, so he was getting adequate oxygen at the moment, but the wound could be causing his lung to collapse slowly.

And that's when I decided. I couldn't just sit there and wait until Calvin found the right angle of attack.

My best bet was to lead the killer away from Vincent long enough for the Cranford County sheriffs to arrive and outgun him.

I glanced over my shoulder toward the crematory, the other small outbuilding, and around the side of the house to the backyard. The latter option would be the wisest choice. I'd have to cover more ground in the open, but it would probably prevent Calvin from passing by Vincent on his way to find me.

I took a deep breath and looked at Vincent again. He was watching me levelly now. His breathing, though labored, was regular, and the bleeding at his shoulder seemed to have slowed.

He would be fine if I led Calvin away, and maybe after this initial shock wore off, he would be able to drag himself back to the relative safety of his truck. If only I could lead the shooter away from him in time.

I had to try.

So I leapt from Vincent's side and darted diagonally across the driveway, through the backyard, and into the woods beyond.

I heard the rifle's report as I fled, but I felt nothing, and I managed to enter the woods unwounded.

I looked around with wild eyes, trying to assess my options. I knew Calvin would follow soon; running prey is much more interesting to a predator.

And, in my favor, a moving target is harder to hit.

I didn't know how much time I had before Calvin got to this section of the property, but he definitely had the advantage. This was his land. He would know the topography, all the places to hide.

What was the best course of action?

Run? Continue to lead the sniper away from Vincent?

Hide and try to get the drop on Calvin?

The Cranford Sheriff's Department was already en route, so I only had to play this cat-and-mouse game for ten minutes. Once I heard the sound of sirens, I could circle back to the home site and start organizing a manhunt for Calvin Ivey.

Yes, I'd keep running until I found a good spot to take cover, and I'd wait out Calvin. But where? There was a wide, well-used path to my right, and I decided to run down it just long enough to put some distance between me and the shooter, and then I careened to the left into a denser section of timber.

Once out of the path, all I could hear as I ran were my own footsteps crunching through the fallen leaves and the rush of my breath. If I kept up this pace, I wouldn't be able to rely on my ears to tell me if Calvin were near, and I might not even hear the sound of approaching sirens and thus my salvation. So I slowed, keeping my eyes on the forest around me.

I kept close to trees and weaved as much as I could.

Where was Calvin?

I scanned the surroundings unceasingly, watching for anomalies in the pine forest. A snatch of color. The sound of footsteps. Anything.

Once, I thought I saw a flash of camo to my left, and I hit the ground until I was sure it had been my imagination and then started moving again until I could find adequate cover.

Finally, I squatted beside a large pine to check my watch. Only about five minutes had passed.

And that's when I heard Calvin's voice. "Drop the pistol."

I turned my head to the right and saw him standing boldly in a clear spot in the woods, his hunting rifle trained on me. His face was covered in blood, and one eye was blackened.

Bravo, Mrs. Twilley! I thought as I assessed his injuries.

But my bravado fizzled as I caught the expression in his eyes and thought of Theo and Fred. There was no doubt in my mind that he would shoot me in cold blood.

For a brief moment, I had the urge to take the bastard out immediately. Just raise my pistol and hope I could get a shot off faster.

But Jesus, I had recently suffered a concussion. I couldn't trust myself to take a risky shot.

Also, I was no sniper. I couldn't guarantee a perfectly clean shot in the T-box, near the eyes and nose, that would disable the jackass's motor functions. Not using a .40 caliber handgun at this distance.

With a concussion.

And Calvin wouldn't miss. Not at this distance with a rifle, even after taking a beating from Mrs. Twilley.

Besides, there was too much time left. The sheriffs weren't here yet. Calvin would be able to kill me, go finish off Vincent, and then disappear into the woods before the police arrived.

I couldn't let that happen.

It might not be smart for me to shoot the bastard, but I had to do something.

Change of tactics.

"Okay, okay," I said, lowering my gun and dropping it on the leaf litter around me. "Let's work this out, Calvin."

"Stand up and walk over here," he ordered.

"I know this isn't your fault, Calvin," I said as I complied with his demands and walked very slowly toward him. "We can work this out."

"Yeah," he sneered. "We'll talk. I've got just the place."

I glanced back in Vincent's direction, which was ridiculous because I'd gone quite a distance into the woods and couldn't see him.

"Don't worry about your boyfriend there. If he's not dead when I get back, I promise to finish him off. That way he won't suffer." He waved the rifle at me. "Let's go. You don't want him to suffer more than he has to, do you?"

For the second time in as many days, I'd let myself be taken hostage by a lunatic with a gun, but at least I knew I had backup coming, and I'd drawn Calvin away from Vincent.

Still, we could both be dead before help arrived.

Instead of taking me toward the outbuilding that housed the crematory, which was what I'd expected, Calvin pushed me back toward the wide path that I'd first used when I entered the woods.

"I never liked guns, you know," he said as he walked me forward, "and I only used this thing on your boyfriend because I had to. But I'm a good shot. Would have got you both if I'd been able to use my dominant eye and that damn wall weren't in my way."

I didn't respond, trying to think of the best way to talk a lunatic out of killing me.

"I've always preferred to use a blade anyway," he continued. "It's so much more poetic, don't you think?"

"Look," I said as Calvin came close enough to nudge me with the barrel of the rifle. "We're just insurance fraud investigators. All you've got to do is tell me you had nothing to do with Theodore Vanderbilt's life insurance fraud, and I'll gather up my boyfriend and get out of your way."

He laughed. "First of all, I didn't have nothing to do with that guy's insurance fraud. And second of all, how stupid do you think I am?"

Calvin continued to push me forward. The woods opened into a large clearing, and I took in my surroundings, hoping to find something I might be able to use to escape.

At the far end of the open area stood a front loader, which had obviously been used to dig the large hole that gaped in the ground before me.

The hole was clearly our destination, and I deliberately slowed my steps as he shoved me toward it.

"Calvin, why are we in this situation? And how can we get out of it?" I asked, going back to the old faithful hostage negotiation techniques I'd tried with Kathy Vanderbilt.

"Oh, come on," Calvin said with a combination of rage and sarcasm. "Does that ever work on anybody?"

I glanced over my shoulder at him and winced at the cold expression in his eyes. Still, I managed to quip, "To tell you the truth, Calvin, I'm beginning to have my doubts about some of this stuff myself, but I really do want to try to help us find a way out of this."

Without anyone dying, I added mentally.

"Yeah, yeah, don't act like we're in this together or that you're here to help me. You ain't here to help!"

Well, he was right. I wasn't here to help him. I was here to save Vincent's life and to help the poor families of the deceased men and women whose bodies Calvin had wedged in the crematory building.

We trudged on, and soon I was looking down into the pit.

I sucked in a breath at what I saw, and all pretense of hostage negotiation flew out of my head.

"What is this?" I asked.

"What does it look like?"

It looked like pure hell. Bodies in various stages of decay were piled one on top of the other, and their limbs were tangled together. I closed my eyes against the discolored flesh and the frozen faces that were somehow crying out for help even in death.

"Mass grave," I whispered.

"And you are about to join them."

I stepped back involuntarily into Calvin's rifle and looked at him over my shoulder. His eyes narrowed at me, and I thought it best to keep moving—keep him off balance as much as I could—so I began to walk around the edge of the pit, trying to get him to think of something other than shooting me and dropping me into the hole.

"You didn't kill all these people, did you, Calvin?" I asked, and then rushed to answer for him. "I know you didn't. I saw the crematory."

"Hell, no, I never wanted to kill no one or nothing," Calvin said, turning me so I could look him in the eye, as if he wanted me to understand. "The only killing I ever did was because he forced me to."

I remained silent for a moment and then asked, "Who? Who forced you to kill?"

"Daddy," he admitted, surprising me.

"Your father made you kill these people?"

His eyebrows dropped menacingly. "I didn't kill these people."

"But you have killed before?" I thought of the knife in his belt line and the surgical precision of the wound that had killed Theo. Calvin had trained as a mortician. Maybe he wasn't the best embalmer, or maybe Morton underestimated his skill, but clearly, he knew how to exsanguinate a person with one cut. "You killed Theo Vanderbilt."

"I had to."

"Why?"

"My daddy would have found out the secret, and I couldn't have that. It was better to do it this way, protect the secret."

"About the broken crematory?" I asked. "And the bodies? What happened to start all this? The crematory looks like it's in pretty bad shape. How did it get into that condition?"

"The crematory hasn't run in two months," he said. "I figured I could fix it, so I just stored the bodies until I could order the parts. At first. Then, I had to give the families something. So I gave them campfire ashes, cement, whatever I could find."

"It sounds like you've had a hard road," I said, moving again, but this time facing him. "But I can help you out of it."

"No, I don't want help. I can do this myself."

I did not like the way Calvin's face was beginning to contort into a sneer. "Why don't you just put the rifle away?" I suggested. "You don't like it anyway, and besides, it sounds like you can resolve this with your father."

"Oh, I'll put the rifle away," he said, "but I don't think you'll like my knife any better."

"You don't have to do this," I said.

"That's where you're wrong." Calvin's voice was resigned, and the sound sent fear pricking up my spine. I knew I wouldn't be able to stall him much longer. "I've never had a choice. I have to kill. I've been surrounded by death since I was a kid."

He appeared to be about to wax poetic about his childhood and give me some sob story about how he'd turned into a psycho killer, and, frankly, I didn't give a good goddamn.

Time slowed down as I reached forward with my left hand, pushing the barrel of the rifle away from my chest and grabbing Calvin around the back of the neck with my right hand. I raised my knee to his abdomen and yanked his head down as hard as I could.

I had landed a few good blows with my knee, hoping it was enough to lay him out, when I felt the rifle fly from my grip, and suddenly Calvin's hands were on my throat.

Tears leapt to my eyes as he crushed my windpipe, and my hands scrabbled at his, trying to find purchase so that I could tear him off me. I tried to use my knee to drive him backward, but soon breathing became impossible, and the world began to dissolve into a tiny pinprick of light.

I felt Calvin turn me in his arms, sparing me momentarily, and I gasped for air as I felt the knife come to my throat.

I could feel blood dripping from my neck now, and I was sure I was going to die.

With one last burst of energy, my hands grasped at the knife, and I threw my weight forward, trying to unbalance Calvin enough to gain some sort of advantage.

And suddenly, Calvin dropped like a sack of grain.

Totally shocked, my hands flew to my throat, and I knew my eyes were wild as I turned to look at the dead man. He'd fallen in a heap beside the mass grave he created, and his head was turned as if he were staring down at the bodies he'd collected.

But Calvin saw nothing now; the bullet had landed between his eyes, leaving them completely sightless.

I knew Calvin Ivey was well and truly dead, but my momma didn't raise no fool. I pulled the knife from his unresisting grip and picked up the rifle from the leaves where it had fallen in the struggle.

Only then did I look around for the shooter. Had the Cranford Sheriff's Department arrived and found us? Did they have a sniper in the department?

Who shot Calvin?

Then I saw movement in the underbrush and heard a rough voice say, "Here."

And in the next heartbeat, I was running through the brush toward Vincent.

Before I reached him, I heard the sirens of the sheriff's cars, and they were a sweet sound to my ears. I threw myself onto the ground beside Vincent. He was lying prone on his stomach, his Sig clutched in his left hand.

"Can you turn over?" I asked hoarsely and then helped him roll to his back.

He looked like hell. The wound on his right shoulder was bleeding more heavily now, and his face and lips were turning blue.

Even though I'd just heard the sirens, they didn't know about Vincent's condition, didn't know we needed an ambulance. So I grabbed for my cell phone and dialed 911. "Officer down," I shouted into the operator's ear. I calmed enough to identify myself to the dispatcher and provided my location. The operator assured me that EMS would be on the property within minutes.

After disconnecting, I tried desperately to staunch the blood flowing from Vincent's shoulder. My hands were coated in blood—probably some of mine and some of Vincent's—but I needed something to absorb it and keep pressure on the wound. So I yanked my new sweater over my head, pressed the woven cloth into his shoulder, and held it there.

"Listen to me, Mark," I said as I leaned onto his wound. "You're going to be okay. The paramedics are coming. The sheriff's department is already here. I heard the sirens."

Honestly, I don't know what I said after that, but I'm fairly sure it was a tight race between thanking him for saving my life and chastising him for dragging himself off that driveway.

Soon the EMS crew appeared all around me, trying to remove my hands from the sweater on Vincent's shoulder, pushing me aside. "Okay, ma'am, we'll take it from here," I heard a female paramedic say, but I never looked at her. I felt her hands taking over my place on the wound.

Then she said to Vincent, "Sir, can you hear me?"

He groaned in response.

And even though the EMS personnel were huddled around him, Vincent was looking only toward me, his blue eyes hazy and seemingly unfocused.

"Tell me what happened," a male paramedic said, breaking my eye contact with Vincent.

"Shot once. Clean through, I think," I said. "He can't breathe."

"Collapsed lung," the female said, followed by a string of medical jargon I didn't catch. "What about you?" she asked me. "You're bruised and bleeding."

I touched my neck and discovered she was right. "I'm fine," I said even though my throat was burning. "Take care of him first." I directed my attention back to Vincent. "You idiot," I said gently to him. "You came all the way out here with a collapsed lung. What were you thinking?"

Of course, I was probably an even bigger idiot for trying to lead a sniper into the woods and away from Vincent in the first place.

Despite the oxygen mask the paramedics had placed over his nose and mouth, Vincent managed to give me a strong look and say, "Totally worth it."

I smiled. "To me too."

"Ma'am," the male paramedic said, "please step back and let us work."

That's when I realized I was still leaning over Vincent with just my white lace camisole to cover my upper body. It was a modest fit, and no more revealing than a tank top, but still, I blushed as I stood.

I crossed my arms in front of me and looked back down to see Vincent still watching me.

"But now you owe me a sweater," I said to his prone form. "And a meal."

I can't say for certain, but I'm pretty sure Vincent said, "Done."

THIRTY-ONE

"Hello, ladies," Tripp said as he sauntered through the door of Tricia's hospital room a few days later. He was still dressed in his work clothes—suit and loosened tie—and as usual, his presence alone seemed to ignite the hormones of all the women in the room.

No matter their age.

Me included. But only a little.

I may not think of him in a romantic sense anymore, but I'm not dead.

Two out of three of us jumped up to greet him, and my mother reached him first, throwing her arms around him and kissing him on the cheek with a loud, motherly smack. She was just wiping the pink lipstick from his skin when Tricia rasped, "Tripp Carver!" from her place on the bed.

I gave him a quick hug to gain a measure of comfort from his physical presence, but not long enough to savor the scent of his woodsy cologne.

I swear.

"Hey, Jules," he said softly in my ear as he stepped back, pulled one rose out of the bouquet he held, and handed it to me. "You doing okay?"

"Yeah," I said, taking the rose and holding it close to my face so I could inhale its delicate scent. "Thanks for coming by and for the flower."

Then Tripp strode across the room with great ceremony and presented the rest of the bouquet of fresh yellow roses to Tricia.

My sister giggled, and my mother took the flowers from his hand even before Tricia had a moment to enjoy them.

"These are beautiful," my mother said, burying her nose in the blooms and sighing as if they'd been meant for her all along. "Thank you, Tripp. You were always such a good boy, weren't you?"

He winked at her. "Well, that's what I wanted my girlfriends' mothers to believe, anyway."

Now it was my mother who was reduced to giggles, and I rolled my eyes. Tripp was a good boy, and more than once I'd felt guilty for risking his reputation by pulling him into my personal investigation of Tricia's rape.

Of course, it was a bit late for that kind of thinking, given that I'd stolen evidence and already asked Tripp to use his influence in Orr County.

Still, I would never forgive myself if he were somehow implicated in any of my less-than-perfectly-legal decisions. But Tripp hadn't done anything even slightly unlawful.

"Oh, now we all know that's not true," my mother said as she unwrapped the bouquet and began arranging the flowers in an unused hospital water pitcher.

At first I wondered if she had somehow read my mind, but then I realized she was still talking about the past. As usual.

Tripp grinned, but instead of responding, he perched on the edge of Tricia's bed and gave her a little squeeze on the shoulder. "What did you do to land in here?" he asked.

"I just took a tumble down a little staircase. I can't believe it ended up with all this fuss," she said as she gestured around the room, ending on the IV bag of detox drugs that was still properly inserted in her vein and taped down. "I had surgery."

"Then you'll be out of here in no time, so you might as well enjoy the attention while you've got it," Tripp said. "You've got a whole hospital full of doctors and nurses at your beck and call. Have fun with it."

"Great," I said, giving him a gentle shove with my foot from my place in the recliner beside the bed. "Leave it to you to encourage her. Fortunately for everyone involved, Tricia's being discharged today."

And she had been fortunate in sorting out her enormous medical bills. Apparently, a social worker had connected her with a private charity that helped people just like Tricia.

At least that was one less thing for our family to worry about.

My mother finished arranging the flowers and also took a seat on Tricia's bed, again leaving me with the impression of a pleasant family scene.

And if I'd made a few different decisions—like not stealing evidence—this *could* very well have been a family scene. Tripp and I might have married.

But there was no use thinking about that. I couldn't change the past, and I didn't really want to change it. Still, I decided to let myself enjoy the moment. I closed my eyes and just listened as the three of them talked.

If it couldn't be a family scene, at least it was a hopeful scene. My sister was clean, and she was leaving with a prescription to help her through the rest of the transition to sobriety.

Feeling peaceful and secure for the first time in a while, I dozed off in the chair.

Hey, I still had a concussion and, added to that, stitches in the small knife wound on my neck. I was allowed to catnap, right?

When I woke up sometime later, I found my mother gone, my sister dozing too, and Tripp watching TV.

"What are we watching?" I asked groggily.

"Nothing good," Tripp said. "Can I have a word outside? I have news."

At that, I reached out for Tripp's arm and let him pull me into the hallway. "There's news?" I asked, trying to keep the desperate hope from my voice.

"Yeah." Tripp let out a breath. "Atkins gave us the name."

Holy crap, I thought.

I was about to learn the name of the man who had raped my sister. Right here in the middle of the hospital hallway.

My heart began to beat faster, and inexplicably, my eyes filled with tears. I held them back and looked up at Tripp. "Okay, let's have it."

"Before I tell you," Tripp said earnestly, "you've got to promise that you're not going to do anything crazy."

I frowned at him. "Of course I'm not going to do anything crazy. I'm doing everything by the book."

Mostly.

At least from here on out.

He frowned at me in return, and I figured he had probably guessed my thoughts, but he handed me the envelope he'd been holding under his left arm.

I reached for it with a shaking hand.

Here was the end of my life's work—or at least the beginning of the end. Right here in this manila envelope.

How strange that the goals of a lifetime could be so neatly and efficiently packaged.

Unable to prevent myself, I immediately opened the envelope and reached inside, where I found a copy of a police record.

"You got a copy of the file for me?" I asked, surprised. Tripp was always so honorable. I wasn't technically supposed to have this.

"Yeah," he said. "I figured it was okay because you're a state LEO. Besides, you could just find a way to get it yourself. It's not like I'm giving you anything you couldn't get on your own."

I stared at him. What he said was true. I would have found a way to access this information through my DOI connections. It wouldn't have been ethical exactly, since the suspect was not involved in any DOI investigations, but this method involving Tripp wasn't exactly ethical either.

And I hated that.

"Thank you," I said. "But are you sure you want to give this to me? Maybe you should just tell me his name."

He studied me for a long moment.

"Look, don't get too excited over this," he said as he ran a hand through his hair. "There's not much in there. We don't even have an address on the guy, and most of what is there is based on your sister's file, which you already know, and the assault, which you also already know about. A public records request will get you basically what's in that file. My conscience is clean enough."

I nodded, figuring if he was okay with it, so was I.

"But there's a name?" I asked, not caring about the scarcity of the information at the moment. If I had a name, I was one step closer to locating Tricia's rapist.

And once I located him....

"Yeah, there's a name: Clayton Leslie Slidell."

Just hearing the name, a rush of adrenaline washed through me.

No, I had no idea who the guy was. He wasn't some big name in the state or anyone important. He was a nobody. But he was now a nobody with a name.

"You shouldn't really thank me," Tripp said.

Through my adrenaline haze, I blinked at him.

"What?" I asked, frowning. "Of course I should thank you. You worked with the prosecuting attorney about the plea deal."

"Yeah, I did, but he was resistant, and I was just as surprised as you were to find that the deal had been made."

I folded my arms in front of my chest and leaned against the wall. "So how did it happen?" I asked.

Tripp shrugged. "There was outside pressure—a lot of sudden outside pressure—and I don't know where it came from, but it was enough to change the attorney's tune and make him offer the plea."

Outside pressure?

That sounded suspiciously like Vincent's doing, and on that thought, a strange suspension of emotions took over me. It was Vincent. I just knew it. I'd told him in the vaguest terms that I was still investigating Tricia's rape, but he didn't know any of the details. Maybe he had taken it upon himself to look into the matter. It was the kind of thing he would do, especially after meeting Tricia and beginning to understand my desire for justice.

Any normal—non-criminal—woman would feel a hot flush at a man like Vincent strong-arming a suspect for cooperation. But not me. I felt only panic.

This whole investigation was supposed to be personal, and now other people were being roped in. First Tripp. Now Vincent.

And frankly, I wasn't sure I was comfortable with that. At all.

I was just skirting this side of evidence tampering, a felony charge, and I didn't want to take anyone down with me. And whether knowingly or not, they were both now complicit. Sort of.

"You okay?" Tripp asked as he watched me from his side of the hall.

"Yeah," I said. I propelled myself from the wall where I'd been leaning and gave him a big hug. "It's just a lot to take in. That's all."

"I understand. And you should know we've got Slidell flagged in our system. If he shows up anywhere for any crime—including jaywalking—we'll be on him."

I let go of him and stepped back. "I really appreciate it, Tripp."

But I had no intention of waiting around until the jackass decided to jaywalk somewhere.

I was going to find him myself.

Tripp eyed me again, but he didn't give me any more warnings about my investigation. Instead, he only said, "Well, I pulled an all-nighter, so I'm headed to bed." He waggled his eyebrows. "Any chance you want to join me?"

I laughed at his unexpected comment. "Um, no."

"Too bad," he said, and then he was gone.

Thirty-Two

I returned to Tricia's room long enough to tell her where I was going, and immediately I rushed to Vincent's room in the adjacent wing. I'd been dividing my time between Vincent and Tricia since the shooting, so he wouldn't be surprised to find me at his bedside.

"Hey," he said as I entered the room. His voice was low, gravelly, sexy, and though I preferred to imagine that he'd been sleeping, his rough tone was more likely the result of his recent surgery. He'd been lucky, though. Calvin's bullet had gone clean through his shoulder, and there had been no lasting damage to his lung. A bit of cleanup and a chest tube, and Vincent was already on the mend. He'd be released from the hospital soon.

"I came to thank you," I said, getting right to the point.

"You're welcome," he said. Then he paused, eyeing me from his place on the bed. "What did I do to deserve this gratitude? Other than save your life, that is."

He didn't know? Or was he trying to be clever and make me gush about his heroic deed in the shooting of Calvin Ivey?

I pondered that for a nanosecond and came to the conclusion that Vincent's MO wasn't cutesiness or cleverness. He was pretty much up front and in your face.

But just to be sure, I asked, "So you didn't exert any pressure on anyone on my behalf?"

"You mean other than pushing some lab tests and warrants up the line?" He tried to straighten himself in the bed, looking concerned now, much more awake. I watched his arm muscles work and then tore my eyes away.

How did a man manage to make a hospital gown so sexy?

"Yeah, you didn't do anything else?" I asked.

"No," he said. "Should I have?"

"No," I said, probably a bit too quickly.

"Are you in trouble?" Now he appeared extremely concerned.

"No, I'm not in trouble," I said, and then, after a moment's thought, I added, "but I'd like to drop by your place after you're discharged. After you've healed a bit. Just to talk."

He seemed to be trying to figure out what I had in mind. Well, if he could figure it out, then more power to him because I wasn't quite sure yet what I was doing. I just knew that I needed to enter some facts into evidence and let Vincent choose what to do from there.

"Uh, okay," he said. "Are you sure there's nothing wrong?"

"Totally sure. You just get ready for my visit. I'll let you off the hook on that surf-and-turf dinner if you cook."

"Deal."

When Tricia was finally released, I went with her to my mother's house and helped get her settled in her old bedroom. I even stayed for dinner.

But as night fell, I knew I had somewhere I needed to be.

I hurried toward my neighborhood, but instead of turning into my own driveway, I turned into Helena's. Only after I rang the bell and Helena showed up with baby Violet on her hip did I realize that I was wearing another of my new outfits, but after sitting around the hospital and doing various chores at my mother's house, it was in a deplorably wrinkled condition.

"What, no coffee this time?" she asked, and then she looked me over from top to bottom. "Girl, what have you done to those clothes?"

"Oh, good grief," I said with a laugh. If she only knew what I'd done to my new sweater! "It's just a little wrinkled. Besides, no one's going to see me."

She raised an eyebrow and looked around pointedly. "By my calculations, everyone on this street has seen you."

"Well," I said spinning around, "let them have a good look."

Helena laughed and ushered me in.

"Come on in and sit down. I've been dying to tell you all about my new job," Helena began.

But I waved a hand at her.

I wasn't good at this kind of thing, so I decided to speak as plainly as possible. "How did you know about the plea?"

Helena's face fell, but then the disappointment cleared. "Oh, that," she said with a laugh, sliding Violet into her high chair and handing her a plastic spoon. "How did you know it was me? I didn't want you to know a thing about it."

"I was confused at first, but once I thought about it for a moment, I realized it couldn't be anyone else." I paused and looked at her, wondering whether to thank her or warn her off.

I decided to do both.

The thank-you came first, but Helena shrugged it off.

"It was nothing," she said.

Hardly, I thought.

"Besides, I'm an assistant US attorney now. I might as well use the influence where I can, and this was done in the name of true justice. Can't argue with that, can you?"

No, I couldn't. But I wanted to.

"I really appreciate it," I said. "I can't tell you how much."

Now it was my moment to turn away and gather myself as Violet's baby talk filled the room. At length, I turned back to Helena's wide, curious eyes.

"I just don't want to get you into any trouble," I said.

Helena laughed. "I'm not going to get into trouble. Everyone throws their weight around now and then, and if it helps bring a rapist to justice, then so much the better."

A tear slipped down my cheek, and a look of pity swept Helena's features. I opened my arms and gave her a long hug.

"Thank you," I whispered. "But listen," I said, pulling back at the sound of Violet's spoon banging the high-chair tray. "I don't want you to stick your neck out for me."

"I wasn't sticking my neck out," Helena insisted. "I was helping a friend. I ran into Tripp downtown on Monday. He looked upset, and I asked him if he wanted to talk, so we had lunch. Turns out he was working on a plea related to your sister's case. He thought I knew."

I nodded. Tripp had told me as much already.

"He said the defense attorney was the sticking point," Helena said lightly, "and I just called and unstuck him."

I shook my head in amazement. "During your first week at your new job?"

"Oh, no," Helena assured me, grinning. "I waited until the second day at least."

"Hels," I said on a sigh, "I can't believe you did that. It was an awful risk."

She cocked her head sideways and considered my words. "You're supposed to say thanks and then nail the bastard, not act like I did something to damage my career. Because, trust me, I didn't do anything wrong. I just made sure they thought the US attorney's office was interested."

"Thank you," I said again. I looked at her, trying to convey my seriousness through my gaze alone. "I just don't want you to waste your influence on me. Promise me."

She shrugged. "I don't understand, but I promise."

Of course she didn't understand. I hadn't told her about my little evidence cache.

My not-quite-legally attained cache.

And now she was part of this too.

She'd wandered into it unknowingly, and I'd sucked Tripp into it without giving him the full truth either. Of course, they still had plausible deniability—more or less in Tripp's case—because they had no knowledge of my previous actions, and I didn't want to confess now and turn it into a case of what they knew and when they knew it.

Ignorance seemed to be their best defense.

I shook my head at myself. This was getting out of hand. I may have implicated at least two innocent people already.

I could not let that happen again.

Thirty-Three

Almost two weeks later, I was sitting in my SUV outside Vincent's place on Lake Montclair. I'd had plenty of time to think of what to say and how to explain myself.

But as I walked to the front door and rang the bell, I forgot everything I'd planned.

It was a good thing I'd brought props because, based on the way my tongue suddenly stuck to the roof of my mouth, I wasn't going to say anything comprehensible any time soon.

And when the door opened and Vincent stood before me, his large body taking up almost the entire opening, I just gaped.

He was dressed in worn jeans and a t-shirt.

And he was barefoot.

A man shouldn't look that delectable in ordinary weekend attire, but Vincent sure did, and that wasn't making my reason for being there any easier.

There was a good chance that I was about to lose my partner, my friend, my potential...I didn't even want to think it. Vincent was, after all, the quintessential professional, and I was about to confess to violating key protocol.

Like federal law.

I'd done these things in the name of justice, but I was biased. I would do almost anything to see my sister's rapist caught. I would dance around the edges of legality, and, for me, it was the right thing to do. The case would still be cold otherwise.

But not everyone shared my personal bias for my sister. At least not in the same way I did.

"Hello," Vincent said, shaking me out of my contemplation.

I looked up and into his eyes, and before I could change my mind, I thrust the pile of folders I'd been carrying into his abdomen, well away from his healing shoulder.

Automatically, he reached for them.

"What's this?" he asked as I pulled my hand away, trying to ignore how firm his body felt under my fingertips.

"Read it," I managed. "Please."

"Is this about the Vanderbilt case?" he asked.

"No," I said. "But I did find out this week that Kathy Vanderbilt is after Americus Mutual again for Theo's insurance money. Can you believe it? Even facing ten years in jail, she's trying to get her respects."

He laughed, a low gravelly sound. "No," he said, "Kathy wouldn't let a little thing like being charged with attempted abduction, assault with a deadly weapon, and arson—not to mention attempted insurance fraud—stop her from getting her money. She'll be the richest con in cell block C."

"She's a pistol," I said. Americus Mutual would fight Kathy, of course. She and Theo had attempted to defraud them, thus giving the company legal cause to nullify her husband's policy, but that sort of paperwork takes time. And before Americus had gotten a chance even to begin processing the documents, Theo had truly turned up dead.

And since he was murdered by someone other than his beneficiary, the policy was still binding. Therefore, Kathy still had legal grounds for claiming the full million.

That would be an interesting legal battle, I was sure.

I added, "We still haven't learned why Calvin killed Fred Thomas. Our best guess is that he was named in the newspaper article as the first responder on the fire scene. I'm theorizing that Calvin feared Fred might be able to ID the body in the LTD, which would have led to exposure of the defunct crematory and his cache of bodies. Maybe Calvin was planning to kill Mike Symmes, the other fireman, next. And all because of a broken crematory."

Vincent shook his head. "Yeah, if he'd only told his father about the state of the crematory, like any sensible person, none of this would have happened. But Calvin was probably clinically insane."

"Frankly," I said, "I get the feeling the apple doesn't fall far from the tree. Andrew's been telling us all about Morton and his 'training regimen,' what he made those boys do in order to learn to face down death. Morton terrified those boys."

"Well, psychopath or not, Calvin was a sloppy, disorganized murderer. He was leaving bodies—or at least blood—all over Cranford County. We'll probably never know what he would have done if we hadn't caught him so quickly."

"And get this," I added. "More bodies have been found on Calvin's property. It seems he installed a commercial septic tank in a clearing way back in the woods and has been stowing bodies there too. They've found more than 150 sets of remains so far, and they expect to find as many as 200 before they're done."

"Good God," Vincent said. "I knew there would be a lot of bodies, but I wasn't expecting that many."

"Well, the good news is that no more bereaved families will suffer under the negligence of the Eternal Rest Funeral Home. Morton and Andrew Ivey have closed the business, and they've been charged with breach of contract, which was the only law on the books that applied to their situation, but I have a feeling Georgia will be enacting some new desecration of body laws and oversights for funeral homes."

"And Merle Cummings?" Vincent asked. "The final ME report said that she did die of natural causes and her body was released to her family's care. Was she finally laid to rest?"

"Yes. I spoke to Mrs. Twilley, who is just as feisty as ever after her encounter with Calvin Ivey. She now has her great-aunt's remains on her mantel, and she apparently enjoys telling the story to every guest that enters the room."

Vincent laughed again, and I shook my head, partially in amazement at old Mrs. Twilley and partially to help me move on to the business at hand. "But that's not what I'm here about," I said.

His eyebrows lowered as he looked at the folders for the first time. "Your sister's file?"

"Yeah," I said, inhaling the scent of bacon that wafted toward me. Might as well have a last meal. "May I come in?"

Vincent stepped aside to let me pass, but his nose was already in the file as he shut the door behind me and followed me into the kitchen.

He sat down at the table, and I took the moment to distract myself by going to the stove and checking on breakfast. Grits simmered in a pot, and bacon was draining on paper towels.

I picked up a piece and crunched into it.

I glanced at Vincent. "Eggs?"

"Fridge."

So I guess I was cooking them.

I found a pan, butter, and four eggs and got to scrambling. By the time Vincent had finished his first pass through the files, I had breakfast on the table.

"You know," I said as I took the seat across from him, "this doesn't count for our deal."

"Sure it does," he said with a forkful of eggs held aloft. "I paid for this meal. And cooked most of it."

I smiled at him, but it felt hesitant and the expression died on my lips. "So?" I asked, gesturing at my sister's file.

"How did you get this file?" he asked, pointing at it with his now-empty fork.

Panic skittered up my legs, and I froze for a moment.

Was I really going to say it?

Deep breath.

"I stole it."

"Stole it?" he repeated, sounding totally neutral.

"Yes, when I found out I was being laid off from the MPD, I knew I'd lose access to everything. The case was already cold, and I was sure it would never be solved. So yes, I stole it along with a copy of the fingerprint." I paused again for another deep breath. "And a sliver of material containing the suspect's fluids."

"I see," he said.

This was it, I thought. He was about to turn tail and flee.

Well, by God, if that were going to happen, I would make the most of this opportunity to get everything off my chest.

I had to do it sometime.

"Look," I said, using my fork to point at him. "I'm not saying I feel guilty for stealing this stuff. I did it only because I couldn't let my sister's rapist escape prosecution. I had to continue investigating."

"I understand."

"No, you don't," I said, setting the fork down more forcefully than I should have. "When I took this stuff, it was just me I was putting in danger. But now...."

I trailed off and Vincent just watched me, waiting.

"Now, Tripp is involved. And Lia Trent, who ran the fingerprint for me, and Helena. I asked for Tripp's help with the plea, but I shouldn't have. I should have waited. The rapist made one mistake. He'd make another. But no! I had to try to get that name immediately. And Helena ended up using her new position at the US attorney's office to push the defendant to take the plea. I'm slowly sucking everyone into my mess."

"Do they know about the evidence?" Vincent asked, tapping the folder with a finger.

"Tripp may suspect, but none of them knows for sure."

Vincent stood up and walked to the stove behind me for more bacon. I turned to watch him, to try to read his body language, but he kept his back turned to me. "Why tell me?" he asked.

I bowed my head. I couldn't even look at his back as I said, "I didn't want you to get sucked in."

"So you showed me the evidence in order to keep me out?"

I laughed nervously. "When you say it like that, it sounds stupid. But yes. That's exactly it. Now you know everything and you can decide what you want to do. There's no chance of you accidentally being implicated."

His back was still to me, and that made me nervous. What was he thinking? I couldn't tell.

"What if I just turn you in?" he asked.

"I thought of that," I said. "And I don't care. Either way, the secrets end now, and no one else will be wrapped up in this mess."

He turned around then and looked me straight in the eye. "So you are completely willing to face the consequences?"

Was I?

Well, really, there was no question.

"I knew the chances I was taking when I stole the evidence three years ago, so I am definitely willing to accept the consequences now. I just don't want anyone else to face them with me," I said firmly.

Vincent's blue eyes continued to focus on my face, but he said nothing, so I added, "Yes. I am completely willing. And I'm going to keep pursuing this through whatever means are available to me. If I'm charged with a felony and lose my job over this, I'll still keep going. I will find Slidell and make sure he is tried for his crime. I will never stop."

As I said those words aloud, I realized how true they were. I would never stop. If I never found Tricia's rapist, I would be stuck in law enforcement forever. I'd be frozen exactly where I was now. I'd never grow up and figure out what I wanted to be.

I knew this was totally unhealthy and probably an obsession, but that man had ruined four lives. He needed to pay for what he had done.

Vincent was still quiet, watching me.

"Are you going to arrest me now?" I asked, holding out my hands toward him, ready to be cuffed.

He stepped forward and pushed my hands back toward me. "As if I'd make the mistake of cuffing you in the front," he said, returning to his seat at the table and studying me. "You'd choke me first chance you got and escape."

I laughed, but then the silence grew long. I became increasingly uncomfortable under his blatant scrutiny.

"Okay," he said finally. "I'm in."

I blinked. "In?"

"Yeah, I'll help you find Slidell, and together we'll make sure he's arrested and tried for his crime."

"No," I said a bit too loudly. "That's not why I came here at all. I was trying to give you an out."

"Well." He leaned back against the chair and crossed his arms over his chest. "I'm not taking it. I'm in."

I knew my mouth was hanging open, so I closed it, only to open it again and say, "But this could end your career. If they find out about my files and learn that you helped out after you knew about them, then you could lose everything you've earned in this field."

"It could end your career too, and you're not going to stop," he said logically. "But yes, I could lose my job with the DOI. It's a risk I'll take."

"But there's no reasonable explanation for such a risk. Not for you. I have an emotional stake in this. You don't."

He tilted his head sideways and his expression softened. "Don't I?" he whispered.

I looked down, feeling a blush creep into my cheeks. I so did not want to go there. Not right now. Not about this.

He spoke again, his voice firm to my ears, but still I did not look at him. "I understand the risks. You told me everything, right?"

"Yes," I said, and that was the truth. I had revealed my entire self to him. Essentially, I was standing before him totally naked, vulnerable and exposed. "But that's not why I told you. That's not the result I was looking for."

"That's the result you got."

"But I don't want you doing this because you feel like you have to save me." Tripp had been in the saving Julia business, and that hadn't gone well. At all. I didn't want to ruin whatever Vincent and I had—friendship or maybe one day something more—by letting him play the role of protector or benefactor. "I'm not a damsel in distress, and I don't need a knight to come rescue me. I can do this on my own."

"Hell," he said, "this isn't about saving you. You're fighting, and that's what I'm trained to do. I fight. And I'll keep fighting as long as you do."

I looked back up at Vincent. His face was hard now and his blue eyes serious. He was pretty scary looking.

"Are you all in?" Vincent asked.

"Yes," I said with conviction and certainty.

"Then," he said in his strong, solid voice, "So am I."

THANK YOU FOR READING
DEATH BENEFITS!

If you enjoyed this book, please let me know!

Leave a Review: http://www.amazon.com/dp/B0074SRURW
Email Me: http://bectonliterary.com/contact/

JOIN THE LAUNCH LIST
Be notified when the next Mercer Murder is released!
http://eepurl.com/o-leX

Please enjoy the following excerpt from

AT FAULT
SOUTHERN FRAUD MYSTERY 3

Copyright © 2013 by Jennifer Becton
www.jwbecton.com

ONE

I crashed into the car in front of me because I simply couldn't stop myself in time.

That was precisely the way the accident had been designed.

It was late Saturday morning, and unlike most normal people, I wasn't enjoying a leisurely brunch over the newspaper or sipping coffee on the veranda while savoring the moments of my life.

Nope. I was behind the wheel of a decades-old sedan cruising Leonidas K. Polk Highway, one of many Middle Georgia thoroughfares bearing the name of a long-dead and even longer-forgotten Civil War general. With its smattering of gas stations, convenience stores, and crumbling family-owned businesses, the road had just the right balance of traffic and space to serve as the perfect location for a staged automobile accident.

And I seemed to be an ideal accident victim—a woman traveling alone and apparently vulnerable.

This was a bad assumption, however. What criminal onlookers could not possibly know was that underneath my wool coat, I carried a .40 caliber handgun and a badge bearing the name of a state law enforcement agency that most people had never heard of.

I'm Special Agent Julia Jackson with the Georgia Department of Insurance. My job is to investigate insurance fraud and apprehend the criminals involved. Sounds like it ought to be dull, right? I should spend most of my time pouring over spreadsheets and following trails of dollars and cents like an ordinary accountant, and often, that's what I end up doing. But over the past few months, my seemingly innocuous insurance fraud investigations have led me out of the doldrums of decimal places and straight into the realm of violence and death.

But one thing has remained constant: I am the investigator of the crimes, not the victim of them.

Until today, that is.

Today, I'd left my Explorer at the office and commandeered an unmarked DOI sedan, which was registered and insured under my current alias, Janet Aliff.

And voila: I was the bait, sent to navigate this dull section of two-lane highway southeast of Mercer, Georgia.

Driving precisely at the speed limit, I passed a dilapidated, yet still functioning corner gas station, where an older model gray BMW pulled out of the parking lot and into the lane behind me. I felt my adrenaline spike as I watched its progress, and my hands clenched the wheel reflexively as my breath came fast and shallow in my chest.

This is it, I thought, trying to force myself to ease my grip and relax. An injury was less likely if I kept my body as loose as possible.

I almost laughed aloud. Relaxation was asking quite a bit; I was about to rear end someone.

I sucked in a deep, bracing breath as I reached a straight stretch of highway and glanced in the mirror to see the BMW begin to accelerate, a gray missile bearing down on me.

Yes, this was exactly how it worked, a textbook setup. I'd studied this type of staged accident many times in the course of my DOI training, and even witnessed a few in person. Only now, it was going to happen to me.

My fingers tightened and relaxed on the wheel again, and I resisted the urge to speed up as the Beemer closed the distance between itself and my sedan.

To any casual—or not so casual—observer, this kind of fool-headed driving was nothing out of the ordinary. People liked to haul ass despite impediments such as other vehicles or pedestrians.

After letting the BMW ride my bumper for a tense quarter mile, unswerving in my purpose or speed, I watched as the driver hit his turn signal, indicating that he wanted to pass me, and swung into the vacant left lane, pulling alongside me.

I briefly eyed the driver, who did not so much as nod before accelerating past and making his way back into the right-hand lane.

But he didn't continue to accelerate. Instead, his car slowed.

This was also a shockingly normal occurrence in Mercer, Georgia. In larger cities, drivers turn cutting off another vehicle into a viable passing maneuver. They can pass you with mere millimeters to spare, and yet you don't have to apply the brakes because they zip ahead without a care in the world. But in Mercer, where life ambles along at a slower pace, sometimes people cut you off and then proceed to slow down.

It makes no sense, but it happens every day.

Pretending to be annoyed that I'd come into contact with one such driver, I threw my left hand up in a gesture of impatience and slowed my vehicle too. And the two of us chugged along as a sort of sluggish unit through the bright, crisp morning.

That's when it happened.

We came to a yellow light, and instead of buzzing through it with time to spare, the other driver slammed on the brakes.

Even though the goal of the entire exercise was for me to become the victim of this very accident—I was supposed to hit the vehicle in front of me—when I saw those brake lights glowing, my adrenaline kicked into second gear, causing me to jam my foot onto my own brake. Suddenly, I found myself practically standing on the pedal in an effort to stop quickly enough to avoid the collision.

Forget staying loose and calm. I was in survival mode as my sedan pitched and dove forward, and I jerked the steering wheel to the right. Later, I would claim that this was a tactic to make it appear that I was attempting to maneuver my car safely onto the shoulder and avoid a collision, but in reality, my subconscious truly was attempting to save me from an accident.

But no one had to know that.

I felt my sedan skid awkwardly to the right, and the shrill squeal of tires on asphalt transformed into the rumble of loose gravel striking the wheel wells. As dust and the reek of burning rubber filled the air, my eyes closed of their own accord, and I heard the ominous crunching sound of my front left fender impacting the rear right of the BMW.

The force of the impact was minimal, laughable really, and other than a slight jarring sensation, I didn't feel any pain as the car's momentum ground to a halt.

At the moment my eyes opened to survey the scene, I heard a loud pop—an explosion of whiteness and dust in my field of vision—and suddenly, I couldn't see the car ahead of me at all. Or even my own dash. All I could see was the air bag as it smacked into my face and chest with an impact that felt—and sounded—like I'd just been run over by a rampaging elephant.

"Ow," I said, deadpan into the air bag, though there was no one to hear me.

I sat for a moment with my face pressing into the air bag, shocked at its pointless deployment. At such a low speed, it shouldn't have gone off at all.

I sat back to reassess my condition. *Now* I was in pain, soreness burgeoning in my chest and face, thanks to the air bag. Carefully, my hands slid along my ribs. No one spot seemed more painful than the next, so maybe they weren't broken. Or I'd broken all of them equally, but that seemed unlikely.

Next, I checked my face in the rearview mirror and cursed. Based on the swelling that had already started, my right eye was going to turn black and blue before the day was out. Maybe before the hour was out. I touched the flesh around my eye gingerly and winced. I had come through the wreck uninjured; it was the air bag that hurt me.

Damn safety measures.

Groaning, I angled the mirror away. It was useless to sit here gaping at my needless injury; I had a job to do.

I unbuckled my seatbelt, letting it slide slowly back into its slot, and began punching the air bag out of my way. As in a real, unstaged accident, after deciding that I was relatively uninjured, the safety of the driver and potential passengers in the other car became my next priority, so I leapt rather shakily from my vehicle and dashed to the one ahead of me. The BMW was now sprawled crookedly in the right lane.

Well, mostly in the right lane.

I managed a quick peek at the damage to both vehicles—not too bad—as I ran to the driver's already open door.

Halting in the doorway, I knelt to assess the other driver's condition, and I didn't have to feign concern.

From my kneeling position, I looked up at the BMW's driver: my partner Mark Vincent. I was more concerned about him than about myself, even though I'd been the one who was just knocked in the head by an exploding air bag. Only two months ago, Vincent had been shot, resulting in a collapsed lung, chest tube, and surgery. He'd been back on the job for only two full weeks, and already we were testing him physically.

He had assured me he was healed enough for a low-speed accident, but I hadn't been so sure.

Fortunately, Vincent's air bag had not deployed, and under my cursory look, he appeared uninjured, but his usual stoic expression wavered slightly as he took stock of me.

I could tell by his reaction that my eye wasn't even going to last ten minutes before bruising visibly.

Great.

Hazards of the job, I supposed, but now was not the time to deal with them. I had a role to play.

"Oh my God!" I said loudly enough for potential onlookers to hear. "Are you okay?"

"Yeah, I think so," he said, just as we'd planned, only he added in a low, gruff voice meant for my ears alone, "Are you okay? Your eye."

Under his steady blue gaze, I nodded my head quickly.

"It was just the air bag. It's fine," I managed to say before I heard footsteps approaching from behind.

The runners had arrived.

Keep Reading *At Fault* (Southern Fraud Mystery 3):
http://www.amazon.com/dp/B00C179BP0

Acknowledgements

My deepest appreciation goes to everyone involved in the creation of *Death Benefits*. Thanks to Michael Sheehan for providing information on military and police matters, Jennifer and Matt Mathis for arranging a tour of a working forensics lab, Bill Brewer for information on car fires, and Dr. Carey Bligard for sharing details on concussions and other medical minutiae. Also I am grateful to my editorial team—Beverle Graves Myers, Kelley Fuller Land, Octavia Becton, and Marilyn Whiteley—for helping to keep me from making grievous errors. Thanks are also due to Bert Becton, a quasi-member of the editorial team, who was forced to listen to me work on the plot of this book for months. Of course, all mistakes in this text belong to me, but as usual, I will try to foist them off on someone named above.

ABOUT THE AUTHOR

J. W. Becton (a pseudo-pseudonym for historical fiction author Jennifer Becton) worked for more than twelve years in the traditional publishing industry as a freelance writer, editor, and proofreader. In 2010, she created Whiteley Press, LLC, an independent publishing house. *Absolute Liability*, the first in the six-book Southern Fraud Mystery series, became an Amazon Kindle Best Seller and made the Indie Reader Best Seller list for three nonconsecutive weeks.

CONNECT WITH JENNIFER ONLINE

Blog: http://www.bectonliterary.com

Facebook: http://www.facebook.com/JenniferBectonWriter

Twitter: http://twitter.com/JenniferBecton

BookBub: http://www.bookbub.com/authors/j-w-becton

Launch List: http://eepurl.com/o-leX

YOU'RE INVITED!

Get the Inside Scoop on
The Southern Fraud Mystery Series
and
The forthcoming Mercer Murder Series featuring Tripp Carver
By Joining the Welcome to Mercer, Georgia! Fan Group:
https://www.facebook.com/groups/MercerGeorgia/

Made in the USA
Las Vegas, NV
27 April 2021